FROSTGRAVE
GHOST
ARCHIPELAGO

TALES OF THE LOST ISLES

OSPREY
GAMES

W9-BVY-206

TALES
OF THE
LOST ISLES

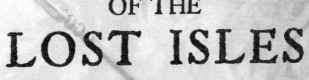

Osprey Games, an imprint of Osprey Publishing Ltd
c/o Bloomsbury Publishing Plc
PO Box 883, Oxford, OX1 9PL, UK
www.ospreygames.co.uk

OSPREY and OSPREY GAMES are trademarks of Osprey Publishing
Ltd, a division of Bloomsbury Publishing Plc.
First published in Great Britain in 2017

© 2017 Osprey Publishing Ltd
All rights reserved. No part of this publication may be used or reproduced
in any form, without prior written permission, except in the case of brief
quotations embodied in critical articles and reviews. Enquiries should be
addressed to the Publishers.

A CIP catalogue record for this book is available from the British Library.

ISBN: PB: 9781472824684
      ePub: 9781472824707
      ePDF: 9781472824691
      XML: 9781472824714

17 18 19 20 21   10 9 8 7 6 5 4 3 2 1
Typeset in Adobe Garamond
Originated by PDQ Digital Media Solutions, Bungay, UK
Printed and bound in Great Britain by
CPI (Group) UK Ltd, Croydon CR0 4YY

Cover and interior artwork by Dmitry and Kate Burmak

Osprey Publishing supports the Woodland Trust, the UK's leading
woodland conservation charity. Between 2014 and 2018 our donations
are being spent on their Centenary Woods project in the UK.

TABLE OF CONTENTS

THE CLOCKWORK
CHART

by M. Harold Page

THE PRICE YOU PAY

by Peter McLean

ISLE OF THE SILVER
MIST

by Howard Andrew Jones

RIVER OF FIRE
(SCENARIO)

by Joseph A. McCullough

THE AUTHORS

FOREWORD

The Ghost Archipelago has returned. A vast island chain, covered in the ruins of ancient and otherworldly civilizations, the Archipelago appears every few centuries, far out in the Southern Ocean. At such times, pirates, adventurers, wizards, and legendary heroes all descend upon the islands in the hopes of finding lost treasures and powerful artefacts. A few, drawn by the blood of their ancestors, search for the fabled Crystal Pool, whose waters grant abilities far beyond those of normal men. It is only the bravest, however, who venture into the islands, for they are filled with numerous deadly threats. Cannibal tribes, sorcerous serpent-men, and poisonous water-beasts all inhabit the island ruins, guarding their treasure hordes and setting traps for the unwary.

INHERITANCE

BY
MATTHEW WARD

The banshee wail of the wind rises and falls in time with the *Moonrunner*'s bucking deck. Lightning splits the sky. The storm's enjoying itself, revelling in every gale-tossed barrage of icy rain. The storm, and no one else. I can't see the rest of the crew through the deluge, but I'll wager they're every bit as drenched as I. Hells, I can't even see the gunwale. It's only feet away, but in this mess it might as well be at the bottom of the ocean. Likely to end up there, if the deluge keeps on. Still, if I can't see my crewmates, they can't see me. All to the good, long as I'm not swept overboard.

No sooner has that thought formed when the storm punishes me for harbouring even that small hope. The ship's plunging bow crashes into a rising wave. I feel the dull *crack* as a tremor in the decking more than I hear it. Water rushes across the deck, then recedes as the bow angles sharply upwards. My cold fingers lose their grip on the rail, boots skid on the slicked deck and then I'm falling backwards, flailing for long-lost balance.

My shoulder cracks painfully into the cabin door. The suddenness of it drives the breath from my body. Could

8

be worse. Six inches to the left, and I'd have split my head open on the cabin lantern's iron stanchion. A foot or so further on, and I'd have been down the companionway to the lower deck without benefit of the ladder. Good way to fetch a broken neck, that. Embarrassing way to go, if naught else. Couldn't meet my old da's eye if I met him in Davy's Tavern.

The *Moonrunner* crests the wave and plunges into the trough beyond. I cling to the stanchion as the deck reverses pitch, and prepare a dash back to my post at the ratlines. Valdim's cabin is off-limits to all but himself. I daren't be caught here. Not now. It'd ruin everything.

So naturally, that's when the storm ebbs.

The wind drops. Thunderheads part, revealing a watery grey sky through thinning rain. There's the suggestion of land off to starboard. Not much. Just a dark, uneven smear that speaks to a cliff face, and maybe jungle beyond. Vaanden's Isle? Maybe. Long overdue, if it is, but that's the way of things in the Ghost Archipelago. Nothing's quite where it should be. It's taken Valdim two decades to find this place, far as I know.

Still ain't fair weather, or anything like, but it's a marked improvement. The *Moonrunner* shudders, and finally settles on something approaching an even keel. I glimpse a half-dozen bedraggled crewmates clinging to rigging and gunwales, all of 'em with the rapturous expressions of men and women certain they've been preserved through the intervention of a higher power.

Only Quezan seems unmoved. The wiry old devil's a pace or two back from the bowsprit – exactly where he stood when the storm arose – with no support save for that gnarled sprig-staff of his. He's as sodden as the rest of us, but otherwise has the manner of a man embracing the warmest of sunshine. I can't see his craggy face, but I bet he's smiling. He's an odd one, even for a Warden. Reckons he's got life all figured out, and maybe he has. Or maybe he just doesn't care.

Time to move. Before eyes turn in my direction. I release the stanchion, and edge out across the deck. Softly now. Nothing draws the eye quicker than furtive footfalls. The heavy hand that falls on my shoulder tells me I'm too late.

'What 'ave we here?'

A hard shove spins me around. It's Theo. Of course it is. His dark eyes brim with resentment for rejected advances.

'Prying 'round the Captain's cabin, Bonnie? You know better than that.'

His lips twist into a self-satisfied leer. He's enjoying this. Maybe I shouldn't have kneed him in the nethers that time. More likely I should've kicked his head off while he was down. Knew he'd hold a grudge.

I force myself to stillness. Panic won't help. Clobbering Theo's a simple enough proposition, but it won't stop there. But maybe there's a chance I can brush this off.

'Don't be daft. Storm flung me here, didn't it?'

Theo grabs my shoulder. Pulls me close. 'You think the Captain'll believe that?'

'I...'

A deep voice cuts me off. 'The Captain will believe *what*?'

Some of the colour fades from Theo's sunburnt skin. My stomach lurches in a way that has nothing to do with the *Moonrunner*'s slackening corkscrew-motions. No way this ends well, not now we've drawn Valdim's attention.

Sorry, da. Looks like I've failed you. Should've stayed home.

I shake the apology away; channel my mounting fears into a two-handed shove that gets Theo out of my face. Then I turn, calmly as I can manage, to address Valdim. 'He's seeing things. Bashed his head in the storm, I reckon.'

Valdim doesn't reply at first, but continues his descent from the quarterdeck. Even drenched to the bone, black hair plastered to his scalp and the rain spilling from his waterlogged weskit and trews, he cuts an imposing – almost regal – figure. A man fully seized of the notion that he's meant for greatness. He doesn't seem to notice the *Moonrunner*'s drunken motions. Not so much as a single booted step falls out of place.

'Your pardon, Bonnie, but my enquiry was to Theo.'

I hang my head, as expected. Valdim adores etiquette. But even that silky tone of his can't disguise the menace bubbling beneath. Not that it's meant to. Valdim regards me in silence for a moment, then those piercing green eyes of his sweep away to transfix Theo. 'Well?'

Theo swallows. Righteous indignation's hard to maintain beneath that stare. 'Saw her at your cabin door, captain.'

Valdim crooks an eyebrow. 'Really?' His tone hovers somewhere between surprise and polite disbelief. 'Did she go inside?'

I hold my breath, fighting to keep a neutral expression. A nasty thought worms its way to the surface. Just how long was Theo watching me? I didn't see him through the storm, but that's no guarantee...

Part of me wants to make a break for it, take my chances in the water. Likely it'll come to that anyway, given how the situation's turned. Better without a slit belly than with. Even if there ain't sharks hereabouts, it's hard to swim with your innards hanging out. A surreptitious glance to either side stalls that idea. We've drawn a crowd. Quezan's still at the bowsprit, seemingly oblivious to the entertainment unfolding aft, but he's the only one letting the moment slide. Too many eyes on me now. Too many grasping hands between me and the gunwale.

Theo's face creases in what passes for concentration. 'No, captain.'

I exhale softly, though I'm sure the rain covers the sound.

Theo shoots me a venomous look. 'But she were scrabblin' at the lock.'

My relief dissipates, snatched away as if by a cold wind. With that lie, I'm done. And it has to be a lie, because if Theo had seen me working the cabin's lock, he'd have seen me slip inside too, and linger there for a good minute or so. You don't cage a lass for stealing if you can set her heels dancing for slitting throats.

And speaking of throats, mine's gone awful dry.

Valdim clears his throat as he faces me. There's a shift in his manner. Theo's words have tipped the balance, and not in my favour. He rests a gloved hand on the pommel of his sword. It's all I can do not to stare at it. I wonder if this is how my da' died.

'Anything to say, Bonita?'

The *Moonrunner* dips. Seawater rushes across the deck and over my boots. There's no shame in playing out the game as long as possible.

'He's lying.'

I don't think the deeper truth shows in my voice, but Valdim's no ordinary reaver. You don't stay captain without seeing round a few corners. Loyalty to the living's one thing, but when you're dead you're dead. No loyalty then. Just look what happened to my da'.

Valdim glances at the cabin's lock, then steps closer. Even now, there's no anger in his face, only polite interest. 'Oh, I'm sure he's still smarting from that disagreement at Sterport.'

Quicker than the eye can follow, he lunges. A fist closes around my bedraggled straw-blonde curls. I gasp in pain as Valdim yanks me towards him. Another tug, and I'm on my knees beside the cabin door.

'But did you really think I'd miss the scratches on the lock?' The first hint of darkness creeps in beneath the gentleman's tone.

I'd hoped he might. I hear tell there's a method of tilting a lock that leaves no trace, but I've never learnt it. 'Let go of me!'

I claw at the hand holding me captive. I already know I can't match him. Valdim may be thin as a miser, but there's not a sea rat on the Southern Ocean can match him strength for strength. That's his Heritor's gift, and he uses it well. The crew watch in rapt silence, practically slavering for what happens next, Theo most of all. I bet they're recounting all the reasons why I deserve it. Tam's remembering how I took my share of the plunder at Sterport, but scrimped on my part of the killing. Ritha reckons I'm too deep in the Captain's confidence for my tender years, or my length of service – she doesn't know the struggle I've had concealing my loathing for Valdim these past months. And there'll be shallower, pettier reasons harboured amongst the sea of faces. I don't blame them for that. Didn't I do the same when Crabbe went in the ocean ten days back? Doesn't take much to tarnish a soul. To turn a blind eye.

Valdim's grip doesn't waver. 'I honestly thought you'd a future with us.' A tug on my hair hauls me upright. A gloved fingertip traces my cheek. 'A face to charm the drowned dead back to the shore, and a wit to make 'em dance. Such a shame.'

My mama's looks, and my da's cleverness, in other words. Were it the other way around, I'd have been chum at our first meeting. 'I meant nothing by it.' My pleading tone comes naturally. 'Got curious, is all.'

He shakes his head. 'I wish I could believe you. Truly I do.'

The wind picks up. Angry clouds swallow Vaanden's Isle. The rain lashes down with renewed vigour. With a mighty crash, a wave breaks across the *Moonrunner*'s bow. The deck dips. Theo grabs at the ratlines for support. I keep my footing mostly due to Valdim's grip, and even then it all but costs me a hank of hair.

Valdim doesn't move an inch. 'See to the ship! I'm not plunging to Davy's Tavern because you're longing to see the colour of her blood!' As the crew scurry away, Valdim spins on his heel and glares sternward. 'Quezan! Strangle the cursed storm! What am I paying you for?'

'It is young and restless.' The Warden's bellow is half-lost to the renewed gale. 'Its spirits are not easily tamed.'

He strikes the deck with the foot of his staff, and begins a low-rumbling chant in the Drichean tongue. It rises and falls like the *Moonrunner*'s heaving deck, the disjointed syllables barely audible. I'm not really listening. I've no attention for anyone but Valdim. With the crew banished to the business of keeping the ship upright, there's no audience – no obstacle between me and the side of the ship. Now there's only the matter of Valdim's vice-like grip, and I've an answer for that.

'Now then, young Bonnie... arrgh!'

Valdim's cry of pain masks the sound of my boot knife piercing his forearm. His clenched fist spasms open. All at once, I'm free. If only his heart had been in reach.

I stagger away, the fear of the previous minutes bleeding away into bravado. 'Jac Cochran sends his regards.'

Valdim stares, his mouth agape in a rare moment of wrong-footedness. 'You're Cochran's brat?'

I grin. This is a good moment. Not the one I imagined it'd be, but I may as well enjoy it. I dip a hand to my weskit pocket and produce the prize I wrestled from Valdim's strongbox not five minutes earlier. Even in the darkness, the medallion gleams. 'Come to claim my inheritance.'

I hardly see Valdim move. But for the *Moonrunner's* sudden lurch, he'd have had me. As it is, he barrels past with an animal growl, slamming into the companionway rail.

I ride the momentum of the heaving deck, cursing my cockiness as I slip the medallion safely away. I've come too far to botch this now. But Valdim's not the only one with the waters of the Crystal Pool in his veins.

Valdim's sword scrapes free of its scabbard. 'A hundred crowns to the one who lays hold of her!'

The nearest crewers respond at once, staggering like drunkards across the bucking deck. Theo's amongst them. Truth be told, they'd kill me for a lot less than a hundred crowns.

Taking a deep breath, I draw upon da's gift. *My* gift. At once, I feel the prickling beneath my skin. The pain comes close behind – the same pain that held me back from trying this before. Now I've no other choice. It's worth it as soon as I hear the first confounded cry. Right now, I love the storm. My birthright needs a backdrop to mimic, and the downpour's just heavy enough to count.

'Hey! Where'd she go?' yells Tam.

I drift carefully past his shoulder, catching a glimpse of my reflection in the cabin door. I'm no longer flesh and bone, not to look at. I'm part of the rainstorm, a thousand dancing raindrops, kin to the spirits Quezan seeks to quieten. If I concentrate, I can just about make out the curve of my brow, the outline of my jaw – the dark hollows where my eyes glint like morning dew. But I know what to look for. My erstwhile crewmates don't. Tam stares right at me without ever knowing I'm there.

Then I'm past him, heading for the starboard gunwale.

Predictably, Valdim gets it first. 'She's a shifter!' he roars. 'Watch for her footprints!'

Clever. Then again, he and da' tore down many a flag before their falling out. Course he'd know what I'm about. Easier to watch for the imprint of water sloshing around my boots than the rain-cast hollow I leave in the air.

The *Moonrunner* rolls into a trough as I pass the companionway. I grab at the rail for support. My hand grows smooth and dark, mimicking every knot and blemish in the wood beneath for as long as it's in contact.

Ahead of me, Ritha's flailing at raindrops like a woman trying to find her way through a darkened room. I slip behind her, unable to suppress a smile at how ridiculous she looks.

The pain intensifies, burning like fire in my veins. I can't keep this up much longer. I won't have to. I'm nearly there. Then all I have to do is keep from drowning. Does Vaanden's Isle still lie to starboard? There's no way to tell if the *Moonrunner*'s kept its heading. I hope it has, otherwise I've come a long way for nothing.

Something strikes me from behind, bearing me to the ground. Something heavy. I roll clear, and up onto my knees.

'She's here! I've got her. I've...'

Theo's exultant shout ends in a cry of pain and a shattered jaw. Hard to block a blow you can't see coming, and I've a wicked elbow. But I've no time to crow. My birthright's fighting me now, burning me from inside out. I need to get off this ship.

'Hold her, you imbecile!' Valdim's an onrushing shadow in the rain, his face full of fury. Likely it's been years since someone played him for a fool. 'Don't let her escape!'

''ee 'oke 'y yaw,' moans Theo, both hands cradled to his mouth.

I dive for the gunwale. The *Moonrunner* heaves. I collide with the outer rail, hip cracking painfully against the tar-stained timber. The shock of it breaks my grip on my birthright. The fire recedes, and the illusion fades. Flesh and blood once more, I stare down into the maelstrom of white wave crests, and reflect how this seemed a much better plan a few moments back.

Valdim slows his advance. Reckon he knows what's in my mind. 'Give me back the medallion, girl. We'll put you ashore, call it evens.'

'Like you did my da'?' I brace my back against the outer rail, and slide upright. 'Sorry "uncle". I'll take my chances with the deep.'

Valdim roars and lunges for me with outstretched hand. He's a lifetime too late.

Bracing my feet against the deck, I tip my shoulders back. Gravity does the rest. The murky black flank of the *Moonrunner* rushes away above, and the cold waters of the Southern Ocean welcome me to their embrace.

The fire's naught but thin grey ashes when I awaken. My clothes are still wet from the desperate swim for shore, my shirt sleeves ragged from clambering over rocks.

I'm still not sure how I made it here. Part of me's convinced that all of this – the spent fire, the sunlight glimmering at the cave mouth – is one last hallucination before I drown. But only part of me. The rest's too sore to agree. I'm lucky to be alive – not least because the storm gasped its last scant minutes after I struck the water. At least I *think* it was minutes. Truth be told, there's a lot of last night still jumbled in my head. Lots of gasping for breath before the next wave hits. More praying for salvation than I care to admit. Maybe I *am* drowning, after all.

Nah. Drowners don't get hungry, and I'm starving.

I take a moment to inventory my possessions, and even that's luxury. Doesn't take long to tally up a knife, tinderbox and medallion. I tilt the latter into the sunlight at the cave mouth, examining it properly for the first time.

My da' described it a hundred times before he took that last, fateful voyage, but seeing it for real still sends shivers down my spine. The imagery's crude, geometric. A stylised sun eclipsed by the moon, surrounded by Drichean lettering. I can't read the latter, but I know what da' thought it meant – the medallion's a key to the greatest treasure in the Archipelago, hidden in a temple vault on Vaanden's Isle. I grew up on his tales of plunder and mystery, of gold and glittering gems. Swore he'd make me and mama rich, one day. Never did happen, though.

Problem was, 'Uncle' Valdim didn't want to share.

Broke my mama inside when she heard what passed between 'em. I never saw the messenger who brought word. I only witnessed the aftermath. She took to her bed, and never rose. I'm made of sterner stuff. I'll beat Valdim to his prize, then I'll kill him. Simple as that. Then maybe I can go home.

Or it was simple, anyway, back when I'd timber under my feet. Everything's chancier now.

Never mind. I'll get da's treasure – be it gold, gems or whatever, and I'll return home rich. Wash my sorrows away in splendour, you'll see.

Breakfast is fruit, harvested from trees near the cave mouth. Sour apples and sourer bananas. Not my first choice, but castaways can't be choosers, and I've no time for hunting. If this *is* Vaanden's Isle – and gods, I hope it *is* – then there are bound to be Dricheans prowling around. Not sure what they'll make of me, and I'd just as soon not find out. Da' never credited those mariners' tales of cannibalism and flaying, but he's not here. I am, and I've taken enough risks of late. As low a profile as can be managed, that's the way to go.

I'm getting my bearings outside the cave when I realise I've less time than I realised. The tide's all to hell and gone since I arrived – a golden beach stretches away beneath the cliffs. And anchored in the bay, patchwork sails reefed, lies the *Moonrunner*.

Stifling a curse, I squat down behind a bush. Two tiny figures haul an upturned jolly boat beyond the tidemark. Three others stand apart. Quezan's staring out to sea, distant as ever. Valdim, gentleman's coat flapping in the coastal breeze and thunderous mood written clear across his brow even from this distance, glowers inland just as intently. And the third? He's stripped to the waist and staked to the sand a short distance away from the abandoned jolly boat. It's Theo — there's no mistaking that shock of black hair. Too many failures in too short a time. He's in for a deal of trouble when the tide comes in. If he lasts that long. There's a reason I got well clear of the water before collapsing, even bone-tired as I was. Crabs hereabouts are a mite larger than the norm, and predatory with it.

No tears for Theo. He'd have done worse to me, given the chance.

Of course Valdim followed me here. What else could he do? It was that or give me — or rather, the medallion — up as lost to the seas. Does he think I'm strong enough to have survived? Or is it more that he's hoping his treasure's still in reach? Five years since he sent my da' to Davy's Tavern, and Valdim's spent every day in between searching for a way through the shifting islands of the Ghost Archipelago. Course he's desperate. Must be in a right state.

Bad news and good, same as usual. Sure, it'd be easier without Valdim here, but at least he's left half his rogues aboard the *Moonrunner*. Better yet, fortune's fair wind has me ahead of my former comrades. They'll be making for the temple, hoping to beat me there or at least catch me opening the vault. If my luck holds, I can reach the temple ahead of them.

Keeping low, I ease back from the cliff face, and head inland.

* * *

The air's thick and oppressive beneath the canopy. Every breath's a hot wind in my chest, damp and bitter. Still, better that than making the same journey under the open sun. The sunshine's brilliant where it pierces the leaves – however hot it is down here, it's worse beyond. And anyway, the heat's nothing compared to the constant avian shrieking amidst the treetops. I'm sure those birds are having a fine time of it, but they're giving me a headache. They're also masking any sound Valdim's lot might be making. My former captain could be paces behind, and I'd never hear him.

After what seems like an age, I finally stumble across the first of the sunken statues – little more than squared-off blocks stacked one atop the other. The uppermost stone always bears the eclipse symbol present on the medallion. The others are covered in broken Drichean lettering. Are they warnings? Instructions? Signposts on a long-abandoned pilgrim trail? I've no way to know. But I've never forgotten Da's tales. The statues'll lead me to my prize, long as I'm still headed uphill.

I fancy I'm making faster time than Valdim's company, but I've no proof and a whole trade scow's worth of insecurities, so push myself harder, just in case. I've stopped jumping at every rustle of undergrowth by the time the beach is lost to sight. Whatever else Vaanden's Isle holds, it apparently has a limitless supply of timid, short-furred monkeys who bolt at the first sign of anything larger than themselves. Sadly, there's no ignoring the caterwauling from the treetops. It's enough to wake the dead.

Impatience lends confidence to my stride. Every sense I have is trained on the path behind, seeking some sign of Valdim's pursuit. It's an easier proposition than scouring the undergrowth to either side, which grows increasingly tangled the further behind I leave the shore.

The trail swings eastward at the next statue. This one's larger. Plaited flowers and scraps of worked gold are dotted around its base – offerings, I suppose, to whatever gods the Dricheans see fit to honour. I leave the tributes well alone. I've enough going against me without inviting divine wrath.

A few paces beyond that, the birds at last fall quiet.

My gratitude's brief, extinguished when the undergrowth comes alive with the dozens of desperate bodies scampering for all they're worth. Not away from me, as they have before, but towards, past and over me, in a torrent of tiny hissing voices and razor-sharp claws. Almost too late, I realise what's happening.

They're running from something.

A larger, darker shape crashes through the jungle from further uphill. I twist aside, the wind and the musky stench of it barrelling past my shoulder. Balance, already fragile from the simian assault, escapes me completely. I crash into a tangle of branches and go absolutely still.

Standing in the centre of the path, inches from where I'm lying, is an enormous, bipedal lizard, its leathery hide a mix of mottled browns and green. The snapperjaws the Sterport wealthy use as guard animals worry me enough. This thing's easily four times their size. Hells, it's only a little shorter than me, crown to heel. Its teeth are longer than my fingers. And its foreclaws? They make my knife look like a toy.

The lizard dips its head into the branches. Something screeches and falls silent.

Heart in my throat, I embrace my birthright. As the fire in my blood grows, my limbs fade into the undergrowth, taking on the gnarled texture of tree bark, and the waxy, luscious greens of the bushes. My hair, spilled across my face during my fall, becomes pallid fronds.

I daren't even breathe, the creature's so close. I silently urge it to leave, to chase down the rest of monkeykind its presence set to flight.

The lizard doesn't budge.

It spins around, thick muscular tail whipping at the branches. Blood still trickling from its jaw, it tilts its head in a curiously bird-like gesture. One tawny yellow eye, slitted like a picture-book demon's, stares into mine from inches away. Leathery nostrils twitch, sifting my scent from its regular prey.

I tell myself it can't see me. But it's clear it can smell something amiss.

Icy fear mingles with the rising fire in my veins. Every instinct I have is telling me to run for it. Every rational thought warns me I won't get three paces.

I still daren't breathe, daren't do anything that'll break the illusion. Sure, I've a knife, but that beast has five on each foot, and a hide thicker than leather to boot.

I try not to think about the delicate green serpent twitching its way across my thigh, or the beetles using my brow as a handy shortcut between two favourite feasting sites. I'm hoping neither creature takes the lizard's fancy, because a bite directed at them will take a chunk of me alongside.

At last, the lizard's eyes trump its sense of smell. Issuing a thin hiss, it lopes away downhill. I don't breathe until its outline's lost amidst the branches, and I don't let go of my birthright until the birds strike up their yawling once more.

* * *

I take things slower from that point on. I confess, that lizard still has me rattled. It shouldn't. I came through the raid on Sterport in one piece, and that was a bloody mess in every sense of the word. It was the beastie's eyes, I think. Intelligent, but without the inclination to bargain. Nothing but hunger in its gaze. Not so different from Valdim, come to that.

The path's long since lost all pretence of directness, crossing a dried-up crevasse of a streambed, and looping back on itself as it crawls up the unforgiving hillside. I've just inched my way across a bridge of fraying liana ropes when a desperate cry draws my gaze down the sheer hillside.

Tam stumbles out of the undergrowth and pitches face first into the streambed. He doesn't move – less thanks to the fall, and more to the black-shafted arrows buried in his back. Ritha leaps over his corpse, broadsword falling from her grip as she claws at the opposite bank.

A powerful, leathery shape crashes through the branches. At first, I wonder if it's the same lizard from before. Then I realise it's wearing a leather harness. The arrows in Tam's back make the rest of the connection. It's a hunter's pet.

A single leap carries the creature effortlessly across the crevasse and onto Ritha's back. The luckless woman screams. Slitted yellow eyes gleam. Needle teeth sink into the base of Ritha's neck. The scream chokes off. Lizard and prey tumble into the crevasse, the former's tail thrashing like an enraged serpent. The steep banks of the streambed hide the rest from sight. Given the sharp reports of snapping bones, I think I'm glad.

And yet, I can't bring myself to look away. Tam and Ritha are gone, that's for sure. What about Valdim? Could I be that lucky? The next rustle of branches confirms that I'm not.

Valdim stalks towards the streambed with his accustomed composure. A dark-skinned corpse trails from his right hand, its upended quiver spilling a dozen arrows into the crevasse. I know at once his victim's a Drichean, even though I've never seen one in the flesh. With the plaited hair, bronze collar and whorled white tattoos he can't be anything else. There's not a speck of blood on the body, no deep crimson to stain the sky-blue robes, and Valdim's sword is still in its shoulder scabbard. Likely he broke the Drichean's neck. I saw him do similar at Sterport, and plenty of others. Likes to show off his strength.

Belatedly, I realise how exposed I am. One upward glance up, that's all it'd take. Even with the path's tortuous course, Valdim's only minutes behind, and I'd be a fool to bet my stamina against his. He sees me, he'll run me down.

I back away from the precipice just as Quezan emerges. The Warden's bleeding from a handful of tiny wounds, but none of it shows in his face. Then again, nothing ever does. He doesn't even take a step back when the lizard leaps out of the crevasse and lands a pace or two ahead of Valdim. He just plants his staff against a tree root and regards the hissing beast with polite interest. Valdim lets the corpse fall.

I should be running, I know that. Using the confrontation to increase my slackening lead. But I can't look away. Call it whimsy, call it macabre interest, but I want to know how this plays out. My hand drifts to the medallion at my throat. There's something pleasing about the thought of Valdim ending in the beast's belly.

I don't have long to wait. The lizard cranes its head low, hisses anew, and springs. It's a blur to me, a rush of teeth and claws as inevitable as the death they bring. Not so for Valdim. He sidesteps the beast's charge. His sword slides free of its scabbard and hacks down, the killing edge slicing so deep that it all but splits head from shoulders. The lizard screeches and stumbles, momentum sending its dying body into a tangled-limbed tumble that stops a pace short of Quezan. Tail and claws thrash wildly at thin air, the motion so wild that Quezan takes a careful step back. Valdim mutters something that I don't catch. Then he thrusts the point of his sword down. The thrashing stops.

As Valdim dips to clean his bloody sword on a tuft of grass, I do what I should have done ages ago: I scramble back from the precipice, and follow the trail upwards as fast as I dare.

* * *

The trail comes to a halt almost without warning, emptying out into a vast, leafy clearing. Directly ahead, a colossal stone ziggurat reaches skyward, the obelisks on its wide, flat summit silhouetted against the brilliant blue sky. Vines and twisted bushes cling tight to gaps weathered deep into the rock by centuries of wind and rain. I know how they feel. I'm clutching tight to the hope that this won't all be in vain. I've come so far. To fail on the steps of the very temple I've been seeking...?

For a change, I've a fairly good idea how far behind me Valdim is. The screams have chased me on for the last half hour – them and the deep, angry calls that echo through the winds, summoning other Dricheans to the hunt. At least, that's what they're supposed to be. Judging by Valdim's laughter, they're more calls to the slaughter.

I wouldn't mind – what are the Dricheans to me, after all? – but he's got the whole hillside alive with spears. I've spent more time hiding beneath illusion than not; pressing breathless against a tree trunk while Dricheans tracking parties thunder past, praying their hunting lizards don't sniff me out. Already, I'm well beyond what I reckoned were my limits, and it's costing me. By the feel of it I'm burning from within, flesh searing as beneath a brand. But I can't stop now. Valdim won't get Da's prize. He won't.

But all the determination in the world can't alter the facts. There's a deal of open ground 'tween me and the ziggurat stairway, and a long climb to the summit. It's only going to get worse the longer I wait.

I let my grip on my inheritance slide. The sweet relief of the fading fire is almost enough to make up for the unshakeable and irrational feeling of nakedness. Not that it matters, open ground and direct sunlight don't play well with my gift. I'd be tiring myself out for nothing.

Hoping that the flanks of the ziggurat are as empty of Dricheans as they appear, I break from the cover of the treeline and run for the stairway.

The steps are as worn as the rest of the ziggurat, but their treads are deep. Doesn't stop my knees from aching before a score of steps have passed away behind me. I press on, climbing on all fours so that my arms take some of the strain.

Fifty steps on, twice that to go, and I feel like I've been climbing forever. I sink against the stairway, the exertions of night and day come to claim their toll all at once.

'There she is!' bellows a familiar voice. 'I'll slice you to ribbons for this, my girl!'

I peer down the ziggurat's slope. Valdim's racing towards the stairway, sword in hand.

Quezan follows at a steadier pace, unconcerned as always.

Valdim's threat is all the reason I need to redouble my efforts.

The weather shifts as I reach the summit. There's no warning. Blue skies turn to thunderous greys, and the rain hammers down. The fluxsome weather of the Archipelago at work once again, no doubt.

One hand scrabbles on suddenly slick stone but the other keeps its purchase. I haul myself off the stairway, knees cracking against stone. As far as I can see through the rain, the ziggurat's top is almost completely flat, spoilt only where blocks have succumbed to the elements, and where a slender statue of dark stone rises from a pool at the very centre.

I've seen that statue before. A hundred times in my da's stories. A woman with a leopard's face, arms raised in salute of a sun now hidden by clouds.

I'm here. I'm finally here.

Which is why it's so unfair that I'm not alone.

Three Dricheans stand between me and the statue. Two are plainly warriors, their sky-blue robes supplemented by segmented armour plates that gleam dully in the rain-haunted twilight. The third, standing between them, is old bordering on ancient. He leans heavily on a crooked staff, his back even now bent like a tree in a gale. The way I feel, he's the only one of the three I could take in a fight.

I clamber to my feet, shifting my weight for the inevitable fight to come. A fight I'm sure to lose. I keep my knife in an underhand grip, the blade concealed flat against my palm. They have the numbers. Surprise is my only advantage now. I recall my escape from the *Moonrunner* the previous night. The rain's almost as thick now as then. If I can hold onto my gift long enough…

'We know why you have come.' The old man's words are thickly accented, almost guttural, but they cut through the hiss of the rain. 'But only the worthy may claim what you seek.'

What is he babbling about? At least his guards haven't moved. Waiting for me? Polite of them.

'My da' wanted me to have your treasure, old man. That makes me worthy enough, I reckon.'

A quizzical grey eyebrow twitches. 'And what does your companion say?'

My heart sinks. I want to believe this is a variation on the old 'look behind you' ploy, but I know it's not even before Valdim's voice cuts through the rain.

'Well, well, well. Bonnie Cochran. Fancy meeting you here.'

I twist away from his grasping hand, but exhaustion slows my reactions. An iron grip closes around my wrist, drawing me in. I slash at him with my free hand, but Valdim twists the knife away, sending it clattering across stone.

'Let me go!'

I'm done. I know I'm done, so what harm a little defiance? The Dricheans are watching us with dispassionate interest. Damn them anyway.

He transfers his grip to my throat. 'Should've come to me honest, Bonnie. Now you'll end up like old Jac. Squeamish fool that he was.'

His remorseless black stare meets mine. I know I'm staring into death. There's a sharp tug at my throat, and then Valdim shoves me towards the ziggurat stairway. Bronzed arms enfold me, holding me still.

'Keep her fast,' Valdim barks at Quezan. 'Some things should be savoured.'

I don't know exactly what he means by that, but the possibilities range from brutal to horrific and back. I almost don't care. The sight of the medallion dangling lazily from Valdim's fingers breaks my heart.

'That's my da's!'

Valdim shakes his head. 'Did him no good though, did it?' His gaze shifts behind me. 'Can't you do anything about this storm?'

'I've done all I can,' rumbles Quezan.

'Fine Warden you are.' Valdim shakes his head in mock amusement, then spins on his heel to face the Dricheans, medallion held high. 'Let me past, old man.'

Two spear hafts strike stone.

'You are not worthy.' The old man's tone brooks no argument. It's almost serene.

Valdim takes a step forward. 'These are the Southern Isles. Strength *is* the only worthiness. Stand aside.'

The guards start forward. Valdim's already moving. Twisting aside from a disembowelling spear thrust, he locks both hands around the shaft, drawing the Drichean towards him. There's a sharp *crunch* as the guard's knee shatters beneath Valdim's heel. The Drichean screams, toppling into Valdim's waiting arms. A sharp twist, and the guard's neck snaps like a rotten bough.

The second guard roars a guttural cry, half challenge, half loss. Valdim's sword blurs free of its scabbard. The

Drichean collapses, blood spraying from a gashed throat. Valdim advances on the old man, the blade's bloody point outstretched, medallion still hanging carelessly from his other hand.

'I think I'm worthy, don't you?'

The old man's expression doesn't waver. He reminds me of Quezan, one step removed from everything that goes on around him. 'No.'

Valdim's low chuckle ripples through the hissing rain. The old man's unarmed, he's no match for Valdim. He's scarcely an obstacle, but Valdim's going to kill him anyway. Just like he killed my da'.

The fire accompanying that thought burns through my weariness. I feel it gutter almost as soon as it flares, but for one glorious moment I'm more angry than tired. Anger begets strength – strength enough to twist loose and bury an elbow in Quezan's belly. I know it's a weak blow even as it lands, but the Warden gasps and doubles over all the same.

Looks like something finally surprised him.

Boots skidding on the wet stone, I run at Valdim. He turns too late. My shoulder slams into his chest. A heartbeat later I'm lying on my back in a puddle, breath struck from me. Stupid. Stupid. I'd have had more luck charging an oak tree.

Valdim grins. 'You should know better, Bonnie.'

He's right, I should. Just like I should know better than to expect the old man to help me as I just tried to help him. What does he care if a couple of outsiders kill one another? More of a surprise is that Quezan's back to his role of impassive witness. Likely he thinks Valdim doesn't need the help. Hard to fault that opinion, all told.

Valdim's sword thrusts down. I roll aside, calling on my gift as I do so. Fire boils up in my blood. For once, I welcome it. If I can feel pain, I'm still alive.

Steel *chinks* against stone. Valdim spins on his heel, searching for my telltale outline in the rain. 'Hiding, Bonnie? Just like dear old Jac.'

I don't answer. He's trying to taunt me into saying something – to give away my position. Instead, I circle clear. The fire's burning deep. I've used my gift too much of late. I can feel it slipping. I need a weapon.

My eyes settle on a guard's spear, inches from his lifeless hand. Feet away from me.

'Old Jac, now he got himself an attack of conscience too. We both know how it worked out for him, don't we?'

I grab the spear. It's heavy. Reassuring. Valdim turns. He's staring straight at me, but he's no idea I'm there.

This one's for you, Da'.

The moment I lunge is the same moment in which the fire in my flesh gets the better of me. I stumble, my charge faltering along with my illusion. The thrust meant for Valdim's heart glances off a rib, ripping open his coat and gashing a bloody wound across his chest. He roars in pain, his fist clubbing at my head. It's not a deliberate blow, more the instinctive flailing of a wounded animal, but it's enough to knock me sprawling, head and shoulders over the ziggurat's edge.

Valdim lurches towards me. I've hurt him, at least.

There's something in that. 'Give Jac a greeting for me, will you?'

I will my body to move, but it's had enough. I've put it through too much.

I glare defiantly up. 'Hells take you.'

A sharp smile. 'You first.' He sweeps the sword skyward. Even now, bleeding and weary, Valdim's a showman, performing for his tiny audience.

Lightning arcs from angry skies, striking the upraised point of Valdim's blade. He doesn't even have time to scream. There's a sharp *crack-hiss*, then two odours wash over me – one almost sweet, the other the unmistakable stench of burnt flesh. Thunder cracks the skies. Valdim's body teeters above me. Then the wind catches it, and the seared mass topples past me, coat blazing like a torch.

I've just enough presence of mind – and just barely enough coordination left – to snatch the medallion from Valdim's lifeless fingers. Then he's gone into the stormy darkness of the ziggurat's slopes.

Good riddance.

I haul myself upright on quivering limbs, half-expecting another bolt of lightning to send me to join Valdim. Quezan and the old man watch me in silence, their expressions well-matched in inscrutability. Then Quezan taps his staff twice on stone, and the storm clears. Sullen clouds roll away as if they'd never been, and golden sunshine caresses the ziggurat.

I stare at Quezan, mouth agape, thoughts crashing together like waves. The good fortune of Valdim's death now seems like anything but. If the storm was Quezan's doing, then so was the lightning that slew Valdim, but why?

Quezan meets my gaze, then stares at the old man and tilts his head.

The old man nods. 'She is worthy.'

He bows to Quezan, then shuffles away across the summit, walking stick tapping on stone. He begins his descent of the stairway without a backward glance, not at me, not at Quezan – not even at the bodies of his guards.

I turn the medallion over in my hands as Quezan approaches. 'Why?'

'You are worthy. He was not.' He shrugs, as if nothing could be more straightforward. 'I'm glad to have brought you here.'

'What do you…?' I fall silent as my thoughts catch up with my mouth. Last night. The storm that gave me cover to reach the cabin, and again to escape the *Moonrunner*. 'You knew? All along, you knew?'

Quezan offers a knowing smile. The first such smile I've seen on his craggy features. 'Of course. Your father would be proud.' He gestures at the statue. 'It is time to claim your prize, Miss Cochran.'

Bruised, sopping wet and with fire still raging beneath my skin, I stagger towards the statue. After a moment's searching, I find an indentation on the plinth. It's a perfect match for the medallion. As I press the disc home, there's a rumble of distant machinery. Statue and plinth sink into the floor. A gout of dust and a dry, musty smell herald a new plinth rising in its place. A stone casket sits silent and proud where the statue once stood. I have the strangest sense that it's waiting.

This is it. My da's prize. My inheritance, and my revenge. I reach out. The casket's lid creaks back.

So many years, I'd wondered what I'd find. Gems, gold. Treasures of the Southern Ocean. But the casket contains none of these, merely a weathered fragment of parchment – a scrap of doggerel scrawled hastily by an undisciplined hand.

I sink back onto my haunches, disappointment coursing through me. 'That's it?' I glare at Quezan. 'I suppose you're going to tell me my "worthiness" is the true prize.'

He gives a tiny shake of the head. 'No. Worthiness is not absolute. It is a vessel that must be refilled by thought and deed. Look again.'

I stifle a scowl, and do as instructed. This time, I see there are shapes beneath the scrawl. Shapes that almost look like… islands? Disappointment fades. 'It's a map?'

'Part of one,' he agrees. 'The most sought after map in all the Southern Isles. One that points the way to the Crystal Pool.'

'That's a myth…' I protest, but the response is rote, automatic. Of course the pool's not a myth – or not just a myth, leastways. My gift proves that. The Heritor bloodlines didn't come from nowhere. Quezan's right. If this map truly shows the way to the Crystal Pool, it's worth more than gold, more than a hold's worth of gemstones.

Assuming, that is, I can find it.

Excitement builds. Possibilities. I pour over the fragment, but it's no use. There's nothing on there that I recognise. I need the missing portions to make sense of it. 'So where's the rest? The map, I mean.'

'Prove yourself worthy once again, and I'll lead you there.'

Just like that, I realise I've no idea what it was I did to prove myself worthy. Was it standing up for myself? For that wizened old Drichean? For provoking a brawl, I couldn't win? Knowing Quezan, it could be something else entirely.

'Again, what do you mean again? How?'

I look up, but Quezan's gone, as if he was never there. Can't say I'm surprised. Not with everything else. What was it he said? About worthiness being refilled by thought and deed? Cryptic nonsense typical of a Warden, but it's all I have.

But first, what I need – what I *really* need – is a ship. And the *Moonrunner* needs a captain. I doubt the survivors'll feel much loyalty to Valdim, not now he's gone.

Looks like I'm not going home. Not yet.

UNCERTAIN FATES

BY
DAVID A. MCINTEE

Gurbin rested his hands on the rail next to the ship's wheel, as he gazed at the horizon. He could almost feel his hands merge with the wood, as if he were part of the ship, and could feel its speed. Speed that wasn't enough. Gurbin was lean and dark, with athletic limbs, and many pockets sewn into his silken garb, all secured with a fastidious bow of ribbon. His britches reached only to his knees, and his sleeves to his elbows, and his shins and feet were as bare as his forearms and hands. Long knives were strapped to all four limbs.

'Nervous, Gurbin?' a voice asked from behind him. It was a tall and wiry man, his leathery skin tattooed with serpentine designs. He wore a jerkin and trews of sharkskin leather, and was festooned with vials, gourds, and an albatross feather in his broad hat. Unlike Gurbin's velvet scalp, his ponytail bunched somewhere under the back of the hat, helping to keep it wedged on in the breeze.

'Cautious, Tomms. Tense perhaps,' Gurbin admitted, 'but I wouldn't say nervous.' He pointed to a smudge on the azure horizon off to larboard. 'Someone's following us.'

Tomms smiled thinly, but didn't even look at the distant ship. 'They've been following us for two nights.'

'Do we know who they are?'

'Who do you think?' Tomms snorted. Gurbin couldn't blame him; they had fled from Tlanti's men on that last moonless night less than a week ago. She wasn't the sort of person to let such a trespass go without a response, and she had never been known for lazy responses.

'I hope those soldiers you hired are good at what they do, then.'

'I only engage the best for my expeditions, Gurbin. You of all people should know that.' Tomms beckoned Captain Pavius over. The ship's captain was stocky, with a thick beard and fists like hams. 'How close are we to the island?'

Pavius grunted. 'The lookout should see it within an hour or two at most. Then we only need a couple of hours to make landfall.'

Gurbin looked in the direction of the speck on the horizon. 'Do we have a few more hours?'

Pavius glanced skyward. 'Depends if they have a sea or sky witch with them. If not, then absolutely, no problem. If they do, though… All bets are off.'

Tomms nodded. 'You'd know, Gurbin; does Tlanti's crew have a Weather Warden among them?'

Gurbin shrugged. 'Not unless she's hired one for the chase. Which would depend on how much time she had to prepare,' he said.

Tomms nodded thoughtfully. 'The equation's simple enough, I suppose: would the time a trustworthy Warden could gain them in the pursuit outweigh the time taken to find and recruit such a person before getting underway?'

'It's not impossible, but probably unlikely.'

'You mean it's unlikely, but not impossible,' Tomms corrected him.

'Do you want to take the chance that she didn't?' Captain Pavius asked. 'She must have known it would be in her interest.'

Tomms flashed Gurbin a grin. 'Let's not, and say we did.' He turned, his eyes searching for the cabin boy, and called out to the lad. 'Boy, go below and tell my retinue to arm.' The boy nodded hurriedly, and dashed through a door in the sterncastle. Gurbin turned his own attention back to the ship on the horizon. Something about the persistence of the speck left him in no doubt that it was the *Aerys*. She was too far away to make out her ensign, but he knew what he would see if it was in range: the spider with the skull-shaped body.

* * *

Wrapped in sufficient layers of leather jerkin, teal woollen doublet, and brightly coloured cloak as proof against the stiff breeze, Tlanti stepped onto the deck of the *Aerys*. Above her fluttered the arachnid flag of the ship's master, Captain Wolfram.

The Captain himself was standing by the helmsman, looking ahead at the horizon through a spyglass. He was a tall man with a forked and greying beard, and wore black trews and boots and a deep red leather doublet.

There were bracers on his forearms, a blue sash around his waist, and a weather-worn leather hat with a large ostrich feather curled around the band was jammed on his head. He half-turned with a faint smile at the sound of her boots on the planks, and handed her the spyglass without being asked. Tlanti peered through it, focussing on the black smudge far ahead of the Aerys's bowsprit. She was delighted and excited to see that Tomms's ship seemed larger now than it had the last time she had looked through the glass. 'When will we be within boarding range?'

'Less than an hour; the wind has been freshening at our backs all morning. We'll be in ballista range a little earlier.'

'Still plenty of time for them to notice us and take action.'

He shook his head. 'They'll have noticed us sometime ago, unless Pavius is drunk under a table, but they won't take action.'

'If they have a wind or wave witch aboard—'

'They don't. If they did, they'd have put more distance between us. They could turn and fight, but I doubt they will. The advantage is all with us. Cowards.'

Tlanti lowered the spyglass. 'It's not cowardice: They won't turn and fight, because Gurbin isn't stupid, and neither is Tomms.' She grinned. 'Luckily neither are we, so that's all to the good.'

* * *

'Land ho!' the lookout called. Tomms and Gurbin rushed across the deck to the fo'c'sle, half-a-dozen soldiers in mail-shirts and kettle helmets following. Another mail-shirted man was already at the rail, returning his breakfast to the waves. Tomms doubted it tasted any worse coming back up than it had going down.

To the naked eye, the island didn't look that impressive – a greenish cut across a few inches of horizon, as if the sea and sky were splitting apart. Through a spyglass, it was a little more solid-looking, with thick tree cover. Tomms knew that islands didn't generally have much of an inland; they were crescents or rings of land, with a lagoon in the centre, which made him wonder how this one could require the length of march that had been hinted at to him by various sources.

Tomms turned, to check on the position of the *Aerys*. She was a little further to one side, but also a little smaller, to his eye. He hoped he wasn't imagining that. 'They're dropping behind,' he exclaimed. 'We're pulling away—'

'No,' Captain Pavius corrected him, 'They're cutting across, stealing the wind from our sails.' He hurled the wheel frantically around. 'We'll get slower and they'll get faster. Throw in that we'll have to slow and tack as we approach the island to avoid beaching ourselves, and they'll have us for sure.'

'So be it,' Tomms snapped, 'I believe the traditional phrase is prepare to repel boarders!'

'That depends on whether they decide to simply sink us,' the Captain growled back.

Tomms shook his head. 'They won't. There are things they want.'

'Which,' Gurbin added, 'they'll find a lot harder to get from the sea bed than from a ship that still floats.'

'I hope nobody's too keen on making it that hard for them,' Pavius said, 'but we don't want to make it any easier either.'

Tomms regarded him icily. 'I shouldn't make jokes like that if I were you, Captain; it's not good for the crew's morale, and it's not healthy for anyone's confidence in your loyalty.'

* * *

Taking the wind from their sails? That's a great trick!' Tlanti was clearly happy, but Captain Wolfram shrugged it off. She was almost bouncing up and down on the balls of her feet, making things rattle slightly in all the purses and pockets.

'It's a pretty standard thing, and has its uses.' He leaned to call down to some of the men on the main deck. 'Wind the ballistae, and prepare firepots!' Then he turned to his bosun, and said, 'Send archers into the rigging, with bodkin and broadhead.'

'I'm looking forward to boarding them,' Tlanti said. 'Your men can bring us close enough alongside?'

'If you can jump across five or six feet you won't even have to wait for the gangways to be put across.'

Tlanti laughed. 'I don't have to.' She stroked the polished claw that hung from a thong around her neck, and her eyelids drooped for a moment. Two saurian creatures stepped out from the hatchway behind her.

Stalkers. The saurians were larger than a man, with long, powerful tails, and viciously curved six-inch talons on their hind legs. Their forelegs were shorter, but carried sharp claws too, and their long, narrow skulls were filled with sharp fangs. Lithe, agile, and as fast as the wind, their feathers had been removed so that their toughened skins could be painted with a fearsome pattern in her colours – in this case, red, black and purple.

The sailors shuffled aside nervously, except for Captain Wolfram and the man on the wheel, who paled, but stayed at his post.

Tlanti didn't mind them being afraid of her pets. It kept them focused, but also meant they were confident in a fight against anyone else. Who wouldn't be, with such beasts on their side?

* * *

'They're coming!' the Sergeant-at-arms shouted. He and his men all hefted their swords and axes, looking uncertain as to what use they would be right now. The *Aerys* was coming in directly now, her prow aimed amidships. Tomms eyed the white water under her bowsprit, looking to see if there was a ram there. It looked very much as if there was.

'They're going to ram us,' he warned.

'Three-quarter starboard!' Pavius was already shouting. The deck tilted, the sail and ropes creaked loudly, and there was a strange thunking sound that Tomms couldn't place – until one of his men-at-arms tumbled with a scream, a bodkin-headed arrow nailing his thigh to the deck.

More arrows were falling, burying their tips first in the planking, and then, as the ship tilted, in some of the soldiers and sailors. One of Pavius's archers fell from the crow's nest, splashing into the churning waters between the ships. Tomms and Gurbin dropped, pressing themselves against the wooden rail that encircled the deck, while the men-at-arms ducked into what cover they could find. Mail was no protection against the needle-tipped shafts dropping from on high.

Something shattered somewhere, and burning oil sprayed across the sterncastle. Sailors dashed around, trying to both stay out of the way of falling arrows, and find buckets of water to throw on the fire. A second crack came from above, and fire began to lick at the mainsail. The helmsman screamed, trying to brush off splashes of burning oil that had dripped onto his shoulder. As he thrashed against the wheel, the ship banked more, turning further to starboard.

'Ware the wheel!' Gurbin yelled to Tomms.

'We're getting further out of their way,' Tomms shouted back. 'Sounds good to me!'

Pavius shoved past them. 'Too far! There's a reef before we make shore.' The Captain threw the helmsman to the deck, where he rolled around in an attempt to put out the flames. Pavius then grabbed the wheel, hauling it back to port as the shoreline and beach grew steadily larger beyond him.

* * *

'Right where we want them,' Captain Wolfram said to Tlanti. 'Between us and the reef.'

'Try to take the ship intact. What it's carrying is worth a lot.'

'Those are the magic words. Boarding party ready!' At the Captain's word, small knots of pirates, armed to the teeth with swords, axes and daggers, began to gather at the rail, while the archers in the *Aerys's* rigging loosed another volley.

* * *

There was a rumble of thuds and a few more screams, and then the rain of arrows ceased. Moments later, a shadow fell across Gurbin, as the *Aerys* came alongside, her ram missing the hull by a few feet. Gurbin glanced at the rails on the other ship, which was almost close enough to touch. Pirates were slamming boards down, braced against deck and rail, forming short ramps.

'They're going to hit! Brace for collision!' Everyone momentarily froze, grabbing on to the nearest post or piece of the ship's structure, ready to steady themselves.

That was when the first pirate boots thudded onto the deck. Half a dozen of them had hurled themselves from the makeshift ramps against their ship's rail, crossing the last couple of feet between the ships in the blink of an eye.

There was a solid thud beside Gurbin, and he turned, expecting to see another pirate. A stalker's maw hissed right into his face, carrying a stench of putrid meat. It straightened back up with a flick of its tail as a second stalker landed on the back of Tomms's bosun, nailing him to the deck with its claws. The bosun's scream barely started before it was cut off.

Gurbin held up a hand, instinctively trying to ward off the stalker, even though he knew the beast would probably just take the hand first, as an offering, but it flicked itself around before he'd finished the thought, and darted at a sailor who was using a boathook as a spear against one of the pirates.

A terrible judder ran the length of the ship with a tremendous grinding sound as the two hulls scraped along each other. At least with the arrows no longer a threat he could stand up and fight. Gurbin drew two long knives from the sheaths on his forearms, and waded into the fray, looking for Tomms, who had almost vanished in the melee of clashing bodies.

A sailor with a face covered in other people's blood lurched in front of him with an axe raised. Gurbin ducked under it, cutting the sinews of his arm with one knife, and stabbing him in the armpit with another. He didn't even know which crew the man had belonged to. He saw Tomms standing between two mailed soldiers as they held off three pirates, and made his way towards them. Tomms met his eye, and Gurbin found himself stabbing one pirate in the kidney and cutting his throat before the man even knew he was there.

The other two pirates backed off, but one of the stalkers darted in between them. It took a sword-thrust in the thigh, but merely screeched and took the arm off the soldier who had wounded it. He fell, screaming, as Tomms raised his hands in a warding gesture. The stalker stepped backwards, shaking its head as if to clear something from its nose or eyes. The remaining soldier kept the two pirates busy, while Gurbin grabbed Tomms's arm and pulled him aside.

'We need to get off the ship,' he told Tomms.

'I'm so glad you're here to think of these things,' Tomms grumbled. 'We need a few minutes to get a boat lowered. That means we need to win this fight.'

* * *

'Half a point to starboard,' Wolfram called out to his helmsman. 'Push her onto the reef!'

'What about us?' Tlanti asked. Running the ship aground wasn't part of her plan.

'The *Aerys* is built to allow estuary and river operations. Shallower draught, so their keel will catch on the reef before ours ever would.' As he spoke, the more musclebound of his sailors were hurling grappling hooks at Tomms's ship, and hauling on the ropes to hold the two ships together.

'Time to take charge,' Tlanti said, and marched down to the main deck. There was a terrible screeching and groaning; a sound of creaking muscle from some leviathan awakening in the depths of hell. Tomms's ship heeled to one side, spilling men painfully to the deck. 'We've struck land,' she heard someone call out on the other ship.

Incanting with the polished claw amulet in hand, she stepped through a gap in the rail just as the enemy ship rolled back, its deck sliding far enough that she could step down onto its deck. Two of the pirates, armed with sword and shield, fell into step behind her, and the stalkers scrambled to meet her. One was limping, and she could feel her blood boil. The desire for revenge was strong, but she knew it wasn't worth thinking about, for the simple reason that the stalkers didn't leave woundings unpunished. Whoever or whatever didn't kill them had always made the biggest and last mistake of their lives.

'Find Gurbin,' she said, 'and I want him alive. Tomms you can kill.'

'Aye,' the pirates responded, and the stalkers nodded their heads as if also agreeing.

* * *

Gurbin dispatched another pirate with a grimace, and then saw the new arrivals through a gap in the melee: the stalkers having regrouped around a short and curvy, raven-haired figure in layers of garb that he knew would deflect cuts from a knife, as well as keeping her belongings and impedimenta concealed from other spellcasters.

He hesitated for a moment, his eyes flicking from Tlanti to Tomms. Tomms caught his glance and frowned, his head turning in Tlanti's direction. She saw him at the same moment, snarling, then her eyes fell upon Gurbin, and she jabbed a finger towards him. Immediately, the pirates with her, and one stalker, started towards him, barging people out of the way. Gurbin stepped back involuntarily, and felt his hip bump against the ship's rail.

'Run,' Tomms shouted. 'Get off the ship now!'

Off the ship? Gurbin thought. His muscles took over, responding immediately. He vaulted over the rail, gathering his thoughts, bringing in his self, and feeling the power start to buzz in his veins, just enough to know he was making the right effort. His soles hit the water, but no further, and he bent his knees and rolled on the surface of the water, which squished beneath him like a good mattress. 'Meet me at the treeline,' Tomms shouted down to him. Gurbin glanced up, grimaced, and nodded once.

Then he bolted, knowing he only had a few seconds. This type of skill was the most difficult, and a layer under his skin felt as if he was burning already. He had perhaps a few more seconds of running across the surface of the sea before he would have to let go of the density of his body, and he would plunge into the water and have to swim.

The damp sand seemed so very far away.

Gurbin gulped in air and pushed his muscles harder – more difficult than ever, now that he heard the splashes of several bodies crashing into the water. Curses and the sounds of thrashing and coughing erupted around him, as pirates dropped from the rail into water that was considerably more than ankle-deep to them.

* * *

The stalkers darted for the stern, following their fleeing prey, and Tlanti could feel their desires, and the tensing of their legs, ready to spring and run. She hissed a quick incantation, turning her hand, and they slid to a halt, claws gouging the deck. She knew the stalkers were strong enough swimmers, but if they had tried to run across the water and found themselves immersed, it would have thrown their focus.

Tomms was still aboard, and she pointed the pirates and stalkers to him. 'Kill that bastard!' They hurried to obey, but Tomms's soldiers closed ranks around him, their longswords, and even a couple of pole-axes, forcing them to keep their distance. As the fight raged, Tlanti could see Tomms and another soldier slashing at ropes holding a boat over the water.

She sent one of the stalkers round to flank the soldiers, but it was too late, the boat fell.

* * *

The ship's longboat hit the water with a flat smack on the opposite side from where the *Aerys* was butted up against her. Tomms and his remaining four soldiers put away the knives with which they had cut the ropes holding the boat aboard, and scrambled over the side. Despite their mail and helmets, the soldiers climbed down with as much agility as did Tomms.

The *Aerys* was still pushing against the ship, which in turn was forcing a swell of water out, threatening to push the longboat aside before they could clamber in. A wave splashed Tomms's boots, and he braced his feet against the side of the hull, to kick himself far enough out to land painfully in the rocking longboat.

Thankfully, he saw, all four soldiers were safely aboard, and – more importantly – still fully armed, if somewhat unsteady on their feet. He bent down and lifted the ends of two oars, shoving one into the hands of the nearest soldier. 'Let's get going. Quickly! Gurbin will be ashore by now.'

The soldier settled himself, and he and Tomms used the oars to push the boat away from the ship, while the other soldiers picked up the remaining oars and used them to point the boat at the beach.

* * *

Tlanti swore profusely, and gestured her forces back to the *Aerys*. The stalkers ran back, leaping over the rails and back onto the pirate vessel. Most of the pirates remained, since they had a prize of their own now.

'Captain Wolfram!' Tlanti called. 'A longboat heading for shore; I want it sunk.'

The Captain shook his head. 'It'll take too long for us to detach from their ship.' He looked up at his archers in the masts. 'A longboat is making for shore! A silver piece for whoever kills anyone aboard it!' He turned to his bosun. 'Prepare a longboat, and volunteers for a shore party.' He stepped below decks for a moment, and was strapping on a belt with two long, curved swords when he returned. 'You don't mind if I stretch my legs ashore, do you?'

Tlanti grinned. 'Not at all. An extra sword is always a good thing, and two are awesome.' She took the spyglass again and surveyed the beach.

* * *

Gurbin swung himself around the trunk of a tree, out of sight of anyone on either ship, and dropped to his knees. He gasped for breath, every inch of his skin burning as painfully as his lungs. His veins felt as if they were on fire, his limbs trembled, and he knew he'd been lucky to make it to shore.

When he had recovered a bit, he looked around, to see a boat making for the beach. He knew it was Tomms, as his soldiers' armour glinted in the sun. Sighing, he pushed off from the tree, and began to make his way towards the part of the beach where Tomms would land.

* * *

Tomms welcomed Gurbin's arrival with a wide grin. 'There you are! Safe and sound?'

'More or less.'

'Good,' Tomms said with a nod. 'Then there's no time to lose. The days are long in these waters, but we have far to travel.' With that, he tossed Gurbin an arming sword, and hefted a hand-and-a-half bastard sword himself. The soldiers drew their weapons also, and Tomms turned and led them into the undergrowth that was already thickening around them as they left the beach.

* * *

On the far side of a low headland, another longboat juddered to a halt, her simple plank seats barely tilting from the horizontal. Captain Wolfram was first out, and everyone took a hand in dragging the boat up the beach so that it wouldn't float away at high tide. 'And what's your plan, lass?'

Tlanti looked expectantly into the rolling breakers. 'The same one I contracted you for: I'll take a warband and separate Gurbin from Tomms. Permanently.'

'Snatch and dispatch? Before they find what they're looking for?'

'That would make things easier.' She watched as the pair of stalkers emerged from the water's edge. Unlike dogs, they didn't bother to shake themselves dry, but were already looking around alertly. Tlanti nodded to two of the pirates. 'Go and find their boat, and either steal it or smash it.' They ran off immediately, in the direction of where Tomms must have landed his boat.

The rest of them – Tlanti, Wolfram, a grizzled, shaven-headed pirate called Klegg, and a muscular pirate called Ironhand, walked towards the edge of the trees inland. There was a faint scent of dust in the air amidst the sea spray, but also an aftertaste of rot and mildew. They paused after passing the first couple of trees, and Captain Wolfram raised an eyebrow. 'What are we looking for, by the way?'

'Well...' Tlanti hesitated, then admitted, 'I'm not quite sure.'

'That doesn't make finding it any easier. And don't give me any of that "we'll know it when we see it" bilge, either.'

'I wasn't going to, because we won't. We'll know it after *they* see it.'

'What?'

'Gurbin, at least, knows what he's looking for. That's why we can't just rely on finding it first. Since Gurbin is still with Tomms and not us, we need them to find it first.'

'So we don't even know if they're looking for a lead to the Crystal Pool?'

'Of course we know *that*!' Tlanti snapped tightly. 'Everybody on these seas is looking for that. But I don't know what form this clue takes. A map? A witness? A relic? A spell? Only Tomms and Gurbin know.'

Wolfram nodded. 'Aye, he keeps his cards close, that Tomms. Always has. Fair enough, though, it has kept him alive longer than...'

'He deserves?'

'I was going to say longer than most people could expect in this line of work, but you're not wrong either, that much is true.'

* * *

'This looks promising,' Tomms said, as the sun, hidden above the murky green tree canopy, was approaching its zenith. He used his bastard sword to chop down some of the undergrowth ahead of him, then sheathed it and pulled the torn vines and branches aside. Two of the soldiers ripped the vegetation away further, revealing a wall of ancient Cyclopean stones; a sand-coloured edge to the world, almost as tall as the mainmast of a ship.

'Promising?' Gurbin echoed. 'Frustrating, you mean.' He looked along the wall in both directions. 'Whoever built this doesn't seem to have put any gates in it.'

'Then we climb, I suppose,' Tomms said. He gave the order to his soldiers, who spread out a few yards apart, divesting themselves of helmets, mail and weapons, which they placed carefully on the ground. Then two began ascending the closest trees to the wall which they could find. A third soldier approached the wall itself, and reached out to seek hand and footholds with which to haul herself up. After a moment, one of the tree-climbers shouted down, 'There's no branch close enough to jump over!'

'Same here,' the other one shouted.

The soldier on the wall shuffled herself sideways, back and forth, before descending. 'There are no handholds within reach of the top,' she said.

Tomms sighed. 'And this is the only route...'

'To where?' Gurbin asked.

'To where we're going.' Tomms turned to his soldiers. 'Did you see the top from those branches?' One of them nodded. 'How thick is this wall, do you think?'

'As thick as the average man is tall, I reckon.'

Tomms smiled, and patted Gurbin on the back. 'If you were quick enough...'

'You can't be serious.'

'I've seen you do it before.'

'When a wall is much thinner, and I knew there was open space on the other side. The top edge might be only the width of a man's height at the top but there's no way to tell what's on the other side at ground level. A wall that high has to be thicker at the base than at the top.'

Tomms nodded thoughtfully, then looked up. A colourful bird jinked between the branches, and swooped overhead. Tomms reached into a leather tube on his belt, and drew out a couple of feathers. He spread them into a fan between finger and thumb, and began to incant. The trees were a green carpet below, and the wall thick but crumbling. It seemed to encircle the entire centre of the island, and beyond, at the heart of it, was a lush, verdant dome. Cracked steps and ledges were visible through tiny gaps in the trees, pale spots like pinpoint stars in the night sky.

The winds shifted, and he slid down the edge of a thermal, skimming the thicker air in search of the inner wall. It was buttressed at regular intervals with towers long fallen to ruin, their staircases and guardrooms spilled like a serpent's entrails. At one point a section of the wall's facing had crumbled, and sand, stones and coral were splayed out from it. Then he rose once more, and rode the thermal waft heavenwards.

* * *

Tomms opened his eyes. 'The wall is about three times as thick at the base. Here, it's layers of stone filled with rock and sand, maybe coral. No spaces.' He walked over to the wall, Gurbin following in spite of himself, and patted the rough, ancient surface. 'I trust that doesn't pose any problems?'

'It shouldn't,' Gurbin admitted.

'Good; I'd have regretted bringing you into our partnership otherwise.'

'A partnership that won't last, unless there's a gate somewhere in this wall. Otherwise you're going to be stuck on this side.'

'There's a tower with a staircase against the inner wall a few hundred yards in that direction. We all head that way, you climb the stairs and lower a rope for us to climb.'

Gurbin nodded slowly. 'You'd better be right.' Something rustled in the undergrowth, and everyone turned at the sound of a strange huffing. Gurbin's eyes widened; it was one of Tlanti's stalkers. The soldiers, already re-armoured, drew their weapons, while Gurbin froze. If he ran, would they chase him? Or could he outrun them?

'Go,' Tomms snapped. 'We'll hold them off.' His eyes narrowed as he turned to face the stalker, ready to fight. Gurbin found himself running. His blood heated, and he risked a glance in the stalker's direction, half-expecting to see it following. It flicked itself around its own tail, and shot off into the forest, but it was too late for Gurbin to stop, and he hit the wall full-tilt.

Everything went dark, but he could feel himself still moving. There were strange tensions in his torso and limbs that came and went; buzzing sensations and tickles, and the sense of swimming through treacle. Then his blood sang, light burst into his eyes, and he stumbled to a halt amidst a small clearing. He turned slowly, catching his breath, and looked at the crumbling wall behind him. As he oriented himself, he started through the trees in the direction of the tower that Tomms had mentioned.

* * *

The stalker ran, homing in on its mistress's enemy. If it was surprised to find itself facing Tomms again, it didn't show it. He approached it carefully, his soldiers keeping their distance this time. The stalker watched him, attuned to the stink of his fear, and the allure of warm blood in his veins. It was tensed to spring, because it was always tensed to spring, yet it didn't.

Tomms stopped a few yards away, making a noise under his breath, not unlike the way in which its mistress did. It could almost taste his blood already, but somehow couldn't move. He motioned with his hand, and the armoured soldiers began to shuffle to either side of it. 'Oh, my little friend,' Tomms said, 'you surely don't want to leave us so soon?' He risked a couple of steps closer, his hand trembling. 'There are a lot of lizards in the world. Tlanti can always find another to replace you.'

* * *

Tlanti had stopped walking, and was focused entirely on incantation. 'Trouble?' Wolfram asked.

'One of the stalkers has found Tomms, but he's... He's trying to steal it.'

'Steal it?' Ironhand echoed. 'How—'

'He's a Beast Warden, as I am. He doesn't have the talismans that I do, but he has skill. Klegg, take your bow, and run five hundred yards that way.' She pointed. 'Take a shot at Tomms. Doesn't matter if you kill him or not, so long as he notices.'

* * *

Gurbin had gathered up some long vines, looped into thick, natural ropes, to add to the rope he had brought through the wall with him. Now he pulled himself up one of the broken tower staircases, and clambered on to the wide walkway at the top of the wall.

As he tied the ends of his ropes to suitable pieces of stone, he found himself wondering who had built this wall. Serpent Men? Dricheans? The Empire of the Blue? Who and why, he wondered; was this a treasure trove or a garrison, uncounted years ago? Either way, there was no sign of any men having visited it recently.

The thought led him to another, more pressing, question: Why wasn't Tomms already below, haranguing him to help them ascend? After all, Tomms and his soldiers hadn't needed to collect ropes on the way, so they should have got there first.

* * *

Tomms was within five paces of the stalker, and it hadn't run or attacked. It remained under his power, which suggested that Tlanti was still pretty far away. That would be her loss shortly, he decided. She had a much better connection with her stalkers than he ever would, so he had no illusions about being able to control it in the long term.

All he had to do was keep it where it was until it could be killed, and his soldiers were just about close enough to do it now—

With a thunk, an arrow appeared out of nowhere, and buried itself in a tree bole next to his thigh. Startled, he looked round for the archer, his concentration broken for an instant. What felt like a solid log slammed into his ribs, pitching him to the ground. The stalker's tail had done him a favour, as a second arrow shot past his head, the fletching cutting a nick in his ear.

He rolled flat, and saw the stalker disappear into the foliage, while the soldiers took cover, both from the archer and in case the stalker came in again to attack.

No more arrows came, and nor did the stalker return. A furious Tomms gathered the soldiers around him, and set off for their rendezvous with Gurbin and his ropes.

* * *

The stalker came into view a couple of minutes before a panting Klegg. Tlanti nodded her thanks to him, while applying a healing ointment from a pouch to a couple of small cuts on the stalker's sides. 'Tomms?' she asked.

'I'm not sure,' Klegg admitted. 'First shot was a near-miss, the second might have got him. He went down, but the lizard there had hit him at the same time. I couldn't tell.'

'Doesn't really matter, I suppose. The important thing is we didn't lose my friend here, who heard all about the plan to have Gurbin lower ropes from the wall to carry them over it.'

'Well,' said Wolfram, 'assuming that Tomms and/or his soldiers are continuing with that plan, how do we get through that wall? They're not going to leave the ropes for us to follow.'

'We swim.'

'Swim?'

'There's an underground channel that Tomms doesn't know about.'

'How do you know about it, if we're only following them without knowing where they're going?'

'The stalkers always know where to find fresh water. They can scent the path of the channel. We'll follow them to an entrance.'

'And if the channel is filled to the ceiling, with no air?'

Tlanti didn't answer.

* * *

Captain Wolfram was the first to surface, after the longest minute of their lives. He guided Tlanti upwards as Ironhand and Klegg surfaced behind them, and she saw that they were in a low, dark cave. Only a hint of phosphorescent lichen cast any light, but it was enough to see that slope of shingle led from the pool up into a narrow, winding passage. One of the stalkers was there, its eyes glinting in the dark.

The roof was too low for them to stand up straight, so they crouched as Klegg and Ironhand manoeuvred the sealed barrel onto the shingle. Wolfram prised it open, and they availed themselves of dry clothes and weapons, the darkness preserving their modesty.

The tunnels and crevices were narrow, with painful and sometimes jagged obstructions, but somehow the four of them, plus the two stalkers, squeezed and crawled past all of them, until a glimmer of sunlight cut through the gloom and stabbed painfully at their vision. Blinking like newborns, they emerged into a narrow, overgrown gulley, which widened into a game trail of some kind. They straightened their backs with clicks and groans, and looked back to see that the gulley had emerged from under the foundations of a thick section of the wall. The line of a broken stone staircase showed that they were inside rather than outside the wall.

'We'll have to work our way around to where they're crossing,' Tlanti said. 'Hiking time!'

* * *

The clearing was more than just a clearing. A mere few yards away, the far side of it wasn't bounded by vegetation, but simply dropped away into endless depths. The edge curved away to either side, forming the rim of a gigantic pit at least a thousand yards across. Streams and pools here and there had caused channels to crumble away, while in the centre of the pit, a towering column of rock, a couple of hundred yards across, stood only slightly higher than the level of the clearing.

Below, in the uncountable depths, there was only mist and darkness. 'Is this what they were looking for?' Ironhand asked.

'It's definitely what that wall was meant to protect,' Captain Wolfram said. 'Still, this is probably a good place to camp down if need be. We don't have to worry about anything coming up that cliff, so fewer approaches to watch out for, but less of a bottleneck than the tunnel.'

'I completely agree,' Tlanti said with a nod. 'Now we just need to find that elusive little pixie who can walk through walls.'

* * *

They hadn't been moving long, when a soft, gravelly clinking came through the undergrowth, and Tlanti held up a hand. They froze in place, as best they could; the sound couldn't be mistaken for anything other than a group of men with weapons, marching in unison. 'Tomms's men?' Wolfram whispered.

Tlanti shrugged as one of the stalkers crept forward and out of sight. Then she shook her head. 'Men in bronze armour, with round shields.'

'Dricheans,' Klegg muttered. The nearer stalker turned its head towards him, its beady gaze emotionless. Tlanti nodded, without looking round, and the stalker echoed the gesture. It bared a quarter inch of teeth, a grim and cruel parody of Tlanti's smile. Klegg shivered.

* * *

Gurbin didn't envy the mail-clad soldiers in this heat and humidity, but they showed no sign of being any more weary then Tomms or himself. 'Where are we going?' he asked.

'Nowhere in particular,' Tomms admitted blandly. 'We're marking time until a rendezvous I—' Without warning, several men leapt out of the undergrowth, two blocking Tomms's and Gurbin's path, others knocking the unprepared soldiers to the ground and kicking their weapons aside. A handful of other men stepped out and arrayed themselves in a loose perimeter around the group.

The newcomers all wore bronze breastplates, helmets and greaves, and carried round shields and a mixture of short swords and javelins. 'Dricheans,' Gurbin exclaimed. One of them, whose helmet sported a bristling red plume, stepped forward. 'Why have you infiltrated our patrol area?' he demanded, his accent peculiar and archaic.

Tomms smiled broadly. 'Isn't it obvious? To meet you.'

'You are no Dricheans; you can have no legitimate business with us.'

'That's sort of true,' Tomms admitted. 'But I do have business with your orders.'

'Our orders?' the leader echoed, in spite of himself.

'The last sealed orders you – or more likely your ancestors – received before you ended up stuck behind this wall.'

'Our orders do not concern you. Apart from the sections about killing our enemies.'

'Who am I talking to?'

The Drichean with the tallest plume on his helmet looked Tomms up and down, as if debating with himself whether he owed a foreign civilian any introduction. 'You may address me as Lochagos.'

'Lochagos,' Tomms said slowly, 'we were sent to ascertain that you had followed your orders, and were carrying them out properly. When we report back to our and your superiors—'

'Your soldiers are not Dricheans, and our superiors would never send others to inspect us.' He raised a hand, and said, 'Kill the soldiers, and capture the runner and the Warden! They have questions to answer...'

The two soldiers with the javelins drew back their arms, and threw.

Gurbin didn't see the throws, but heard the rasp of leather and metal as the men moved. The focus came instinctively, as reactions had to, and suddenly the world quietened, branches no longer slapping at him or tugging at his robes. First one metal shaft flew under his field of vision and dug into the ground, then another. He darted left to avoid running into the quivering javelins that had just passed harmlessly through him, and then jinked right. He knew he couldn't keep himself insubstantial for much longer, not while running full-pelt, and he certainly didn't want to stop running while he was in range of the Dricheans' bronze-tipped arrows and javelins.

He had only the slightest moment to register movement out of the corner of his eye, before another Drichean pushed with his javelin instead of throwing it, slamming the wood into Gurbin's face. Everything went black.

* * *

'This is our chance,' Tlanti shouted, rushing forward. The Dricheans were expecting an attack from the flanks even less than Tomms was, and two of them were down and being rent by stalkers before anyone could react to their presence.

Wolfram and Tlanti darted for three Dricheans who were carrying a bundle, tied up in a couple of cloaks. The Dricheans were struggling with the bundle, which was struggling as much against them. Wolfram's paired swords took the forearm off one, and impaled the other's skull. Tlanti punched out with the polished stalker claws in her hands, blinding the last and opening up his throat.

Klegg and Ironhand took on the others, but of Tomms and the last of his soldiers, there was no sign. Swords clashed, and blood sprayed, and after a few moments, there was a sudden silence, broken only by distant rustling, heading away from the fight.

Tlanti knew that would be Tomms, protected by whichever soldiers had survived. She directed one stalker to follow the sound, and called the other. Klegg and Ironhand returned too, and picked up the bundle, which had stopped struggling.

They carried it back to the clearing they had found at the edge of the bottomless moat, and then relaxed a little. 'Gently,' Tlanti snapped, and one of the stalkers stepped closer to the men. They laid the bundle down, and Klegg cut the leather bindings with a dagger. The oilskin flapped open, and Gurbin rolled out, thrashing around for a moment until he realised that he was no longer constrained by the oilcloth.

He pushed himself to his feet, eyes wide, and looked around the camp.

'What have you done?' he demanded.

'What I had to do.'

'You fool!'

'What?!' Tlanti scowled. 'Don't mention it.'

'Bringing me here was a big mistake. Tomms will be coming.'

'I wasn't planning on telling him where you are. Were you?'

'I don't have to. He already knows.' Gurbin looked around, searching for any sign that they understood the seriousness of their situation. He saw none. 'As I said, bringing me here was a mistake. Tomms always knows where I am.'

'How?'

'How do you think?'

'Imagine I don't know, and tell me.'

Gurbin opened his mouth as if he was going to say

something, but then his face froze into a rictus. His eyes looked apologetic to Tlanti, but his lips closed, his teeth gritted.

'He means this was a trap,' Ironhand said suspiciously. 'This witch has betrayed us!'

'Impossible!' Wolfram snapped.

'No one has betrayed you,' Tlanti said.

Klegg nodded. 'Aye, she has the right of it there. This fancy-pants was our enemies' leader to start with. He can't betray us if he was fighting us from the get-go.'

Tlanti led Captain Wolfram a few paces away. 'What do you think?' she asked.

'About how Tomms might always know where Gurbin is?' Tlanti nodded. 'He communes with the beasts, as you do. If there's so much as a louse in the Heritor's robes... Is that enough of a beast?'

'For some Wardens, yes. A louse, every leech or mosquito in any stinking swamp... Something else bothers me, though. I'm sure Gurbin was going to tell us... something. But then he—'

'Thought better of it?' Wolfram shrugged. 'Fear of the lash or blade are as good as iron chains and the stocks for most men.'

'Heritors aren't most men, and I've never seen Gurbin show much fear of anything.'

'Showing fear and feeling it aren't the same thing. I've never known man nor woman that didn't have a fear of something, but I've known plenty that would only show laughter or rage to hide it.'

Tlanti nodded, and walked back to Gurbin and the

others. 'Damn you, Gurbin, how long have we worked together? Do you really think I would just let Tomms kidnap you, or force you into working for him?'

'I didn't think you would, but I hoped I'd be able to convince you to hold off.'

'Why?'

'Because I don't want you to end up in the same situation as I am. And, believe me, neither do you.'

'What is it that Tomms is looking for here?'

Gurbin laughed, shaking his head. 'The Dricheans' orders.'

'Good luck getting them to talk,' Klegg muttered.

Gurbin shook his head. 'Sealed orders. That means actual physical scrolls.'

'Maybe with maps and suchlike?' Wolfram suggested.

Tlanti nodded. 'That would make sense. Where would the Dricheans have kept such documents?'

'In their base of operations. It looks like they occupied the southernmost tower. It's the most intact.'

'Do you have a plan?'

'Of course I have a plan.'

'What is it?'

'Well...' Gurbin hesitated, and at least had the good grace to look uncomfortable.

She shook her head, cutting off any continuation. 'Let me see if I can pluck it out of your head. Your plan is basically to lie to me about having a plan until you actually have a plan.'

'I thought you could only read animal minds.'

'Isn't man an animal?'

'Don't even joke about that. Do you have a better plan?'

'Could we make him think you're dead? Or otherwise unreachable?'

'Not with the Fates. They will always be with me, and he will always know where they are. Which means he will always know where I am. And I'd rather not actually die just to put one over on Tomms.'

'Tomms doesn't own you, Gurbin.'

Gurbin sighed. 'He does. I wish he didn't, but...'

'You could have always taken yourself out of ownership,' Klegg grunted, drawing a thumb across his own throat. 'Every slave at least has that option.'

'Do you think I didn't think of that? Do you really?' Gurbin snorted. 'You have no idea. I have no way out.'

'There's always a way.'

'Unless the Fates block it.'

Wolfram barked a mirthless laugh. 'The Fates? The hell with the Fates.'

'I'm in hell with the Fates,' Gurbin snapped. 'They're what keep me in this hell. Klegg would be right, if I had free will of my own. But I don't.'

Tlanti couldn't believe her ears. 'Since when did you become a believer in the Fates?'

'Since they took me, and burrowed into me, and held me. Since the first day I tried to—' He looked away, taking a breath. 'Since the first day I tried to get out, and found I wasn't in control of my own hands anymore. Since the first day my muscles refused to obey me no matter how hard I tried. Since the first day Tomms put those damn slug-things into me.' He opened his shirt, revealing repulsive puckered scars on his chest. 'Three in there and one in my head.'

Tlanti and the pirates drew back instinctively. 'You mean... actual creatures?'

Gurbin nodded. 'I call them the Fates because... well, because I don't know what they actually are, but they're the opposite of free will.'

'That's how he's stopped you from getting away...?'

'Yes.'

'Can't you... I mean, when you do that thing, where you walk through things. Can't you just... leave them behind? Let them fall out of you?'

'First thing you tried, wasn't it?' Wolfram said quietly. Gurbin only nodded.

'Oh.'

'They're part of me now; they change with me. If I walk through something, they walk through it with me.' He hesitated. 'I'm sorry.' And then he ran, bolting away from the edge, and into the undergrowth. In moments he was gone, with not even the rustling of plants to indicate a direction.

Tlanti yelled obscenities after him, and then clenched her fists. Wolfram stilled his two pirates, before they could get far in pursuit. 'Don't bother. If Tomms does know where he is, Gurbin could lead us straight into a trap.' He shook his head. 'Tomms picked his pets well. He didn't do this without thinking it through.'

'Well, things have changed now,' Tlanti said darkly.

'In what way?' Wolfram asked.

'Now he has me to help.'

'There's something bothering me,' Klegg said slowly. The others looked at him, quizzically. 'I may only be an old salt with more rum than brains in my head, but... Were these things stopping him telling us what Tomms wanted?'

'Yes...'

'Then why didn't they stop him telling us what they are and what he did to you with them?'

'Probably out of Tomms's range for such finesse,' Tlanti grumbled.

Captain Wolfram shrugged. 'Let's go and ask him. After all, we know where he's going now.'

* * *

The Southern tower was indeed still intact, draped with Drichean unit colours, and surrounded by a small camp of tents, and perhaps thirty Dricheans, some very old.

Tomms and Gurbin stepped out into the camp, both now wearing Drichean armour and uniform. Tlanti reflected with amusement that one could hardly see the teeth-marks on their appropriated gear. Two of the Drichean guards flanking them were wearing similarly damaged armour, and she wondered where they had dumped their mail hauberks.

'Oh, Milady Tlanti,' Tomms said smoothly. 'What an unexpected pleasure.'

'You mean an unpleasant turn of events.'

'Yes. So, what is it you want, dare I ask?'

'You know what I want, Tomms. Or should I call you Lochagos?'

'Ah...suffice it to say that that isolated outpost has long been due an inspection by their superiors, and we are only a little delayed. As for what you want...I presume my Heritor.'

'He was never your Heritor.'

'No? Perhaps we should ask him? Or at least give him the chance to decide for himself?' Tomms turned to Gurbin. 'What say you, my friend? Should I turn you over to the lady here, and end our happy and prosperous partnership? Surrender you to the one who has hunted us so... unflinchingly?'

'It's hardly a surrender, and you have no right to turn me over to anyone.'

'That's very true.' Tomms raised a forefinger, as if pointing out an idea. 'Here is my proposal. Gurbin, my friend, why don't you simply walk over to the lady, if that's your preference? No one will stop you or harm you.'

Gurbin only frowned, his mouth a tense, thin line.

'It seems to me that he's happy where he is.'

'Well I'm not. But I suppose we all have our wants and needs... and you have your orders?'

'No one gives me orders, Tlanti, you know that.' He couldn't resist a smile, and drew a rolled-up scroll from a pouch around his waist. 'Though, oddly enough, I do have—'

That was when Gurbin punched him, and all the hells broke loose.

* * *

As Tomms went down, Gurbin snatched the scroll, and Klegg began shooting arrows from the trees, every one finding a thigh; Klegg was too smart to aim for the bronze cuirasses that an arrow would simply bounce off from. Dricheans, real and impostors, swarmed towards the two struggling men, and right into the maws of the two stalkers. Out in the cleared encampment before the tower, they had the space to dash back and forth at full speed, tearing flesh from bone, slamming men to the ground with their powerful tails, and slashing with their claws.

While Tlanti darted in and took the scroll from Gurbin, Wolfram and Ironhand seemed to be having the time of their lives. Ironhand's bastard sword slid into armpits and clove bronze helmets as if they were only walnuts, while Wolfram's pair of curved blades spun like a whirlwind, opening arteries and sending limbs tumbling to the dirt.

Tomms backhanded Gurbin across the jaw, rolling aside to throw him off. 'Bad timing, my friend,' he snarled. 'You've outlived your usefulness.' He scrambled to his feet, beginning to tense and focus.

Gurbin knew what would come next – burning immobility and a slow death from whatever weapon Tomms could first lay his hands on. The things he'd done today, however, had given him an idea. He had run through walls, and weapons, and he had also run through trees and plants. And trees and plants were living creatures of a sort. Just as Tomms was.

Focussing with all his concentration, Gurbin lowered his head and charged at Tomms, charged right into him.

His vision was black and red, and for a moment they were one body. Now he focused still more, on himself, and only himself, pulling free from the guts and sinews of the other man. He felt as if he was trapped in quicksand, and then somehow he felt hands grabbing his, and pulling.

He stumbled, jerked forward by Tlanti's grip on his wrists, and he fell before rolling back up onto his knees. 'Run!' she yelled in his ear, and pushed him.

Behind them, Wolfram, Ironhand, and the two stalkers fell back, still fighting. All were wounded and bleeding, but half the Dricheans were dead or crippled already, and arrows were still punching into them. Then they had enough distance to be able to turn, and run into the twilit undergrowth.

They rested in the cave until their shaking limbs had relaxed, and wounds had been tended. There had been no sign of pursuit. 'Are you all right?' Wolfram had asked Gurbin. The Heritor had simply shrugged.

'He will be,' Tlanti said.

'You sure? Those things, the Fates...'

'I'm sure. Tomms will confirm it for us; he'll be here in a minute.'

'What?' He reached for his swords.

'You won't need those. He's come alone.' She led Wolfram and Gurbin out of the cave, and the short distance to the clearing they had used earlier. True enough, Tomms was waiting there, eyeing the stalkers that circled at the edge of vision. He was grimacing, either in pain or fury, or both.

'What have you done?' he hissed.

'What do you think?' Gurbin said. 'The Fates are part of a person, so I couldn't leave them behind myself. Until I passed through another person. They don't mind who they feed on.'

'But I do,' said Tlanti. 'And when I knew they were living parasites, I knew I could control them as well as you could. Well, maybe not as well, since they're not my speciality, but well enough to bring you here.'

'Well, I'm here.'

'We just thought you'd like to know that you were right; the Dricheans' orders have a nice map to a lovely nearby island with an ancient hall of records. Hopefully it has something about the Crystal Pool in it. You hoped that, didn't you?'

'Yes. And now you're going to kill me, I suppose. I would, if the situation were reversed.'

Tlanti walked right up to him, and tilted her head, looking past him at the cliff edge. She shook her head. 'Actually I'm going to let you walk away.' He frowned, confused. She began to incant, and his expression cleared into one of terrified understanding.

'No! You can't!' And, with that, he turned, and took a step towards the edge. Then another, and another. And he kept walking.

THE SERPENT ENGINE

BY
BEN COUNTER

It was Bresk who had died first.

The trapper had been checking the snares near the expedition's camp, when a venomous insect had found an exposed point on his calf and sunk its stinger into him. The poison spread through him and the infection turned the wound a livid, writhing purple. By the time Thaal led them to within sight of the temple, Bresk could barely walk. When they woke the next morning to make the last leg of the journey marked out on the Heritor's map, Bresk was dead.

Now the eight survivors stood on the threshold of the immense stepped pyramid, bellies rumbling because they had missed out on their trapper's nightly catch. The Heritor Akmon Thaal was consulting his map again, checking the profile of the upper levels against the sketchy emblem on the map.

'So,' said Jorasca Pavine, leaning against the bole of an immense jungle tree. 'That's it.'

'Yep,' said Dolth, her fellow crossbowman. 'Reckon it is.'

It could hardly be anything else. The journey from the isolated cove to the interior of the island had taken the expedition past stunted ruins long devoured by the ravenous jungle, but nothing like the temple. Its upper levels reached above the level of the canopy, festooned with eroded carved heads and decorative pillars covered in vines. Stained sandstone blocks on each corner were suggestive of altars where some primitive beings offered sacrifices up to their forgotten gods.

'So,' said Dolth, 'we goin' in?'

'Suppose so,' said Jorasca.

Thaal was consulting with the expedition's Warden, Cirillian. Where Thaal was an immense, ruddy man packed with brawn, Cirillian was a slender and graceful woman. The expedition's crewmen wondered if she was even human. She did not seem to suffer beneath her blue-green robes, even in the sweltering midday. Cirillian took a long look at the tattered parchment map, and nodded.

'Brothers!' shouted Thaal to the rest of the expedition. 'We have reached our goal! The promised riches lie within yonder temple. We have only to take them. Onward, brethren! Onward!'

'Welp,' said Dolth, spitting out the mouthful of tobacco he had been chewing on. 'Here we go.'

Jorasca followed Dolth and the other expedition members as they passed into the shadow of the yawning doorway at the base of the pyramid, and crossed the threshold at last.

* * *

'You've seen this before?' asked Jorasca.

'Not like this,' said Xavion. The knight was examining the carvings of the antechamber hall as the crewmen worked on opening the huge stone door. In spite of the relentless jungle heat and humidity, Xavion wore his breastplate and vambraces as if it was a test of his faith. 'It's not Drichean. Ran across some of them on my last expedition. Very stern fellows. Got us in quite the pickle. But they didn't build this.'

'Quite the pickle' probably meant a harrowing brush with death. Xavion's habitual understatement was one of the reasons Jorasca liked him – that, and the fact that in spite of his high birth, he thought of the lowly crewmen like Jorasca as an equal. That was more than could be said for Thaal. 'You think we're going to find the treasure Thaal promises?' she asked, knowing that of all the expedition, Xavion was the one most likely to give her an honest answer.

'The map says so,' he said. 'Our Heritor went through hell itself to get hold of it, or so I understand.'

'And that's good enough for you?'

Xavion looked away from the wall carvings at Jorasca. A greying moustache clung to his narrowed and battered face, lined and sunken even beyond the years of the oldest man in the expedition. 'It must have been good enough for you, my dear, because you are still here.'

Jorasca was about to reply that she could hardly turn back, that the *Fathom's Faith* they had arrived on would not be heading back until she was laden with treasure no matter how much Jorasca wanted to leave. But Xavion was right. She had joined because there were riches promised, riches that Jorasca's lowly birth and poverty of station had decreed she should never see. She was as hungry for it as the rest of them. She couldn't deny it.

'Stand back!' ordered Akmon Thaal. The crewmen working on the stone door scattered at the sound of his voice. The man had a natural authority that not one of them had questioned out loud since the *Fathom's Faith* had set sail. 'We will starve in here before you rabbit-hearted salts make headway. It is will alone that will see us through!'

Thaal crouched down by the lower edge of the circular stone door. He dug his fingers under its lower edge. Muscles bunched and corded beneath his sleeveless leather jerkin and the ruddy flesh of his upper arms bulged. Thaal grunted as his full, divinely-imparted strength shifted the door with a cracking of stone. The door rolled away from the circular opening with a tremendous grinding of rock on rock.

Thaal stood, panting, looking through the doorway into the magnificent chamber beyond. Enormous pillars held up a soaringly high roof, each one surrounded by a spiralling stone snake. Red and deep blue tiles picked out an intricate geometric pattern on the floor around an immense statue of a lizard-like god, a waterfall pouring from its open mouth into a plunge pool below.

For the first time, Jorasca could appreciate the grandeur of the temple. Its exterior was half-ruined and chewed up by the roots and vines of the jungle. Inside, it was as glorious as the day it was built.

She felt movement through the souls of her feet. Something shifted massively beneath the stone floor of the antechamber. Another movement caught her eye, and she glanced at the wall beside her to see dozens of tiny holes opening up in the dense carvings.

'Run!' shouted Jorasca.

With a battery of high shrieks, a fusillade of darts spat from the walls and streaked across the antechamber. Envin, the swordsman, caught one in the eye and screamed as he stumbled to the floor. Jorasca sprinted for the opening, the rest of the expedition behind her. Darts pinged and clanged off Xavion's armour. Thaal was first through into the chamber as the eyes of the carved snakes slid open and streams of darts sprayed out.

Jorasca ran through the doorway and felt the tiles depress beneath her feet, setting off more mechanisms designed to turn the statue room into a killing floor. The lizard god's eyes were open now and a projectile the size of a javelin thumped out, sailing across the chamber and spearing the wounded Envin through the thigh. Envin stumbled to one knee and a hail of darts snicked into his face and neck before he fell, dead before he hit the floor.

'By the earth, by the sea, bring now our salvation!' Cirillian's black wood staff was in her hand, whirled above her head as a salt wind blew through the chamber. The water pouring from the statue's mouth changed its course as if a sudden blast of wind had caught it. The water flowed out of the pool and around the expedition's crew in a rippling, translucent ribbon, meeting over their heads to form a dome of water. Darts punched into the water, lost their speed and plinked to the tiles on the other side. A thin drizzle of salt water fell as Cirillian held the shield of water overhead and the crewmen crouched within its protective boundary.

Jorasca had drawn her crossbow reflexively, even though there was nothing to shoot. The fusillade of darts kept coming, streaming from hundreds of hidden openings into the shield of water. Then, finally, after what seemed like an hour, they were spent and the last of them clattered to the floor.

Cirillian let her staff drop and the shield of water fell to the floor, soaking the cowering crew.

'Well done, Warden,' said Thaal.

'Not quite as well as I would have hoped,' replied Cirillian. She drew back the hood of her robe and brushed a strand of pale blonde hair from her cut-glass face. 'My profoundest of apologies, Lord Thaal. I had hoped to assist you further, but fate does not seem to will it thus.'

A single dart protruded from the ivory skin of the Wave Warden's neck. For the first time since the expedition had set sail, Cirillian showed discomfort. She shivered and beads of sweat stood out on her face. Veins of red were running across the skin of her throat and face. The dart's venom took hold and her knees buckled. Xavion ran to her and caught her as she fell. Her mouth opened to say something more, but no sound came out.

Akmon Thaal stared down at Cirillian's corpse for a long moment.

'This shows our path is true,' he said, clenching a fist.

'There is something at the heart of this temple worth defending with such trapwork. Something it is our destiny to take. We press on.'

* * *

The next chamber was full of corpses, long dried out and mummified. They hung from the walls in their dozens. Each was impaled by a steel spike and had its eyes and mouth sewn up.

No one spoke as the crew made their way deeper into the temple. They did not flinch as they picked their way between huge statues of spiders inlaid with bloodstone and jade. Their feet crunched through bones so old they turned to dust. They negotiated a half-collapsed stairway, squeezing between the sandstone blocks in near-total darkness before they could light their torches again.

'We're below ground level,' said Dolth as he struck his flint. 'Either they dug down to build this, or the ground rose up.'

'Who are "they"?' asked Jorasca. She rubbed her elbows where the rough passageway had scraped at her.

'Don't know,' replied Dolth. 'Dead now.'

His torch caught and its light licked against the walls of the smaller square chamber the crew found themselves in. The walls were covered in carved skulls, stylised and square-edged but impossible to mistake. Along the lower edge, reddish humanoid figures raised spindly hands to the ranks of skulls above them.

'Hardly a good omen,' said Xavion. Already the knight's

armour, normally kept polished, was scraped and dented. 'More to the point, there doesn't seem to be a way out.'

'Do we turn back?' said Jorasca.

'Absolutely not,' said Akmon Thaal, rounding on her. 'This is but another test. The savages who raised this temple did it so its secrets would be revealed only to those of cunning and strength. What was miraculous to those primitives is simple for civilised folk like you and I. There is some simple trick to this room. Find it.'

The rest of the crew searched up and down the carved walls, trying to find some hidden mechanism. Jorasca ran a hand along the smooth stones of the floor. There wasn't enough space between them to get a fingernail. 'This would be a good place to trap us,' she said.

'Then best get out,' said Dolth. He was examining the ceiling with his torch held high. The skulls continued across the ceiling, staring down with flecks of blood-red pottery in their eye sockets.

'This is a door,' said Thaal. He had one hand against the wall while the other pointed out the faint indentation around a section of it. 'There is no handle or lock. There must be a way to open it.'

'Found it,' said Felhangar, one of the crew's swordsmen. He had found one of the skulls was separate from the rest of the wall and swung forward to reveal a niche with a wooden lever set into the stone. 'Cunning buggers these. Didn't hold us long, though. What you think they're hiding past there?'

'Can't be much more to this pile,' said Arnulf. Like Felhangar he was a mercenary with little in the way of subtlety or skills, just a competence with a blade and a willingness to do whatever he was paid for. He and Felhangar were both crew from the *Fathom's Faith*, salty and crude but reliable in their own way. 'Got to be the treasure. Got to be.'

'Come 'ere, you little sod,' said Felhangar, hauling on the lever. With a crunch of mortar falling away, the lever snapped down.

The door did not open.

'Well,' said Arnulf, 'that's just…'

His voice was cut off as the floor lurched away beneath their feet. Jorasca just saw Arnulf's expression change, from frustration to shock, before her own stomach turned and she was falling. The neat blocks of the floor gave way and tumbled downwards, followed by the crew, into a dense and fibrous darkness beneath.

Jorasca had a sense of the blackness turning end over end before a tremendous force smacked into her and white spots flared in front of her eyes.

* * *

It was some old instinct, ground into her like the dirt beneath her fingernails, that forced her not to just lie there and wait for the flaring pain to die away. It was a tough and unloving life that had brought her to the gangplank of the *Fathom's Faith*. She had scrabbled in the gutter to feed her ailing parents, and when they were gone she did the same to pay protection to the underworld lords of the docks and put bread on her plate. She had scrapped and fought, and taken beatings. She had owed money to bad men. She had fled from shadows in the night, and one day heard the offer of work on the *Fathom's Faith* and bid a bitter farewell to the streets that had forged her.

None of it had taught her to lie down and hope the danger went away. It told her now to get her crossbow in her hands and jump to her feet, and damn the crimson pain flashing in the back of her head. She slid a bolt into the crossbow and cranked it back as she tried to get her bearings.

The faint flicker from a discarded torch on the ground did not banish the darkness of her surroundings. It just outlined them in a fragile firelight. Jorasca had landed in a natural cavern underneath the trapped room. It must have been deep in the foundations of the pyramidal temple. The floor was filthy and the stench of rot and effluent assaulted her. She stumbled, unsteady, as she fought to find her balance in the slime underfoot.

Xavion had landed hard a short distance away. He groaned and tried to roll onto his front, weighed down by his armour. Jorasca hurried to him and hauled on his arm to get him sitting up. His armour was dented where he had landed shoulder-first.

'This place has quite the sense of humour,' said Xavion. He could not hide his wince as he tried to get to his feet. The armour over one knee was twisted and buckled. The leg inside it could not be in good shape.

'Dolth!' called Jorasca. 'Felhangar? Arnulf?'

'Bloody kraken's balls,' spat Felhangar as he emerged

from a heap of fallen masonry. He still had the lever in his hand. 'Where are we?'

''Tis nowhere good,' said Dolth, who had landed relatively unhurt. He picked something up that was lying at his feet and wiped the worst of the grime off it. It was a human skull, brown with age except for the bright white teeth.

'Find a way out,' said Akmon Thaal, who was untouched even by the grime. 'They would not build this place without one.'

'Unless no one's supposed to leave,' said Dolth.

Thaal rounded on Dolth. 'It is such weakness of thought that holds men back,' said the Heritor. 'Small minds make for small attainment. Without me, you would still be rotting in that port city praying for the misery to end! With me, you have a chance at greatness. It is our will that determines our fate. It is your fate to never understand that.'

'We can't all be born great,' replied Dolth.

Thaal's face darkened. 'You dare,' he said. 'All I have, I earned!'

'All you have,' replied Dolth, his voice unchanging, 'you got born with. Your great-great-whatever drunk from the Crystal Pool and now here you are. 'Tis luck, no more. A different roll of the dice and you'd be as low-born as any of us.'

'Your body will pay the bill your tongue has run up,' snarled Thaal.

'Don't care,' said Dolth. He dropped the skull on the filthy floor. 'Take my head if you want. We're all going to die down here.'

Jorasca felt her body tensing, as it always did when she smelled a situation turning bad. She had heard Thaal had keelhauled a stowaway before the *Fathom's Faith* had arrived at her home port, and she had no doubt he would kill Dolth if his anger was stoked enough. Maybe the Heritor wouldn't stop with just Dolth. Jorasca realised how little she knew about Akmon Thaal, the anger that smouldered constantly inside him, the lengths he would go to in his pursuit of riches and greatness.

The growl came from the darkest depths of the cavern, and they all heard it. Low and grinding, like stone against stone. The faint light glittered against something winding through the shadows, stalking between the chunks of fallen masonry.

The shape resolved itself into the outline of an immense reptilian form. It was easily the height of a man, though it walked with its head low, balanced by a long, whipping tail. Its back legs were muscular and taloned and its forelimbs withered almost to nothing. Its head was a horror, with a massive undershot jaw crammed with teeth. It seemed to grin as its mouth opened, and something flopped from its maw, caught on the daggers of its teeth.

It was an arm. A human arm. Arnulf's arm.

Three more jumped from the darkness, arrowing in at the crewmates from all directions. One of them made a hideous sound, half-screech and half-hiss, and leapt at Jorasca. Its taloned foot caught her on the shoulder and knocked her flat on her back again.

She felt the points of its claws piercing the leather of her armour. Its massive jaws snapped down at her face and she forced her head to one side. The stink of its breath was appalling, like a heap of spoiled and flyblown meat. She could see its eye now, with the black slit of its iris bisecting a sickly yellow orb.

Its jaws snapped at her again. Its whole weight was on her and she couldn't draw breath. Jorasca forced her arm out from under it and groped down in the slimy filth on the floor. Her hand closed on the stock of her crossbow. The creature reared back, ready to clamp its jaws down on her head, and she jammed the crossbow between its teeth and up against the roof of its mouth.

She pulled the trigger and the weapon kicked in her hand. The bolt was driven up through its mouth and the base of its skull. Whatever it pierced, it was something the creature could not do without. It thrashed uncoordinated for a moment before rolling off her to scrabble uselessly in the dirt.

Jorasca ignored the red points of pain in her shoulder as she jumped back to her feet. She saw Xavion swinging his broadsword two-handed at a creature that leapt at him. The blade connected with the meat of its thigh and carved off one of its hind legs in a tremendous upwelling of blood. The creature screamed and crashed to the ground where it thrashed its remaining limbs as the blood pulsed out of it. Xavion's reverse stroke buried the length of the blade in the side of another creature's skull.

Xavion struggled to wrench the blade free as another creature stalked at him. A bolt from Dolth's crossbow pinged against the wall as the other crew were falling back, towards the unseen far edge of the cavern. Akmon

Thaal, at the edge of Jorasca's vision, was wrestling one of the reptilian beasts to the ground and wrenching its head around so its spine gave way.

Jorasca ran for Xavion, loading another bolt. Xavion kicked the dead reptile free of his blade and Jorasca fired at the one approaching the knight. The bolt caught it in the chest, just above one of its atrophied forelimbs, but it didn't seem to register any pain. The reptile leaped at Xavion as the knight tried to bring his blade round to bear.

But the sword was too long. The reptile closed too quickly. Before Xavion could slash or stab, the creature's jaws closed around his sword arm and shoulder. Jorasca could hear the metal buckling and puncturing as the enormous jaws' muscles clamped down.

Jorasca dropped her bow and drew the thin-bladed dagger she kept in her belt. She ran to Xavion and stabbed the creature in the eye. It did not let go of its grip and she grabbed its jaws, trying to force them open.

'Go,' gasped Xavion.

Two more reptiles were approaching. One of them had a muzzle covered in blood, presumably from devouring Arnulf. Jorasca was sure it was grinning at her.

'Go, child,' said Xavion again.

Jorasca grabbed her crossbow, and ran.

She looked back, once. Xavion was trying to fend off the blood-muzzled reptile. Pinned down by the weight of the dead creature still clamped to him, he could only jab feebly at the creature. Jorasca turned away as the reptile darted inside his guard, its jaws yawning open, ready to bite down on the knight's unprotected head.

Jorasca plunged into the noisome darkness as she heard Xavion crying out. She forced herself to keep running as his cries became quieter. Finally, the knight's screaming stopped, and there was only a seething silence around her.

* * *

They halted at a wall of infernal heat, pulsing from beyond a half-fallen wall covered in carved figures. It was an image of despair and abandonment, for the portions showing the heavens had collapsed long ago and the carvings' prayers were offered up at nothing.

Akmon Thaal had halted, confident the huge lizard beasts were too content with devouring the dead to pursue. He leaned against the wall and consulted the map again as Dolth and Felhangar reached him, panting with exertion and the sudden heat.

Jorasca's lungs burned. She suddenly felt pain flaring all over her from her close encounter with the lizard, as if the pain had been left behind when she fled and was now catching up with her. She took in a scalding breath and the heat was like a weight pressing down on her.

'We go on,' said Thaal, his face dully lit by the ruddy glow coming through the doorway beside him. 'We are nearly there.'

'How do you know?' said Jorasca.

She hadn't willed the words to come out. They had emerged of their own accord. Another, angrier woman inside her had decided to speak her mind.

Thaal turned to her and held the map up in front of her face. 'Everything that was written has come to pass,' he said. 'As I always knew. As you should have accepted.'

Jorasca had glimpsed the map from a distance, but this was the first time she had got a proper look at it. It depicted the island the *Fathom's Faith* had reached, with an oversized diagram of the pyramidal temple. The way through was stylised, bearing little actual relation to the path the crew had taken, but the symbols of a hail of arrows and a fanged maw suggested the perils they had already encountered. Beyond that was a sea of flame inked in red, and beneath it, a circle with the emblem of a gleaming gemstone. The map was covered in annotations in a language Jorasca couldn't read. In one corner was stamped an emblem of two dragons intertwined.

'The mark of the Athenaeum Noctis,' said the Heritor, indicating the emblem. 'The greatest seat of learning in the world. It was from their libraries that I acquired this map, at greater cost than you can imagine. And every line has been proven true. Is that enough for you?'

The braver woman inside Jorasca had retreated, leaving her only with the immense presence of the Heritor Akmon Thaal bearing down on her. 'What is the treasure?' she said, forcing the words out.

'Something beyond mere wealth,' replied Thaal. 'The map tells of a treasure of knowledge that will unlock true greatness for whoever grasps it. Something of such immense import it was locked away in this temple and protected by all the dangers we have survived, so the jealous god of the builders would never have to share it with a mortal. But I am not mortal, and I will take it.'

'How to find the Crystal Pool,' said Dolth. He spoke, as ever, without inflection, as if he was observing a bug on the ground.

Akmon Thaal shot Dolth a dark look and folded the map back up. 'As I said, we are nearly there. Stay here if you will. The guardian beasts will have your scent again soon enough. I shall press on.' He stepped through the doorway and into the heat beyond.

'You stayin'?' asked Felhangar.

'Depends on whether what's past here is worse than what's behind us,' replied Dolth.

'I can't imagine anything worse,' said Jorasca.

'Yeah, well, I got a good imagination,' said Felhangar. He had a habit of snarling every other sentence, revealing black and broken teeth. Perhaps, Jorasca thought, it was how he smiled. 'But there ain't nothing back there I can buy me own ship with, so I'm going with him.'

'Nought for me back there either,' said Dolth. 'Too few left to sail the *Faith* even if we did get back to shore.'

And that was the decision made for Jorasca, because as much as she feared what lay beyond, she wasn't going back through the temple alone.

She followed the crew through the doorway, and saw what they were up against next.

An immense natural cavern lay in front of her, almost entirely filled with a sluggish, glowing river of orange-red molten rock. Some volcanic system below broke through here and the lifeblood of the earth poured up through a great upwelling at one side of the chamber, to vanish in a churning lavafall at the far side. Thaal stood on the shore of volcanic sand, looking up at a building little larger than a townhouse perched improbably on four slender pillars rising from the lava. A bridge of stone lengths, like a grand staircase torn from a palace, led from the shore up to the chamber. The segments of the staircase hung from chains attached to the distant stone ceiling, and each part swayed in the buffeting of superheated air.

'Well, that's just bloody brilliant,' said Jorasca.

'What did you expect?' said Dolth, to which Jorasca had no answer.

Akmon Thaal took the first step onto the stairway. His clothing flapped around in the scalding wind pulsing up from the molten rock.

The ground beneath Jorasca's feet shuddered. The edge of the molten river encroached on the shore as the river's flow seemed to speed up suddenly and the whole cavern shook. Fragments of rock pattered down.

'Bugger this,' said Felhangar, looking down at the shore being rapidly eroded by the molten flow. He ran at the stairway and jumped, landing just behind the Heritor on the first section of stone steps.

A huge chunk of masonry fell from high above and thudded into the lava. The slow wave of its ripple approached the shore and Jorasca realised it would obliterate the thin spit of sand. She followed Felhangar and jumped, hitting the stairway. Her feet slipped from beneath her and she splayed out her arms and legs, clinging onto the narrow stone.

'Dolth!' she yelled.

Dolth hadn't been fast enough. He never had been the lightest on his feet. Now the lava between him and the first steps on the staircase was too wide to jump.

He didn't cry out or beg for help. That wouldn't have helped anyone. He just looked up at Jorasca as the air between them shimmered and distorted with the heat. The way back was cut off, too, leaving Dolth standing on a shrinking island of black sand.

The hot air roared in her ears. She couldn't tell if Dolth made any sound as the heat set light to him. His clothes burst into flame and he thrashed around, tumbling over and into the lava. In an instant he was gone, vanished beneath the surface. The last Jorasca saw of Dolth was his boots as the molten rock closed over them.

Akmon Thaal hadn't even noticed Dolth dying. He carried on ahead without glancing back, picking his way up the swaying staircase towards the treasure chamber. Because that was what it had to be – the heart of the temple, the final stop on the journey laid out by the map. That stone chamber, perched high above the lava river, contained the treasure this temple had been built to keep hidden.

The chamber shuddered again. Fat bubbles of lava welled up and burst, spraying the staircase with embers. Jorasca felt their points of heat pricking at her skin as she clambered up behind Felhangar, who was making better progress than she was.

One of the chains holding up the stairway snapped. Jorasca saw the length of it plunging past her into the lava. Her length of stair suddenly swung to the side, and she clamped her arms and legs around it as it tipped sideways and threatened to pitch her into the river.

Felhangar cried out, a curse strangled in his throat.

Jorasca saw Felhangar tumbling past her, arms and legs flailing as if he had fallen into water and was kicking for the surface. His body was spun and buffeted by the rush of the hot air, and then he plunged into the molten rock and was gone.

Up ahead, the Heritor was struggling to hold on as well. He was almost at the doorway to the treasure chamber and was forcing his way towards the threshold step by step. Of all of them, of course the Heritor would make it. Not because he was stronger and faster, with the blood of his blessed ancestors running through him. It was simply because he was who he was. He was fated to get there. He was the Heritor Akmon Thaal. The rest of them were just there to die and illustrate Thaal's strength. History would not remember their names. It would not remember they existed at all.

The section of stairway swung again, wildly. Jorasca felt her legs kicking over nothingness as her grip faltered. The section of stair slammed into one of the pillars holding up the treasure chamber and Jorasca's hands were jolted free of the stone. She hit the pillar hard and threw her arms around it. Her fingers clamped onto the deep carvings and she halted her descent as the rest of the stairs plunged past her and vanished into the lava.

Her crossbow, dislodged by the impact, slipped off her back. She saw it spinning away below her, and then like everything else it was gone. A handful of bolts followed as they spilled out of her quiver.

Jorasca started to climb. The treasure chamber was the only solid ground left in the immense chamber. Hand over hand, feet slipping off the edges of the sculpted detail, she pushed herself towards the doorway of the chamber above her.

Akmon Thaal had one foot on the threshold. For the first time, Jorasca saw him smile.

A section of the ceiling as big as the *Fathom's Faith* detached in a shower of rocky fragments. Thaal was revelling too much in his triumph to notice it as it plunged towards him. In a great fall of darkness, like a plummeting shard of night, the slab of rock sheared past Jorasca. It thudded into the lava with enough force to shudder the pillar she clung to. When she looked up again, Thaal and all that remained of the staircase were gone.

Jorasca kept climbing. There was nothing else to do. If she stayed there, her arms would weaken and she would fall. So she climbed for what seemed like an hour, and eventually her hand found the lower edge of the chamber's doorframe.

Gasping and coughing, Jorasca pulled herself into the chamber and rolled onto her back. The skin of her face and hands, she now realised, were red and scorched from the superheated air. The chamber was strangely cool, as if insulated from the roiling heat beneath it. In the centre of the square, plain room was a stone casket the size of a coffin, covered in finely-rendered sculpted skulls.

There was no sign of Thaal. Somehow, even though Jorasca was certain he had not dived into the chamber at the last moment, it seemed impossible the Heritor could be dead. Confirmation of it seemed to stick in her mind, like a piece of proof against some deeply held faith.

Jorasca got to her feet and walked to the casket. She ran a hand over its lid, which was carved into a map of the island. The temple itself stood in the centre, its structure delving far below the earth. She pushed against the lid and felt it give. With what felt like the last of her strength she shoved against it, and it slid off and landed on the floor with a crack.

The casket was empty. Jorasca touched the floor of the empty cavity and felt nothing there but dust. No hidden compartment. No treasure of such astonishing value it would make her a queen of any land she sailed into. No secret at the end of Thaal's quest. No map to the Crystal Pool.

Jorasca could not help the laugh that forced itself up out her lungs. It didn't stop, even when the first of the venomous snakes squirmed out of the eyeholes of the skulls on the casket's sides. Suddenly, it all made an appalling sort of sense.

Jorasca was still laughing when the snakes swarmed over her feet and legs, and the first of the fangs sunk into her flesh.

* * *

The first thing she saw when her eyes opened again was a man's face. An unfamiliar man, and one who had seen better days. Pinched, malnourished, with a scraggly beard and hair. He had the look of a man who had spent years in a cell, familiar to her from her own brushes with the authorities.

'You're awake,' he said. 'Good, good. They didn't kill you. They're paralytic, these ones, you see. The snakes, I mean. Not lethal. But, well, sometimes if they're too enthusiastic they can…' He smiled weakly. 'Sorry. I'm Devlin.'

Jorasca tried to reply and demand to know where she was, but her body wouldn't obey her mind. She forced her eyes to focus on the looming shapes behind Devlin and they coalesced into a pair of horrific creatures, taller than a man, with humanoid bodies up to the neck. Their long, sinuous necks and heads were those of snakes, with cowls like cobras. Their bodies were covered in intricately patterned scales and they wore complex armour of lacquered and decorated plates held in place by leather harnesses. The narrow slits of their eyes were focused on Jorasca and their forked tongues flickered as if anticipating the feast she might provide.

'What was it that brought your lot here?' said Devlin. 'Was it the Explorer's Guild map? The Diary of Belisarian?'

Jorasca's mind swam. What was this Devlin talking about? Then she realised. He was talking about Akmon Thaal's map.

'Noctis,' she slurred through numb limps. 'Something… Noctis.'

'The Athenaeum Noctis!' Devlin's sunken eyes sparkled. 'That was my finest work! Do you have any idea how difficult that seal is to forge?' He paused, perhaps sensing confusion in her face. 'I was a forger,' he said. 'Before they… before they took me.'

He indicated the hideous snake men behind him. One of them hissed at him annoyedly, and brandished a curved bronze sword.

Jorasca turned her head a little. She was in the temple, but a part of it she did not recognise. Painted beasts and nightmares covered the walls.

'Listen, we have a deal, me and them,' continued Devlin hurriedly. 'I forge maps for them that bring folks like your crew to this temple. And in return they… they don't kill me. They're not so bad, as long as you're useful.'

'Why?' gasped Jorasca.

'Sacrifices,' replied Devlin. His face fell. 'They want sacrifices.'

There had been no treasure, of course. The map, a cunning fake by this Devlin, had brought Akmon Thaal and his crew to a temple designed to kill them. The temple was as fake as the map – not an ancient place where primitive humans worshipped, but a machine for processing naïve treasure-hunters into sacrifices for the snake men's gods.

It made such appalling, complete sense that Jorasca would have burst into laughter again, had she the strength.

'What can you do?' asked Devlin. 'There must be something. What are you good at?' There was an urgency and worry in his face, and Jorasca realised the snake men were ready to make her the final sacrifice if there was no reason to keep her alive.

They wouldn't have much use for a competent crossbowman, she thought. There wasn't much else she could do well.

'I can… I can steal,' she stammered.

Devlin smiled with relief. 'That's great! You can get my maps into places I can't. And get some of those seals and signatures I need! Yes, that's perfect. They'll like that. Now listen, they'll inject you with a venom, something to keep you loyal. They'll give you the antidote if you keep them happy. Don't try to escape, don't refuse them anything, or they'll…'

One of the snake men shoved Devlin aside and hauled Jorasca up off the floor, slinging her over its shoulder. It stank of unwashed animal and heady spices.

'They won't hurt you!' Devlin was saying, though there was no certainty in his voice. 'Do what they want! Bring more of you here! They'll let you live!'

The snake men carried Jorasca through the rooms of the fake temple, past the deathtraps and secret passages that funnelled sacrifices towards their deaths. Jorasca knew that whether she helped these creatures or not, whether Devlin's fakes continued to flow into the hands of the world's Heritors, the snake men would have their sacrifices.

There had been many sacrifices before Akmon Thaal's crew.

And there would be many more to come.

A NICE LITTLE NEST EGG

BY
JONATHAN GREEN

The prow of the *Mermaid* bumped against the surf-lapped beach, the seasoned larwood of the hull grinding against the wet sand. Lagan the shipmaster dropped the sail and brought the boat to rest, as Captain Sinzar leapt from the deck to the gunwale and onto the seashore, his boots sinking into the soft, silvery sand.

Standing tall, hands on hips, he surveyed the beach and the lush green growth of jungle beyond. Taking a deep breath, he savoured the briny scent of the surf, the hot silica smell of the beach itself, and the sharp-sweet loamy aroma of the fetid forest that covered much of the island.

Second to shore was Kaseem of the Earth – who was also now known to the crew as Kaseem the Seasick, or Kaseem the Weak-Stomached, since the rough crossing from the mainland. He landed with a splash amidst the foaming breakers and staggered up the beach, eager to be away from the water, until his unsteady legs gave way under him and he fell to his knees on the sun-warmed sand.

'Thank the Earth Mother, dry land at last!' he almost wailed, kissing the carved stone pendant hanging from a cord around his neck and then prostrating himself and kissing the beach too. 'Thank the goddess a thousand times over!'

Behind him came Haroun, an unkind sneer doing nothing to improve the already unappealing set of his features, although the sword-cut scar bifurcating his ratty features meant that he could never be considered handsome anyway.

'I'll never understand why you ply the straits of the Archipelago,' he laughed. 'The Earth Mother clearly never meant you to leave the land.'

'While it is true that I love the earth more than I love my own mother, goddess rest her soul,' Kaseem replied, 'I also have a duty to preserve the bounty that she offers from deep within her ample crust.'

'And it is there that you and I share a common purpose,' Haroun laughed. 'Isn't that right, my friend?' he said, addressing the hulking, dark-skinned islander lumbering up the beach after him.

The one known to the rest of the crew as Taboo merely grunted.

Rumour had it that he was a native of the Archipelago but Taboo would never tell, not since he had clearly had his tongue cut out long ago and there was no indication that he could read or write either. The myriad tattoos that covered his near-naked body, and that made his already dark skin even darker, didn't give away any clues either. He had joined the crew at the same time as Haroun, and it was the former street-rat who had told the others the big brute's name was Taboo. Whether he had meant that the islander's name was literally Taboo, or was something that should never be spoken aloud, none of them knew. What they did know was that what Taboo brought to the group – along with the tattoos, various bone piercings, and growled speech – was a fierce loyalty.

But despite the strange inked patterns, pierced flesh and animal grunts, Taboo was not the member of the party who left the rest with the greatest sense of unease. That dubious honour went to Manu, the one also known as 'the Shark', with his sharpened teeth and the gill-like cuts on his neck.

Manu had never revealed whether the scarification was self-induced or whether it had been forced upon him as part of some tribal initiation rite. And then there were the rumours of cannibalism, stories which Manu had neither contested nor confirmed.

What Sinzar did know was that he had seen Manu in battle and as well as having made effective use of both his boarding axe and a marlin spike, the pirate wasn't averse to using his teeth either. Sinzar had seen opponents stumble away from him, screaming, clutching at their throats, blood pouring from between their fingers. And none of them had survived.

Three members of the crew were pulling the shallow-keeled boat up to the tideline of seaborne detritus that had collected halfway up the seashell-white sands.

'Scrimshaw!' Sinzar called, summoning a tall, wiry man, with skin the colour and texture of old leather and wild white hair, from where he was helping haul the boat ashore.

The near toothless Scrimshaw was clearly the oldest of them, but it was impossible to tell whether he was fifty-five or seventy-five. Despite the crow's foot wrinkles at the corners of his eyes and straggly white beard, he was also lithe as a lemur and his wiry form belied a strength born of years at sea. In fact, Scrimshaw himself claimed to have been born at sea.

'Yes, Captain!' he said, almost saluting as he joined Sinzar.

'Let's see that map of yours again. Are we sure this is the place?'

The older man pulled the cracked and creased parchment from where it lay, tucked within his smock shirt, and unfolded it carefully.

Sinzar considered the brushstrokes that delineated peaks and trees and coastal coves – absent-mindedly stroking his close-cut beard as he did so – looking up at the highlands visible beyond the dense jungle now and again, in an attempt to compare the map to the landscape of the island.

'You see that crag over there,' Scrimshaw said, pointing north-west, 'that looks like a bird's beak?' He pointed at a spot on the map. 'That's here, and we're here.' He indicated a crescent-shaped bay close to the bottom edge of the map.

'Agreed,' Sinzar said, 'so this is the place.'

It had been no mean feat to find the actual isle they were looking for amidst the magically-shifting island chain. And who knew how long it might remain within the Southern Ocean, before returning to wherever it vanished to for centuries at a time? But that was why it paid to have a Warden among your crew; they had proved themselves able to navigate the Isles time and time again, when even experienced seamen found it nigh on impossible.

'And what does this say again?' Sinzar traced a line of unintelligible, angular marks that looked to him more like marks made in clay with a chisel-tipped stick rather than something recognisable as script.

'It's Drichean,' the old sailor said. 'This mark here means "fortune", and this one means "lies" or "buried". And this series of symbols means "this place". So, in other words, it reads "Treasure buried here."'

'I'll take your word for it,' Sinzar said. 'Now we just need to work out precisely where "here" is.'

He looked back down the beach. 'Vasquez!' he called. 'Are you ready?'

'Yes, Captain Sinzar,' the eager young sailor replied. Lagan the shipmaster's niece, Denara Vasquez, was the youngest, most petite, and most attractive member of his crew, although she chose to dress like a bilge-rat, favouring a waistcoat and pantaloons over flowing skirts. In fact, Sinzar couldn't recall having ever seen her wear a dress. She was also the most determined, keen to prove herself as capable as any of the others, and indeed was more capable than some of them, especially when it came to cooking.

Haroun had made lascivious advances towards her once, but she had soon taught him to mind his manners.

He hadn't been able to walk straight for a week!

Sinzar knew that, but Lagan didn't, otherwise the shipmaster would have thrown Haroun overboard long ago. And although the Captain felt much greater fondness for Lagan and his niece, Haroun brought his own unique skills to the group – skills he had picked up growing up on the streets of Mandrabar. But more importantly he also brought Taboo, with his great strength and indefatigable stamina.

Vasquez tossed the mooring rope into the boat and joined the others up the beach, leaving her uncle to mind his precious *Mermaid* alone.

Sinzar had once sailed with her father, Jando Vasquez, until a kraken did for him, and Sinzar could see him in her, not only in the twinkle in her eyes and the olive Castigon-cast of her skin, but also in her stubbornness and dependability.

The Captain adjusted the buckled belt across his chest that held his cured leather shoulder-guard in place, over his left-hand shoulder, and tested the scabbards of various knives and other blades – from his scimitar to a stiletto throwing-blade – weapons collected from myriad cultures across the world, a collection started when he joined Captain Bautista's crew aboard the *Daggerfysh*.

'Is everyone ready?' he asked, eliciting nods and grunts from the party. 'Kaseem?'

Kaseem, with a handful of dust in his fist, touched it first to his lips, then to his forehead, and back to his lips again, before letting the sand trickle through his fingers back onto the beach. His offering to the island and the

Earth Mother made, he heaved his pack onto his back, adjusting the shoulder straps to balance the bundle that included digging tools and a tent, and, under its weight, staggered up the shifting sands to join the rest of the party. 'Ready.'

'Then we'd best not delay any longer. Let's bag ourselves a nice little nest egg.'

* * *

As soon as Captain Sinzar's party passed from the beach into the forest, they found themselves enveloped by a preternatural green gloom. The susurrus of the surf was replaced by the echoing cries of unseen birds and the hooting of gibbons hidden by the canopy of leaves high above.

The seven sailors, with Sinzar leading and the Shark bringing up the rear, trekked through the sweltering jungle – only Lagan having stayed behind to mind the boat – following what the Captain took to be animal tracks through the undergrowth. They hacked at the overgrown vegetation with machetes and hand-axes, keeping their swords and sabres sheathed, wanting to keep carefully honed and oiled blades clean of sap and vegetable matter, and most importantly sharp, for when those same weapons might be all that stood between them and a swift demise.

Within minutes they were drenched with sweat, their clothes sticking to their skin in the humid atmosphere.

Fat flies droned past, their bulbous bodies like iridescent jewels, their vibrating wings slivers of stained glass. Kaseem batted the insects away, both anxious and irritated in equal measure, while Haroun just sniggered.

'Look at them!' Kaseem snapped, already on the defensive. 'They're massive! You don't want to be stung by one of them or you'll end up with a boil as big as an ostrich egg!'

'You think they're big?' Haroun laughed. 'I've battled hornets as big as eagles, with stings like sabres.'

'As multitudinous as the grains of sand upon the beach are, the swivings I do not give for your past feats of bravado,' he muttered under this breath.

* * *

Sinzar eventually called a halt at a spot where a vast tree, its buttressed trunk having rotted away to nothing inside, had fallen in the forest, creating a hole in the overarching canopy and allowing sunlight to spear down to the forest floor. As his crew thirstily refreshed themselves from their canteens, Sinzar took his machete to the knot of ancient vines smothering an ancient carved stone, chopping the persistent tendrils free of their tenacious hold on the statue that was revealed beneath.

Time and the jungle had both taken their toll, but it was still possible to make out the exaggerated features of a great ape carved into the rectangular pillar.

Scrimshaw assiduously checked the sweat-damp parchment of the map again, tracing the path they had followed with a finger, to the scratchy illustration of what might have been a gorilla. 'We're still on the right track,' he said, and a minute later the treasure-hunters continued on their way.

From the jungle-claimed stone ape, the path brought the explorers to the edge of a precipitous gorge, the sandstone cliffs gripped by the roots of more trees. A little way further on, in times past another giant tree had fallen, the liana-draped trunk now bridging the void between the towering cliffs. The party cautiously crossed the tree-bridge as a river thundered by far below, hidden by the spray-mist and shadows lurking at the bottom of the ravine.

With the party safely across, Sinzar resumed his relentless march through the oppressive forest, the air thick with the complex, layered scents of bird-eating pitcher plants, the peaty compost smell of decaying vegetation, and the droning of the ever-present overgrown insect life.

And then the Captain chopped through a last obscuring veil of vegetation and emerged from the trees into a clearing, from which rose what was left of a vine-choked temple. It seemed as if the ruins had grown from the bare escarpment of a rocky promontory, and indeed, in places, it was hard to tell where the rocky highlands of the island ended and the fractured, dressed stone blocks of the temple began. Twisted creepers, some as thick as Taboo was broad, also did their best to obscure the boundary between the endeavours of the ancient people whose gods must once have claimed dominion of this place and the mountain. But those same gods had not outlived the Earth Mother and Father Forest.

Yet the memory of them remained. The dressed blocks had been arranged to create the impression of an ape-like face, its mouth open in a roar of primal rage, the gaping maw forming the entrance to a tunnel that led into the ruins and to whatever secrets lay hidden within.

A profusion of low-growing succulents covered the floor of the clearing and beyond them, where lush vegetation gave way to cracked and parched earth, someone had staked out a line of crudely-planted posts. Adorned with the fleshless skulls of humans, primates and even serpentmen, these posts marked the boundary between the vibrant living jungle and the deathly dustiness of the temple ruins.

Not even the presence of the flesh-picked skulls caused Sinzar to stop, now that he had the forgotten shrine in his sights, and he set off across the clearing towards the open mouth of the ape, certain now that the treasure they sought lay within. But it was then that the scowling faces appeared between the trees, teeth bared in ape-like grimaces, and the indigenous population of the island made themselves known to the interlopers.

They emerged from the forest as if they were the forest, shadows taking on physical form as they slipped from between the root boles of towering trees and stepped into the clearing, growing arms and legs as they did so. One moment there was no one there and then they were, as if they had always been, a line of mud-painted warriors, wielding branch-formed clubs and arm-lengths of wood studded with napped flint teeth. In this manner they barred the explorers' route to the ruins.

The whites of their eyes and teeth flashing in the sudden sunlight, amidst mud-smeared faces, made them appear even more threatening, and yet the threat they posed wasn't any worse than a hundred such encounters the crew had endured between them on a dozen voyages within the so-called Ghost Archipelago.

The mystical chain of moving islands was littered with the remnants of once mighty empires, now reduced to isolated island-bound pockets of de-evolved humanity. Civilisation had reigned here, in some bygone era, with a golden rod, but where there had once been kingdoms and hegemonies, now all that remained was all that ever remained when the veneer of civilisation was scraped away, and those relics of cultures long gone were as red in tooth and claw as the wild beasts that also called the Isles home.

A figure emerged from the line of islanders, his arms bound with animal skin, and wearing a crude mask carved from tree bark and clearly supposed to make him look even more like a primate than he already did. This ape-man capered about in front of his fellows, hooting and shrieking and beating his chest in mimicry of an old silverback, directing his aggressive display at Sinzar's crew.

'Alright then, time to turn back,' Haroun said, turning on his heel.

'Are you serious?' Kaseem exclaimed in genuine surprise.

'Of course not, you old goat,' the rogue grinned, unsheathing his sword and turning to face the tribesmen's spears with Castigon steel bared. 'I wouldn't miss this for all the gold in the Archipelago!'

'Would you settle for a share of whatever lies within that?' Sinzar pointed with his drawn scimitar at the gaping ape-mouth entrance to the temple ruins.

'Go on then,' said Haroun with a wry smile.

'Very well, then what are we waiting for?' said the Captain, his weapon raised high, feeling the blood quickening in his veins. 'Do you want to live forever?'

With that he led the charge against the tribesmen.

The tribesmen responded in kind, racing towards Sinzar's band on short, stubby legs, running with the gait of apes rather than that of men.

Forged steel met stone-tipped spears and flint-set clubs, as the primal, territorial fury of the tribe clashed with a trained body of skirmishers. Captain Sinzar's crew might not enjoy the benefits of a formal military schooling but they had fought for their lives, side by side, on enough occasions that they worked well together as a fighting unit, and would even give a Drichean warrior cadre a run for their money. It really was perennially fascinating how motivating the desire for gold or the need to save your own skin could be.

Sinzar met the most eager among the savages, those with the most to prove to their fellows – either that they were worthy of joining the warrior elite of the tribe or perhaps to prove that they still deserved to join the next foray into enemy territory, and not be left alone to guard their womenfolk. But all they proved that day was that they were no match for the blade of Heritor Sinzar.

To his left, Taboo met the charge of another furious tribesman, snatching the warrior's spear from his grasp and hurling it aside, before picking the man up, raising him above his head, and throwing him against the trunk of the nearest tree.

To Sinzar's right, Scrimshaw met the flailing clubs of the primitives with a fencer's grace and skill, dancing out of range of their frantic attacks before leaping back in with a lethal thrust of his own.

Manu met the tribesmen's attacks with a bestial ferocity. Out of the corner of his eye, Sinzar saw an islander stumble back, screaming in shock and pain, a hand clamped to his throat, dark blood spurting from between his fingers with every beat of his panicked heart.

The Captain turned his attention back to the thick of the fighting occurring around him, and it was in that moment that another opportunistic primitive almost did for him; it was only his lightning-fast reflexes that saved him. He twisted at the waist, the thrusting spear passing in front of his face.

But Vaquez had his back, just as her father used to have his back when they sailed together. She ducked in under the tribesman's thrust, her twin swords slicing through the air before her and opening the warrior's belly just as effectively, splashing the thickly growing succulents with his viscera.

While the others engaged the enemy head-on, Kaseem hung back from the fray, taking out any who tried to encircle the party with well-aimed stones, taken from the bag that hung at his waist. He launched them from his open palm with nothing more than a thought and a gesture, but every one of the rock-hard projectiles found their target, tribesmen dropping left, right and centre as the polished pebbles struck unprotected temples with skull-cracking force.

The treasure-hunters were outnumbered at least five to one, even though they had already felled a dozen primitives between them.

Haroun suddenly cried out and his legs buckled beneath him. A descending flint-studded club had found his left leg, the razor-sharp stones opening the flesh of his calf as effectively as a butcher cleaving a joint of meat.

'Fall back!' Haroun cried between teeth clenched in a rictus of pain. 'Fall back!'

'No!' Sinzar countered him. 'Don't fall back! We keep pushing forward. We can better defend ourselves inside the ruins.'

With their captain's encouragement, the crew pushed on, forcing the thinning line of warrior tribesmen back until, with a last, almighty effort, they broke through, Taboo dragging Haroun with him as the treasure-hunters crossed the boundary demarcated by the skull-mounted stakes.

The instant they crossed the line, the indigenous islanders broke off their attack, casting uncertain looks at one another and the retreating explorers, fear writ large on their faces for the first time since Sinzar's crew had trespassed within their ancestral lands. They began to retreat across the clearing, and just as quickly as they had appeared from the forest they melted back into the jungle, taking the dead and dying with them.

Gasping for breath, Captain Sinzar's treasure-hunters took shelter within the cool shadows of the ape's-mouth archway, Taboo's belly fat rippling as he dropped onto his rump on the dusty ground beside the groaning Haroun.

Kaseem kept watch, searching the treeline for any sign that the primitives might be about to return, convinced that the warriors would be back at any moment, having overcome their fear of whatever consequences they imagined would follow as a result of the strangers' desecration of the temple complex.

Manu kept watch from the other side of the arch. The look on his face wasn't one of anxious anticipation but hungry expectation, a sinister glint in his almost white-less eyes and a wide smile on his face that exposed the sharpened points of his teeth. Without blinking, Manu wiped a hand across bloody lips.

Kaseem had witnessed what the Shark had done to one wretched islander and couldn't help wondering if he had developed a taste for their blood and was hoping to drink of it for a second time.

Behind them, Haroun continued to groan as Vasquez did her best to tend to his leg and dress the wound, while the silent Taboo held him still. Scrimshaw was distractedly dabbing at a gash that had been opened in his shoulder.

'Any sign?' Sinzar asked, suddenly at Kaseem's side.

'Not yet,' the Earth Warden said warily, not wanting to tempt whatever deities might still lurk within the ruins to prove him otherwise.

'Then let's get moving,' came the Captain's pragmatic reply. 'Haroun, can you walk?'

The former street-rat winced, as he tried to stand, and let out a bitter gasp of pain. 'No,' he moaned.

'Never mind, Taboo can help you,' Captain Sinzar decreed.

And then they were on their way again, Taboo supporting Haroun, as he limped on, favouring his right leg. The explorers followed the high-and-wide passage as it wound into the temple and up the rugged peak from which the edifice appeared to have hauled itself, Sinzar leading the way, Kaseem's pulse thumping in anticipation as something called to him from the heart of the ruins.

* * *

Sinzar led the party through the temple, the tunnel they were following seeming to wind up towards the summit of the peak, suggesting to him that whoever had built the temple had merely added a layer of dressed stone to either a natural cleft in the rock, or one rough-hewn from the crag by eager, pious hands.

It was never truly dark in the tunnel either, light spilling in from above as well as from the ape-mouth entrance below, and even through fissures where probing vines and lianas had pushed their way between the slumped stones that formed the ceiling. And by that half-light he could see images of apes rise in bas-relief from the more ornatelydressed stones. In some scenes, the apes appeared to be waging war against their enemies, the monkey-men clad in armour and high-domed helms, while their more human foes fled in fear. Further on the humans were shown prostrating themselves before a huge ape seated upon a mighty throne, either in adoration or because they had been subjugated into slavery.

The tunnel eventually opened out onto a large courtyard, the hot sun beating down on the stone-flagged space, while the hooting of gibbons and croaking bird cries echoed from the sculpted stone walls. It looked to Sinzar as if the courtyard might be cruciform in shape, with alcoves and transepts hidden away out of sight that would only be revealed when he advanced further into the space. Set in a geometric pattern around the shrine enclosure were carved stone columns, some of them over thirty-feet tall and not unlike the vine-clad, time-worn way marker they had come upon in the forest.

Everywhere the angry faces of apes glared at the treasure-hunters with accusatory stony stares, mouths locked in silent roars of rage that humans should dare infiltrate this holy sanctuary.

But the temple was not the glorious edifice it might once have been. The courtyard was littered with all manner of detritus, everything from fallen masonry to denuded tree branches, drifts of dry leaves, bones picked clean of flesh, and what looked like crushed pieces of plasterwork or shattered marble bowls. The courtyard was open to the sky, exposing the explorers to the unkind attentions of the blazing noonday sun, but the towering pillars and the tumbled stones gave Sinzar the impression that the space might once have had a roof, or at least more of a covering than it had now, but one that had fallen in long ago. Not all of the supporting columns were still intact. Some lay on the courtyard floor, their disassembled component parts now looking like the broken vertebrae of some colossal stone giant.

And yet, despite all the damage, detritus and decay, there was still one object that dominated the space, leaving Sinzar and the others in no doubt as to which lonely god still claimed dominion of this island.

The statue had to be twenty-five feet tall at least, both terrifying and awe-inspiring in its aspect, being, as it was, that of a giant gorilla. The great ape was standing on its hind-legs, its bunched fists raised above its head, as if it was ready to bring them crashing down and flatten the trespassers at any moment. The blunt fangs that filled its mouth were of ivory, while it glowered down at the explorers, its brow knitted in stone-locked anger, through glittering emerald eyes.

Haroun whistled through his teeth upon catching sight of the sparkling green gems, the agony of his injured leg abruptly forgotten.

'By all the stars in heaven!' Kaseem exclaimed.

'They're huge!' Vasquez gasped.

'And worth a small fortune,' Scrimshaw added, gazing into the ape-god's eyes as if hypnotised.

'Well the money we could make selling those back in Mandrabar or Castigon would certainly give us a nice little nest egg,' Sinzar said, stroking his neatly-trimmed goatee, a roguish smile curling the corner of his mouth.

Sinzar approached the statue, boldly meeting the ape-god's furious stare as he gazed up at the statue, hands on hips in a defiant stance.

'So what are you waiting for? Those stones aren't going to prise themselves loose!'

Without further hesitation, overcoming their sense of awe, Manu and Scrimshaw started to scale the statue, Haroun being relegated to watching from his seat on a fallen column, while Taboo gave Vasquez a helping hand up onto the idol, after the other two.

* * *

But as the others worked, under Sinzar's direction and with the occasional unhelpful suggestion from Haroun, Kaseem's attention lay elsewhere. While the others were fully focused on the task in hand, that of removing the jewelled eyes and blinding the god-statue, he was listening to the earth as it spoke to him. He could feel tremors rising up through the stones beneath his feet, like those created by heavy footfalls.

As he watched, broken fragments of marble skittering across the stone-flagged courtyard, his mind returned to something else that had been troubling him ever since they had entered the temple. Why was it that the ape-loving tribesmen had left them alone as soon as they breached the boundary marked by the line of skulls on stakes? Was it purely because the ruins were sacred to them and it was taboo for them to defile the place with their presence? Or was there another reason?

And thinking back to when they had first encountered the islanders, he recalled that it had been the treasure-hunters who had initiated combat. The tribesmen had only barred their way, up until the moment Sinzar's party engaged them in battle. Kaseem couldn't shake the feeling that perhaps the islanders had merely been trying to stop them from entering the temple. But why? Again, was it because the temple was a location they venerated, or was it more than that? Had they actually been trying to stop Captain Sinzar and his crew from doing something they might live to regret – if they lived at all?

And all the time Kaseem was wrestling with these thoughts, the vibrations caused by thudding footfalls increased in strength.

* * *

'That's one!' Scrimshaw called from his perch on the idol's left arm as he popped an emerald free, tossing it down to Sinzar.

The Captain caught the jewel deftly in both hands, feeling the satisfying weight of it in his grasp.

'And one to go,' he said. 'Manu, how are you getting on?'

'Almost there,' the Shark grunted, as he struggled to get the tip of his dagger into the eye-socket behind the gemstone to prise it free.

'Captain!'

Sinzar turned, hearing the edge of fear in the Earth Warden's voice.

'What is it?'

'We're not alone!'

'What do you mean? Are the islanders here?'

But before Kaseem could answer, with a harsh, squawking cry, from across the courtyard there appeared a huge, flightless bird. It moved at a run, on huge scaly-skinned feet, darting between the pillars and leaping over the scattered branches with great lolloping strides.

Gasps and cries of alarm went up from the party, and the bird's sudden appearance even caused Sinzar to take a few steps backwards in surprise.

The animal was huge, at least three times the height of a man. Its beak was so large it seemed as if its head consisted of little else, while its scaly skin and ill-proportioned body made it seem almost reptilian. The stubs of its wings and its tail stump were only patchily covered in feathers, while a black crest rose from the top of its head. The wings were certainly too small to allow the huge bird to fly, and were only any good for helping it gain some height when vaulting the tumbled columns and scattered tree limbs.

Sinzar took all this in in an instant.

The flightless bird was fast and before he could even draw his blade, it had plucked Manu, from where he clung to the statue, with its beak, one crunching bite severing the bloodthirsty pirate in two. Jerking its head back, the bird gulped down the Shark's torso, leaving his twitching legs to fall to the ground, the dead man's intestines spooling after them from his killer's gory crop.

Bellowing in incomprehensible rage, his belly wobbling as he did so, Taboo charged at the predatory avian, even though the top of his bald head didn't even reach up to its thigh.

The bird cocked its head on one side and fixed the dark-skinned sailor with a blinking, beady black eye. A sound like a curious chirrup escaped its flapping throat sac, and then, with a sharp kick from one of its over-sized feet, it floored the big man, trapping him in a crushing cage formed of its huge talons. In another swift strike, it took the man's head from his shoulders with one sharp bite of its deadly beak.

Vasquez couldn't help crying out in shock and for a moment even Sinzar felt a chill shiver of fear. In the space of only a few moments, the monstrous bird had appeared as if from nowhere, and killed two of his crew with savage efficiency.

But Sinzar's scimitar was in his hand now. The blood quickening in his veins, he charged at the bird, ready to separate its over-large head from its scrawny body with one swipe of his keen-edged blade.

It was only then that he became aware of the presence of another of the huge flightless birds.

Scrimshaw and Vasquez were sliding down the side of the huge statue, their precarious position atop the idol leaving them too exposed and vulnerable to attack, when the second monster appeared from behind it.

Haroun, sword in hand, struggled to his feet, the adrenalin-rush brought on by the avians' attack helping him ignore his debilitating injury.

Scrimshaw darted out of the reach of the snapping beak of the new arrival, crying out, 'We have to get out of here! Everyone, run!'

'No!' countered Sinzar. 'Do that and you're dead! You

think you can outrun both of them?'

He dodged a stamping foot and walloped the second bird across the blunt end of its battering-ram beak with the flat of his blade. The overgrown fowl recoiled with a startled squawk.

'A fighting retreat then?' asked Kaseem hopefully.

'Now how would that add to the legend of brave Captain Sinzar?' Sinzar challenged the Earth Warden. 'There's still four of us—'

'Five!' Haroun blurted out indignantly.

'—five of us, and two of them. And we have a Heritor of the Crystal Pool and an Earth Warden on our side.'

With that, Sinzar took off, bounding across the courtyard, approaching a looming stone column at an oblique angle.

As the first of the flightless birds dined upon the choice meal trapped between its talons, opening the carcass with incising pecks, and picking out the choicest morsels – the dead man's rich liver, succulent intestines and meaty heart – its twin, not wanting to miss out, darted forward, head low, wings flapping uselessly, beak yawning in readiness to snap up anything that came within reach.

The sailors scattered, leaving Kaseem to face the avian's charge alone.

With an almighty leap, Sinzar took off, his feet making contact with the pillar, his speed and momentum allowing him to take two more strides up the side of the column, carrying him even higher. Only then did he launch himself from the pillar, with a final, forceful kick, executing a perfect backward somersault – scimitar still in hand – and he sailed over the charging bird's back, lashing out with his blade as he did so.

Kaseem's hands were poised, a chunk of broken stone suspended between them – one above, one below – as the gigantic flightless bird took two more stumbling steps before its dragon-like legs gave way beneath it. It crashed to the ground, its head flopping at an unnatural angle beside its body, blood pooling on the ochre flagstones of the courtyard, Sinzar's blade having cut almost clean through its neck.

The Heritor landed firmly on both booted feet beside the Earth Warden. 'One down,' he said, looking pleased with himself, even though he was panting for breath and could feel the blood burn palsy taking hold of his limbs after his acrobatic feat.

'One to go,' finished Kaseem, letting the stone suspended between his hands drop to the ground even as he dropped to his knees.

* * *

Placing the palm of his right hand against an ancient paving slab, Kaseem closed his eyes and focused on what he could feel through the ground under him.

There was the cracked, cut stone beneath his hand, and compacted sand and earth beneath that. Deeper down he sensed the solidity of bedrock, the sandstone outcrop that formed the mountain peak of which the lost island was the only part visible above the sea. He felt the tectonically-folded strata beneath that, veins of quartz and feldspar hidden in the primordial rock, and then he found it – a fractured seam deep within the earth's crust; a fissure. A fault line.

The tremors that rippled through the deeply dug foundations of the ruins were many times the magnitude of the tremors produced by the birds' giveaway footsteps. As the waves of seismic force rose from deep within the heart of the island-mountain, the still-standing pillars and intricately carved friezes adorning the walls of the courtyard – that had survived who knew how many centuries, or perhaps even millennia – began to shudder and shake and, finally, to fall.

Sinzar braced himself, as did the surviving members of his crew, the ground at their feet behaving more like the rolling seas of the Southern Ocean.

The world darkened abruptly, a looming shadow falling across him. As the temple fell, so, at last, did its guardian deity, and when the stone colossus hit the ground it was with a colossal boom that sent shockwaves of its own rippling through the mountain. The survivors of Sinzar's ill-fated treasure hunt tumbled to the ground – all apart from the Heritor himself and Kaseem of the Earth.

As the ape-god died, so did the remaining flightless bird, crushed beneath the toppled idol, every bone in its body crushed, the meat on those bones mashed, its internal organs pulped.

As the god's head rolled clear of its broken body, the remaining stubborn emerald eye popped free of its stone socket and rolled to a stop next to Sinzar's foot.

'And now we run,' he said, picking up the gem and pocketing it.

The adventurers didn't need to be told twice; Captain Sinzar's cavalier hubris had cost the lives of two of their party already, and none of them wanted to become the third – especially not the hobbling Haroun.

But as Sinzar ran towards the entrance to the tunnel mouth and freedom, feeling the reassuring weight of the eyes of the ape god in his pocket, a new shadow fell across the courtyard, plunging it into premature twilight. The Captain turned his gaze to the heavens as something vast and terrible eclipsed the very sun itself.

And Sinzar realised at last that what he had taken to be shattered marble bowls and crushed plaster littering the courtyard was something else entirely.

* * *

Lagan dozed in the soporific heat of the midday sun, lying in the shade of the loosened canvas sail. His feet up on the gunwale, his slow, heavy breathing occasionally birthed grunting snores, as the gentle breeze coming in off the sea tousled his bushy beard.

He was roused from a lovely dream – in which scantily-clad harem girls fed him grapes and danced for his pleasure, while another nubile maiden made sure that his wine goblet was never empty – by the desperate shouts of his companions, calling his name over and over again.

Blearily opening one eye, he saw five figures closing on his position as they crossed the beach, almost falling over themselves so desperate were they to reach the boat. Three of them were running pell-mell across the momentum-sapping white sand, while the Earth Warden and Haroun lagged behind, the former supporting the latter as he staggered and stumbled across the beach.

Lagan didn't need to hear their urgent shouts to understand what was expected of him. Tumbling out of the boat, he put his shoulder against the keel and pushed, his feet sinking into the soft sand as he fought to get the *Mermaid* afloat once more.

And then the boat almost slipped out of his grasp, as Scrimshaw and the Captain joined him, helping to free the boat of the beach and push it out into the surging surf.

'Denara, get aboard and get the sail up!' he ordered his niece, the girl bounding up onto the gunwale and from there down onto the deck of the shallow-keeled boat.

As Denara did as her uncle commanded, the rest of the crew boarded the *Mermaid*. Kaseem was the last aboard, Sinzar having already helped haul the injured Haroun bodily into the boat.

With them all safely on board, Haroun huddled in a shaking ball beside the mast, the shipmaster took over, pulling on the tiller as Vasquez tied off a rope, the sailcloth snapping tight as it caught the wind at last.

He knew better than to ask what had become of Taboo and Manu.

* * *

As the *Mermaid* put out to sea, Sinzar cast an eye over the survivors of his little escapade, his narrowed gaze fixing at last on Scrimshaw, where the old sailor lay sprawled on the deck, his eyes closed and his chest heaving as he recovered his breath.

'Show me that map of yours again,' he said.

Scrimshaw didn't even bother to open his eyes as he slipped a hand inside his sweat-soaked shirt and pulled out the greasy parchment, holding it out for the Captain.

Sinzar took it and unfolded it, even as he kept one eye on the retreating island. 'You told us there were treasures to be had within the lost temple on that island.'

'And we recovered them, didn't we?' Scrimshaw retorted.

'I don't dispute that, but death also awaited us there. Are you sure you read that inscription right?'

'Well,' Scrimshaw said, opening his eyes at last, 'I've been thinking about that.'

'Go on,' growled Sinzar.

The sailor sat up and, even though he was now looking at the map upside down, he pointed with a smoking leaf-stained fingernail at the line of angular marks inscribed beneath the crude drawing of the topography of the island. He stopped at the second symbol from the left.

'This symbol means "lies" or "buried", but by extension I believe it can also mean "hidden" or "possess" – as in, something you want to keep a safe hold of you hide – and therefore it can also mean "keep".'

Sinzar pointed at the marks that came after it on the parchment. 'And these? You said they meant "this place" or "here", didn't you?'

'Alright, I'll admit I misread that one.' Scrimshaw pointed at one of the angular markings. 'It means "that place", not "this place", but it can also mean "from here" or "away".'

'So "Keep Away".'

'Hmm,' Scrimshaw mumbled in a non-committal fashion.

'Let me guess' – Sinzar pointed at the first symbol – 'this mark here doesn't mean "fortune", it actually means the opposite, "misfortune".'

'Or "danger",' Scrimshaw added, 'but in my defence the written form of Drichean is very hard to decode. There are all manner of subtle nuances. The meaning of a symbol can change with a simple extension of a line here or there.'

Haroun gave a harsh bark of laughter from where he lay half curled around the mast. The makeshift bandage wrapped around his leg was stained red with blood. 'Danger, keep away!'

'I found us a nice little nest egg though, didn't I?'

'True,' admitted Sinzar, 'but at what cost?'

'I think we're about to find out,' Haroun said, pointing skyward, the smile gone from his face. 'She's not giving up.'

Sinzar looked up as a great shadow fell across the boat.

If a raven could be considered a bird of ill-omen, then the thing bearing down on them now must surely have been considered a portent of certain death. Its vast black wings blotting out the sun, its wingspan was as far-reaching as a Castigon galleon was long.

'By Mermydia!' Lagan gasped, hastily making the sign of the sea goddess. 'What did you do?'

'We killed its young,' whimpered Kaseem, looking queasy.

'And mother's none too pleased about it,' said Haroun, unable to tear his eyes from the black-winged titan. He fixed Sinzar with an accusing glare. 'A nice little nest egg, you said.'

Opening its vast beak, the roc gave voice to a primordial screech and, angling its wings, swooped out of the sky towards the boat.

'Snap out of it!' Sinzar shouted, seeing the trance-like expressions on his companions' faces. 'Arm yourselves! We're under attack!'

Suddenly the deck of the *Mermaid* was a flurry of activity as the crew armed themselves as best they could, considering the size and nature of their foe.

'What are you waiting for?' bellowed Captain Sinzar, leaping onto the gunwale of the boat, scimitar on one hand and gripping the rigging with the other. 'Do you want to live forever?'

As the monstrous bird swept down out of the azure fastness of the sky, Sinzar wondered what price feathers the size of trees would fetch back in the bazaars of Mandrabar.

Now that would make a very nice little nest egg indeed.

BLACK JACQUES'
LEGACY

MARK A. LATHAM

'We've found it, lads, and that's worth drinking to!'

Kassandra Dupont raised her tankard to the cheers of the crew, and drank deep of success. The atmosphere in the tavern was raucous, and Kassandra's men led the revelry. In the Hanged Head tavern, on the fringe of an island group that men called the Serpent's Teeth, sailors of all stripes set aside their rivalries for scant hours of amusement. This was neutral ground, although the unwary might still wake up dead, their pockets empty and their ribs stuck with sharpened steel. Now, drunkards and brigands craned their necks to see what all the fuss was about, but they'd not muscle in on this celebration. This night belonged to her, to the woman known as 'the Owl'.

'Another round, courtesy of the Captain!' The cheers were led by Kassandra's first mate, the hulking Zhembian, Kymba. He stood to his full height, beaming smile and booming voice, tossing a purse of coins to the nearest serving wench.

Kassandra fingered the gold signet ring that hung on a chain about her neck – the heirloom that had set her upon this quest. The only relic of the notorious Black Jacques Dupont to have returned home from the Ghost Archipelago.

Momentarily caught in her reverie, Kassandra became aware of an unflinching gaze upon her. Across the table, her Warden, Kor'Thiel – her guide in the mystical ways of the Archipelago – stared at her, knowingly. Kassandra shook away the odd sensation that the mystic instilled in her, and instead looked to the table before her, where lay an ancient map. It was faded, drawn roughly on brown-stained parchment, its corners weighted down with purses filled with plundered gold crowns. A pretty haul, and one that the crew of the *Nightmaiden* loudly appreciated.

'I still do not understand,' a man standing behind her said. Konrad, her chief scout, always the dissenting voice in her crew. 'The map is old. It is barely legible. What good will it do?'

'It would do you no good,' Kassandra said, coolly. 'Not without me. This map is enchanted; it shows the way to Black Jacques' treasure, but only if you have eyes to see.'

The noise died down as she spoke, to be replaced by a hushed reverence. Everyone – not just Kassandra's crew– knew of what she spoke.

'They say that treasure be cursed,' Konrad said, quietly. 'They say that all who touch it perish.'

'Konrad, the naysayer.' Across the table, Kor'Thiel, the Beast Warden, looked up at Konrad from beneath bushy brows, and all men hushed at his words, for he spoke little. Kor'Thiel stroked his matted, red beard. 'Do not take the gleam from today's victory,' he said. 'Are we not led by the Owl? Our captain is a Heritor – the blood of Black Jacques flows through her veins. Her gift is singular to her line. She will break the curse – it is foretold.'

'Her gift is one that we cannot see,' Konrad mocked. 'She could tell us anything about that useless scrap, and expect us to believe it.'

Kymba moved to intervene on his captain's behalf, the dark-skinned giant cutting a formidable figure, and yet Konrad did not back away. Kassandra placed a hand on Kymba's arm – she knew the ale had flowed freely, there was no call to fall out amongst themselves.

'When the moon rises, what you see as a useless scrap will become our most precious possession,' the Beast Warden said. 'For only then will the Owl see the hidden ways marked upon it, to lead us through these islands, to the treasure that you so desire.'

'And what treasure is this?' Konrad asked. 'Will it be worth the risks?'

'Aye,' Kassandra said, 'and worse besides. But if you ever want to see it, you had best stay close to your captain. Without me, Konrad, you'd be lost.' She stood as she said this, and took a flagon from the tray of the returning wench.

At this jest, the celebrations resumed. Laughter and song echoed about the Hanged Head. Konrad slunk away, back to his cups. Cut-throats melded back into the shadows, eyeing the tavern patrons, though they'd have slim pickings this night.

* * *

Kassandra rubbed at her eyes, and staggered out into the balmy night, the sounds of snoring seafarers and ripe stench of the Hanged Head fading behind her. She slipped between tall trees, down to the clifftop, where a warm breeze carried with it the creaking of rigging-ropes and the smell of salt. The moon hung low over the bay, a shimmering, pearlescent haze masking the horizon. The Ghost Archipelago stood beyond the reach of most mortals. As a Heritor, she was not like most mortals.

She stood upon the clifftop above the bay, wind sweeping at her tousled brown hair and myriad silk scarves. Kassandra allowed her powers to rise, just for a moment. When night fell – and especially when the moon shone – the world changed for her, when she allowed it. She saw the life-force pulsate through every blade of grass; the magical energy of the islands flowing around her in a twisting, iridescent display; the sea shimmered in colours that few had ever seen. Few outside of her bloodline.

She unfurled the map. In the moonlight, hidden paths were revealed to her preternatural vision. Coastlines were marked, dangers indicated, treasure troves recorded. The map came alive with silver trails and scrawled notes. It was not for nothing she was called the Owl, for her gift was to find what was hidden in the darkness. The map had been made by her ancestor, 'Black' Jacques Dupont, one of the first Heritors. And on the map was marked his final destination; his tomb, long forgotten. Finding the map had been perilous in itself, and finding Jacques' resting place probably more so. But it would be worth it.

'I'm coming for you, Jacques,' she said to the night. 'I'm coming for the stone.'

'The stone?'

A voice interrupted Kassandra's private moment. An all-too familiar voice. She wheeled about, reaching for a dagger.

'Vance!' she hissed.

Before her stood a tall man, square of jaw, golden of hair. Behind him, a group of swarthy brigands and seasoned soldiers stood, weapons readied. At Vance's feet crouched a Warden, swathed in simple robes, touching the earth, eyes rolled back into his head, white. The Warden trembled, ending the enchantment he had been working, and stood, unsteady from the exertion.

By virtue of her gifts, Kassandra was nigh impossible to creep up on in the dark. The Warden had been masking the life-force of Vance and his men from her, and now she was trapped. She blinked away her moon-sight, lest the toll upon her began to tell, and the blood price be paid.

'You have led me a merry dance, my love,' Vance smirked. 'To think, I almost passed by this rat's nest, and yet my little birds sent word. Word of a pirate princess, addled with drink, crowing of her latest plunder. A map that leads the way to Black Jacques' treasure. I see you have it with you.' Vance held out a hand and beckoned Kassandra hand the map over.

Kassandra's eyes narrowed. She had sailed across the world to escape this man, and yet here he was. Instinctively, she rolled the map and held it close. She took a step back. Her feet dislodged some stones, which skittered down the cliff. She peered over her shoulder. The drop was too sheer, the rocks below too jagged.

'There's nowhere to run, Kassandra. Give me the map – you know I can take it if I want it.'

'What if I tear it up and throw it into the sea?' Kassandra said, defiantly.

'You won't – I know what the legacy means to you. But… if you did, I would just have to content myself with taking you. We are still betrothed, are we not?'

'We are not!' she snapped. The thought of marrying this man made her nauseous.

'Your father thinks otherwise. He's paid a pretty penny to the man who brings you home. I hope to win his favour by saving him that ransom and taking you back myself – once I've found the Crystal Pool, of course.'

'My father favours you quite enough already, I think.' Kassandra was stalling – she had to think of some means of escape. Or perhaps her crew would realise she was gone. The ale-induced fug still gripped her – and she was a Heritor. The grog did not affect her so much. Her men would be sleeping like babes, wenches in their arms, until dawn came.

All but one.

She saw him now, moving with surprising stealth for a big man, Kymba, his dark skin and black silks made him a shadow. His old life, hunting sabercats in the jungles of far Zhembia, made him quiet as he was strong. Kymba melded in to the treeline, vanishing from sight. He could get around Vance's group easy enough. There were ten men arranged before her – Kymba had faced worse odds. But Vance was a Heritor, too, and unlike Kassandra, his gifts were very much suited to battle.

'Look here, men,' Vance was saying, 'I have a reluctant bride! An extra ration of grog to the man who delivers her to my cabin.'

As one, the men stepped forward. Kassandra's heel slipped on the cliff's edge. She held her breath, waiting for her moment, as hands were almost upon her.

With a roar, Kymba launched his attack. Two of Vance's men were flung bodily through the air. Another fell as a great ham-sized fist struck him. The men fell over themselves so quickly to turn upon their enemy that Kassandra almost teetered backwards, regaining her balance with a theatrical flourish of her arms. She drew her dagger and sprang forward through the crowd, ducking a sword-stroke as she went.

'Don't hurt her, you idiot!' Vance cried. He waded through the press of men, barging them aside. Kassandra lunged at him with her dagger, hatred in her heart. He parried the blow effortlessly with a forearm, his skin hard as iron. Vance grinned devilishly as he registered Kassandra's surprise. He shoved her hard, into the embrace of two of his knaves, where she struggled in vain.

Kymba lunged into the fray, barging one man so hard he toppled over the ledge, screaming as he fell. At the sight of his man's death, Vance stopped his smiling. His chiselled jaw clenched. A strange, amber glow surrounded him, an aura of power. Kymba either saw it not, or did not care. The Zhembian swung his mighty arm, fist connecting with Vance's face. Kymba grunted in pain, his fingers crunching with the impact. Vance barely moved.

As Kymba staggered, Vance stepped forth, his own fist clenched, preparing to strike.

'Vance, no!' Kassandra yelled.

Vance looked to her. 'No? What is it worth?'

'My compliance; I swear it,' she said. 'Do not kill him… Please.'

Vance's infuriating, mocking smile returned. Kymba had stood, oblivious to what was transpiring before him. He looked as though he would strike again, and Vance turned to face the giant. The Heritor opened his fist, and struck Kymba hard in the chest with the flat of his hand.

With a look half of pain, half of sheer surprise etched upon his scarified features, Kymba flew through the air, crashing into the trunk of a great bronzebark tree. Vance's power was his physical strength and resilience, and he made a show of that power for all to see. A bully.

Kymba again tried to stand, and it was Vance's turn to be surprised.

'You have heart, giant,' Vance said. 'But the odds are against you.'

Undergrowth rustled. More figures emerged onto the clifftop clearing. All-too familiar figures. Kymba looked around in confusion as he was assailed from all sides. Kassandra struggled against her captors, tears stinging her eyes as she saw what was happening.

Konrad stood over Kymba, a wicked gleam in his eye. 'It is over, big man. You have lost.'

'Konrad! What are you doing?' Kassandra snarled.

'Collecting my reward,' he said.

With a smirk, Vance searched Kassandra, taking her coin purse, her jewels, and snatching the ring from her neck. 'You won't be needing these, love,' he said. 'After all, what's mine is yours. Or, rather, his.'

Vance tossed Kassandra's purse to Konrad, and her jewels and precious ring. Konrad picked them up from the dirt and nodded thanks.

'Konrad here has left us a trail since you landed on the east isle three days ago,' Vance said. 'When he signalled us tonight, we knew you had struck gold. The wretches down at the cove told us all about your boasts. Kassandra, my love – you were too rash, too careless.' He marched over, and snatched the map from her hand. 'You are going to lead us to Black Jacques' treasure, my betrothed. And remember, you promised compliance. Not that I should trust you these days – you are a pirate now, after all.'

At this, the men laughed. Kassandra seethed.

Vance shouted to Konrad. 'Where is her Warden?'

'Escaped, like a thief in the night,' Konrad said. 'Must have seen it coming.'

'Ah, the gift of foresight. Pity it did not save his captain.'

'What shall I do with this one?' Konrad asked, jerking his head at Kymba.

'Kill him, let him go… it's all the same to me. You have done well. Take the ship – Miss Dupont will no longer be needing it. Split the treasure however you see fit. Our business is concluded.'

And with that, Kassandra was dragged away, her night of victory sundered as her past caught up with her.

* * *

If the first two days had been hard, the third was harder still.

Kassandra had struck out for the Ghost Archipelago as a rebellious young woman, escaping a life of privilege and plenty. She had known what lay in store, or at least thought she had.

Now, ascending a barely-trod track up the side of a great mountain, with the baking sun beating down, she was not so sure. Every step was taken in bitterness, for she had brought Vance and his men this far, her own desire to claim her birthright weighed against her reticence to share that birthright with Vance. He was a soldier born to soldiers. She was a noble born to merchants, who had grown fat off the legacy of their Heritor blood. Their match, the augurs said, was written in the stars. So why then did Kassandra loath Vance so? Perhaps it was his lack of compassion, his cruelty to man and beast, his avarice. Perhaps it was his perfect teeth and sculptured profile, or the way he managed to stay clean even here, in the sweat and toil of a climb across mountainous terrain, with humid jungle all around.

There was no denying it: she hated him. Or maybe she hated what he represented. Right now, they were the same thing.

He walked ahead of her, his Warden, Bharquist, and most trusted soldiers around him. Behind, the rest of the crew hauled equipment and weapons, and pulled the tethers of recalcitrant pack-mules. Sometimes they looked at Kassandra with a gleam in their eye, flashing toothless grins her way. She shook her head at the ignominy – first a lady, then 'the Owl', captain of her own modest ship, and finally a prisoner on a forced march.

At the head of the column, a Drichean guide forged the path. Sure-footed, heavily muscled, skin like tanned leather, the Dricheans were honourable to a fault. Kassandra had little doubt that they would soon learn how treacherous the people from across the sea could be, just as their ancestors had, two hundred years ago.

After several hours, with the sun beginning its descent in a rose-blushed sky, the trail began to flatten and broaden, and a jungle plateau revealed itself before them. Steam rose from vine-twisted trees; creatures not heard by civilised men in centuries called from the dark tangle. The jungles of the Ghost Archipelago were forbidding places, in which even the fauna would conspire to kill the careless.

Vance called for the column to halt, and the men gratefully laid down their packs. Two men came to sit beside Kassandra, like watchdogs. Kassandra stood defiantly. She would show no weakness – these louts would know that a Heritor was worth ten of them.

'Better take some rest, my little brown owl,' Vance said to Kassandra. 'We move in half an hour.'

'You don't honestly intend to cut your way through the jungle?' Kassandra asked.

'It is the fastest route.'

'It is the most dangerous route.'

'We must be at these "Kraken Caves" that Jacques wrote of by moonrise, if your skills are to be of use,' Vance shrugged. 'If we take the long way around, we'll not reach them before dawn, and a day will be wasted. Only you can guide us through the caves, remember?'

'I never forget my own worth,' Kassandra snarled. 'Perhaps you would be wise to remember it.'

Vance tossed back his perfect hair and laughed. 'Priceless, my love. So proud, even covered in dirt and sweat like the rest of us.' His expression changed from amusement to cruelty in a heartbeat, and he drew near, squeezing Kassandra's jaw with a strong hand. 'You are stuck with us – with me – and don't you forget it. Your gift is worthless by day, and barely an asset in this hostile world by night. You have no idea what lies in wait out there, ready to devour such a morsel as you. You have been so long at sea, playing at being a pirate, that you believe your own reputation. But let me tell you this, little brown owl, your reputation was bought and paid for. Do you think your crew followed you through loyalty, or because they were dazzled by your beauty and daring? No, they followed you for coin, and because your family name still bears some weight. They did not follow the Owl, they followed Dupont. And then they betrayed you, because they understood that Vance Autrus is not a man to trifle with.'

He let her go, and she stumbled back a step, glaring at Vance vengefully.

'When we return home,' Vance said, already walking

away, 'there will be changes. I will be the man who claimed the Crystal Pool, and you will be my dutiful wife. There are worse ways to spend your days, love. Think on that.'

'Oh, I will…' Kassandra muttered to herself.

One of the men beside her uttered a pained grunt. Kassandra turned to see him fall, a black-feathered dart protruding from his neck. His fellow rushed to his side, but it was too late. Kassandra could not at first fathom what was happening; only that the man's veins were turning black as some dark poison from the dart coursed through his body. And then she saw movement all around; heard shouts and cries, and screams. She looked about in confusion. Dark forms raced between the trees. Darts whistled through the air. Javelins were thrown. A mule brayed in fear as it was skewered upon a flint point.

A man leapt over to Kassandra, dragging her to the ground. She thought for a second that some tribal warrior attacked her. She struggled and kicked, and then saw that it was not an enemy, but the Drichean, remonstrating with her, trying to hush her.

'Listen,' he hissed. 'Kor'Thiel sent me. Now is your chance. Run. Run that way!' He pointed towards the jungle, to a narrow track that snaked away from the clearing.

'Not yet,' Kassandra said. And dashed immediately in the other direction, towards the dying mule and its precious cargo.

Kassandra paused as a javelin whizzed past her, inches from her face. She ducked the flint-bladed axe of a tribal warrior, rolling away as the axe embedded itself in one of

Vance's pirates. She grinned as the Drichean appeared alongside her, holding up his hide shield as poison darts thudded into it.

'What are you doing?' he cried.

'Retrieving my property.' Kassandra skidded across the grass, snatching up a hatchet from a dead pirate, and set about the lock to a chest that had fallen from the mule's back. The battle raged all around, dozens of fearsome warriors, half-naked forms covered in bright-coloured paint. Monstrous masks, headdresses, pierced flesh.

Vance was already in the thick of the fighting; organising the men into tight formations, forcing the enemy into channels, using his immense preternatural strength. A true soldier.

The Drichean shielded Kassandra from another blow-dart, and hacked down an onrushing tribesman with his mace. Kassandra finally smashed the lock, fumbling about inside the chest. She snatched up the map with a gleam in her eye.

'Go now! The Drichean said. It is almost too late—'

A bone club splintered against the side of the man's head. He spun about and collapsed to the ground. Kassandra rolled beneath the tribesman's second blow, hacked at the back of his leg with her hatchet, and ran. The Drichean had paid the ultimate price for helping her. Who was he? Why had he done it? She could only honour his sacrifice by escaping.

She ran as fast as she could towards the track. The tribesmen's numbers were already thinning. Kassandra swore she heard shouts from Vance's men directed at her.

The distraction of the battle would not give her much of a head start, not once Vance had joined the fray – he had a knack for ending fights swiftly.

Kassandra plunged through undergrowth. Movement all around – fleeing warriors, deciding on easier prey today. She did not stop, keen eyes searching for any landmark that might guide her. She had memorised what she could of the map, but that was the problem with enchantments like these – they twisted and changed as you got closer to the destination. Kassandra's gift was able to unpick the instructions in part, certainly more ably than she'd let on to Vance, but not completely. All she knew was that she had to go north, past something called the Blood Grove, and over the Mermaid-Tail Falls. Names given these strange locales by Black Jacques. Names that meant nothing to their guides, or to Kassandra.

Soon she was beneath dark eaves, the sky blotted out by viridian canopies. All sound was dulled – she could hear only the thrumming of her own heart in her ears, twigs snapping underfoot, her breath loud as a hissing thunder-lizard.

Except, she was sure that was a hiss, and a loud one.

Acting on instinct, Kassandra leapt aside as a tangle of thorny bushes beside her exploded. A sailback roared, its immense scaly hide glistening in the half light, its eyes reflecting the horror on Kassandra's face. She dropped to the ground as a massive claw swept over her head, raking the iron-hard bark of an ancient tree.

And then it stopped. Its yellow, reptilian eyes flashed momentarily red with an inner luminescence. It beheld her. She knew at once: Kor'Thiel. Kassandra returned the creature's gaze, and something passed between them, unsaid – a moment of unspoken communication between Heritor and Beast Warden, through the alien mind of a deadly predator. Kassandra felt a glimmer of hope.

The spell was broken abruptly. Violent cries rose up all around. Kassandra shook the fug from her mind, as Vance charged through the undergrowth, spear levelled at the sailback. The red glow vanished from the creature's eyes and with a roar it turned. Its great tail whipped about the small clearing, swiping Vance aside like he was nothing, and then it was gone, the earth trembling under its clawed feet as it went.

For a moment, Kassandra thought Vance was dead. But as his men arrived, he stood, pushing away those who tried to help him. The subtle aura of his power flickered, at least to Kassandra's eyes, and then faded completely. Vance went down on one knee, squinting his eyes, growling in anger at the agony he felt. The blood burn was upon him. He had used his great strength for too prolonged a period, and now suffered the consequences. It was the Heritor's curse.

'Get the girl,' Vance snarled. His men obeyed, grabbing Kassandra, and dragging her back to the plateau's edge. They half-carried Vance, who thankfully was in no fit state to chastise Kassandra for her escape attempt. That would come later, she was certain.

At the makeshift camp, Kassandra's wrists were bound, and she was placed under watch. Half the men of the party were dead, their bodies littering the ground alongside painted tribesmen. The bodies of pirates and soldiers were looted of useful equipment, and stacked onto a funeral pyre. The dead tribesmen were tossed ignominiously down the side of the mountain, to become a feast for the carrion-birds that already circled overhead.

They rested longer than planned, while Vance recovered his strength. He glared at Kassandra from time-to-time, but said nothing. Only when the sun kissed the distant mountain range, and the sky streaked the colour of fire, did Vance give the order to move out.

The much-depleted group took to the jungle, men exhausting themselves by hacking their way through the foliage, the humid air pungent with sweat. Vance did not sully himself with manual labour – his gifts would have made short work of the morass of jungle, and the looks of his men said that they knew it.

'I must save my strength,' he said to Kassandra. 'Who knows what terrors lie ahead? What if you try to escape, and I must save you from the clutches of some great ape? Stay close, my little brown owl. I shall protect you.'

Hours passed, and night fell. The men formed two teams – half to hack at the undergrowth with axes and broad blades, and half to bear torches, in which myriad hungry eyes gleamed from the darkness. Vance grew increasingly irritable at his men's slow progress, at times forcing Bharquist to use his powers, and bid the forest part the way for their passage. The enchantments seemed difficult – the Earth Warden complained that the ancient magic of this jungle was set in opposition to him.

At long last they came to a small clearing, where the trees pulsated as though alive, and the creepers that wound about them were of the deepest red. Thick red sap dripped from them, like blood, staining the lichen at the pirates' feet. In the light of the flickering torches, it was a hellish sight.

'Blood Grove, I take it,' Vance said. 'So we go north from here. How far did you say it was?'

'I didn't,' Kassandra replied. Vance sighed in frustration, and strode to the men at the front of the line. Kassandra smiled to herself – as long as she had the power still to vex him, she could take some solace in her lot.

From the corner of her eye, she saw movement, something snaking its way through the grass. Ahead, the silvery light of the moon barely penetrated the black canopy of the jungle, but a silver shaft of light fell upon Kassandra's bound hands. It was enough. She shifted her senses, summoning her mystical vision. Around her, the grove was aglow with crimson energy. Deep red luminescence thrummed in every vine and plant. The plants moved, with malign intelligence.

Kassandra hopped aside quickly to avoid a lashing tendril, which snatched instead at the ankle of one of Vance's soldiers. The militiaman let out a panicked cry as he was whipped upwards into the trees. The men at once set about trying to get him down, only to watch in horror their comrade's fate. To Kassandra's eyes it was a grand show of lights, as the man's life-force flared bright, only to be sucked into the entangling vines, and in turn nourish the trees of the grove. At the taste of blood, the plants came alive, rustling, humming with power. Whip-like tendrils snapped across the grove, snatching at their prey. Kassandra saw the entire grove come alive. Her senses were alive. She could see the danger before it struck, but she could not avoid it forever.

'Run!' she cried. She darted away, dodging from side-to-side as hungry roots erupted from the earth, trying to trip her. She ducked swinging boughs with gnarled, grasping hands; she hopped over creepers that snatched at her ankles. Thorny branches flicked at her, scratching her face, tearing her clothes. She did not stop. A man was hoisted into the air before her, and dropped into the maw of some gigantic, monstrous *thing*. His essence exploded in a riot of colour before Kassandra's moon-sight, and then was gone. The blood-curdling screams of the men at her back was motivation enough to run from the Blood Grove, and not look back.

Kassandra ran into the night, until the cries faded and she could see nothing. The moonlight was blotted out, and with it her preternatural senses. She did not know which way was north, or what lay out there in the dark. She was almost grateful that she did not have to find out. Almost.

A strong hand grabbed her arm.

'Running again, eh? I warned you...' Vance snarled.

Kassandra rounded on him angrily. 'Would you rather I died? What good am I to you then, Vance? And you followed me out, did you not? I didn't have to call out to you.'

'No, but I imagine you did so only because you need this?' He held up the map, now secured in a leather case.

Four bedraggled men approached, panting, bloody. One held a torch, bringing much-needed light. A fifth staggered from the darkness – Bharquist. The Earth Warden pulled back his hood, and mopped his tattooed brow.

'Five of you?' Vance asked, dismay evident in his tone. 'The others?'

A bearded sailor shook his head wearily.

'Bharquist, why did you not stop those things? They were creatures of the earth – they were within your dominion.'

'Oh no, my lord,' Bharquist said with a tremulous voice. 'Whatever those things were, they were not of the earth.'

Vance cursed. 'We have not even reached these damnable caves. We still have to make the return journey. But with only seven of us…'

'When we find the treasure,' Kassandra said, 'we shall have all we need. There are said to be items of great power buried with Black Jacques. They will see us well.'

Vance considered this. 'I would very much like to see your ancestor's cursed bones before this night is done, that I might stamp them to dust for the trouble he has put me to.'

'You know how Jacques came to die out here?' Kassandra snarled.

'I care not,' Vance mocked.

'He was betrayed, by someone close to him.'

'Then you are already well on the way to following in his illustrious footsteps, aren't you?' Vance took out his compass. 'We head north, and hope to find some spit of moonlight with which to put you to use.'

* * *

The waterfall was easily two hundred feet high, plunging into a great cleft in the jungle plateau, and splitting halfway down its descent upon a jutting blade of rock. This natural formation created the fish-tail that had doubtless prompted the name, the Mermaid-Tail Falls.

The noise of the cascade was deafening, but Kassandra felt a great relief to be in the open air; to feel the spray of water upon her face. Overhead, the moon shone mercifully bright, although bloated, bat-winged creatures bobbed upon the air currents, doubtless looking for just such tasty morsels as these would-be treasure-hunters.

Vance unfurled the map, and held it in front of Kassandra's face. 'Well? What do you see?' he demanded.

Kassandra took a breath and blinked her moon-sight into focus. Although Vance could see only a hastily scribbled outline upon a piece of stained parchment, the map came alive now to Kassandra's eyes. Paths and groves, caverns and ruined temples, handwritten notes, mystical runes… Warnings. All of these things and more swam across the scroll, coalescing into vivid patterns. But something was not right – the images would settle. Try as she might, Kassandra could not focus on the map – it was as though the lines wriggled away from her sight.

'What's the matter?' Vance said.

'I… I am not sure. It's as though the map doesn't want to be read.'

She turned away, rubbing at her eyes, ignoring Vance's impatient huff. When she looked up, she saw at once what was wrong. The falls ahead glowed with unearthly power. Sigils and secret signs traced upon the rocks centuries ago now revealed themselves.

Kassandra gasped. 'The map continues, all around us,' she said. 'It's beautiful.'

Vance looked to Bharquist, who crouched and touched a hand to the earth, closing his eyes and muttering some strange chant. When he stopped, he said, 'She is right. It is a living map, marked on the landscape itself by Black Jacque's Warden, long ago. This is ancient lore. I cannot decipher it.'

'But I think I can,' Kassandra said. She focused on the sigils that now floated before her in the air, forced herself to pin them down until she could discern their shimmering forms. Some of those signs were familiar. With a laugh, she snatched the map from Vance, struggling to turn it this way and that with her wrists bound as they were. 'Hold it here, like this,' she said at last.

Vance reluctantly agreed, and the map sprang to vibrant life. The sigils upon the rocks were aligned with those on the map, and the entire surface of the parchment twisted and turned, until finally the way became clear.

'It is not really a map!' Kassandra said. 'It's a compass. And it points down there.' She blinked away the moon-sight, already tiring of the effect, and fearing the blood price.

'Behind the falls?' Vance asked.

'Aye. The Kraken Caves. That is where Black Jacques Dupont rests. I would stake my oath upon it.'

'And you expect us to climb down there? With one rope between us?'

155

'What's wrong, Vance – afraid?' Kassandra mocked. She saw indignation flare in his bright blue eyes. 'There is a path,' she said. 'Hidden. I'll show you the way. But it is a difficult climb – you'd best cut me loose.'

'Out of the question.'

'Then I'll fall to my death and dash my head on those rocks, and you'll be without a guide. Come on – what can one slip of a girl do against six brave men?'

'Her job, if she knows what is good for her,' Vance whispered in her ear, cutting her bonds with his dagger.

Kassandra only smiled.

* * *

Soaked to the skin, bedraggled and exhausted, the motley companions assembled in the cave mouth. Its moss-covered walls were soaked with spray, the sound of the crashing falls behind deafening. Torches were lit, illuminating forking passages ahead.

'What do you see?' Vance asked. 'Which way?'

'I see runes,' Kassandra said. 'Jacques marked these passages with magic. One way leads to certain death, the other to his treasure, but only for those with eyes to see.'

'Then lead on. Let's get this over with.'

Kassandra took the right-most fork, ducking low beneath stalactites and squeezing through narrow defiles. The passage twisted and turned, sometimes sloping up, sometimes down. Several times the party emerged into chambers, with several routes branching off, and each time Kassandra carefully led the way. Finally, a shaft of light ahead alerted her to her goal.

'There,' she pointed. 'We've found it.'

Vance's men breathed sighs of relief, for they were not well-suited to the confines of this underground labyrinth. Vance was about to lead the way, when his Warden tugged at his arm.

'Hold, my lord,' Bharquist said. 'I sense danger ahead. Some disturbance rings through the very stone here. A fell presence.'

Vance frowned. 'What do you advise, Warden?' he asked.

'I must converse with the stones, lord, and discover the nature of this evil. Only then will I—'

'Enough of this!' Kassandra said. 'I've waited long enough to claim my birth-right, I shall wait no longer!'

With that, she raced along the tunnel. Vance protested, and at once ordered his men to give chase. He called her back, but she did not listen. Kassandra had no weapon – Vance had allowed her nothing but the clothes on her back – but at least her hands were free. She would take her chances.

She ran into a large chamber, round and dark. One half was taken up by a rippling black pool, crescent-shaped, lapping gently at bare rock. Beside the pool was a rocky mound, upon which lay a ragged skeleton, clutching a small wooden chest. High above, a circular rent in the cavern ceiling allowed a stream of moonlight to penetrate the gloom, and the light fell upon the mound. Around the mound was a circle of glowing runes. Kassandra knew at once that only she could see them – some form of magical ward placed here centuries ago, perhaps to protect the contents of the chest. Was this the source of the so-called curse? This, surely, was the resting place of Black Jacques himself. But where were the bones of his crew?

Footsteps thudded behind her. Kassandra saw the men bearing down on her, and so she ran toward the mound, her moon-sight guiding her, allowing her to formulate a plan.

The men followed, racing full-tilt after her. And at the last, she darted aside, throwing herself to the ground. The men grasped at thin air, but their feet crossed the line of glowing runes.

A mournful groan filled the cavern, sweeping all around them like a winter's wind through a Frostgrave tomb. The men stopped dead. Bharquist began to chant. Kassandra felt Vance's hand upon her arm, hoisting her to her feet.

'What was that? What have you done?'

Kassandra only cried out in pain, wincing. Vance let her go as she dropped to the ground, clutching her eyes. 'The Blood Burn,' she groaned. 'I'm sorry Vance. I could not see. You forced me…' She curled up on the ground, holding her head.

'Weak…' Vance muttered.

A crumbling, cracking noise erupted all around. The rocks gave way, and skeletal forms leapt down from long-hidden niches in the walls, and dug their way from the ground. A handful at first, then a dozen, then a score. The ancient dead assembled in the cavern, taking up swords and shield, beholding Vance's plunderers with hollow sockets and cold, dead malice.

As one, like an army of the dead, the skeletons attacked. Bharquist gestured in the air, bringing rocks down upon the heads of his foes, or rooting them to the spot, but there were too many. The Earth Warden backed away until there was nowhere else to go, and died on the points of blunted, rusty swords.

The other men hacked and slashed at their foes, their swords becoming caught in brittle rib cages, their axes taking off skeletal limbs and yet not for a moment slowing the advance of this immortal foe. One by one they fell.

Only Vance fared well. Kassandra saw his glowing aura like a shining beacon in the thick of the fighting. Ancient blades turned aside on his stone-hard flesh. Skeletal warriors were turned to dust at each strike of Vance's longsword. He roared in defiance, felling his enemies left and right, the power of his arm more than compensating for the inadequacy of a blade-edge against such bloodless assailants.

Kassandra was on her feet now. She skirted the edge of the chamber, staying to the shadows. She had no weapon, she was no threat. She stayed out of sight, looking to the glowing runes that surrounded the burial mound in the centre of the chamber. Biding her time.

'Kassandra! Is this your doing?' Vance shouted.

Perhaps her time was almost up. The skeletons were almost spent. The magic that had animated them was little match for Vance's powers. She cursed, that all of this could have been in vain. That Vance might yet take her birth-right from her.

A-hoot-twoo!

That sound was unmistakeable: the call of a great white owl. It was the creature from which Kassandra had taken her moniker. Now, taking heart from the call of the owl, Kassandra raced toward the central circle, towards the chest.

The last skeleton fell before Vance's blade. His aura flickered as his power waned. His face showed the exertion of maintaining his great strength for so long. Vance moved to intercept Kassandra before the bones had hit the cavern floor. He was fast as a panther, reaching the chest at the same time as her. But both of them were stopped in their tracks.

Before them, a glowing vapour rose from the bones of Black Jacques. It enveloped them, impossibly bright. Kassandra blinked away her moon-sight, and could still see the manifestation before her, terrible and powerful. Vance saw it too, for his eyes widened in surprise – and fear. He struggled, but something had both of them in a mighty grip. The mist coalesced into an ethereal form. A man, bearded and tall, dark hair surrounded a ghastly face, skull visible beneath glowing flesh.

Black Jacques Dupont.

'Who disturbs my rest?' the spirit hissed. 'Do you not know that vengeance keeps me here? Vengeance drives me. Vengeance shall take you!'

Vance tried to struggle, but even at the height of his strength he would be little match for such unnatural forces.

'I… am… a Dupont,' Kassandra croaked, as spectral fingers wrapped around her throat, and the life was choked from her.

'Who you were in life matters not. Only know that you shall serve me in death…' the wraith said, voice like a creaking door.

She was not as strong as Vance. She would die first. Unless…

A-hoot-twoo!

Kassandra turned her eyes upwards. The shadow of the owl passed close overhead. Its eyes flashed red, just for a moment. Kassandra reached out, held her hand open, and felt something drop into it – something cold and metallic. The owl circled away, up to the open sky.

Kassandra held up the ring – the ring that Konrad had taken. Black Jacques let out a mournful sigh at its presence, and released her. She fell away, coughing, rubbing at her throat. Kassandra gathered herself quickly, staggering to her feet, holding out the ring.

'I am Kassandra Dupont,' she said. 'And I come to release you from your curse, and claim what is mine by birth-right.'

'Give it… to me…' the wraith whispered.

'Wait!' she said. 'Promise me safe passage from here.'

'Done. Give it to me…'

'Very well. Although before you go to your final rest, know this: the man you have in your grasp there is an Autrus.'

'What?' Vance croaked.

'Autrus? Yesss…' Black Jacques looked upon the man whose throat he held, and let out such a wicked laugh that a chill ran through Kassandra's bones. At a wave of the Wraith's hand, the surface of the black pool bubbled, softly at first, and then violently. Black shapes, indistinct, little more than shadows crawled jerkily from the pool. They scratched and clambered their way up the mound, until they reached Vance's feet. Only then did Black Jacques release Vance, throwing him to the dark shadows, which clawed and grasped at him, dragging him out of the circle, to the slimy bank of the crescent pool.

Jacques turned once more to Kassandra. She held out the ring, and he took it in an ethereal hand. It floated before him for a second, and then vanished into glowing motes of dust. With it, Jacques himself began to fade.

'Take what is yours, Kassandra Dupont, and go…' he sighed. And with that, Black Jacques faded away, forever.

Kassandra stooped to the chest, and opened it. A light radiated from within – bright as the full moon. She delved inside, and withdrew a sextant, carved from moonstone. An heirloom of long-forgotten power. Forgotten by all but the Dupont family. With the moonstone sextant, and the gift of moon-sight, it was said that Black Jacques could always find his way back to the Crystal Pool whence he gained his uncanny powers. And now Kassandra Dupont would put that claim to the test.

'Help… me… my love,' Vance croaked. He still resisted the pull of the shadows. He was half in the water now, scrabbling at the bank for some purchase that eluded him.

'I am sorry, betrothed, but I am afraid our engagement is off. If only you could see the things I could see now.'

'What…? But the Blood Burn…' Vance said.

'Oh, I am afraid I rather feigned the effects of Blood Burn. I have not been using my gifts since we entered this cave,' Kassandra said, keeping her distance as Vance flailed first angrily, then impotently. 'My powers are much diminished without the light of the moon. In here, however…'

'H… how… did you…?' Vance struggled against his shadowy enemy, his strength at last failing him.

'How did I get this far? Because Black Jacques showed me the way, of course. Silly Vance – as soon as we reached the Mermaid-tail Falls, hidden messages were revealed to me on the map, showing me the way through the caves, and warning me of danger. I memorised it, so I would not have to court Blood Burn by helping you. I lured you into danger so that you would do exactly that. I see your powers wane. Your aura is flickering.'

Vance shouted with anger, and then gasped with pain. His body was wracked by the Blood Burn, the fight was almost gone from him. He could surely feel the cold hands of the wraiths upon him, dragging him backwards, but he could not see them as Kassandra could. Warriors of old, cadaverous, their translucent flesh sloughing from their aged bones. Their armour shone silver, their eyes burned baleful red, burning with demonic fire. Kassandra's blood ran cold at the very sight of them, but she took heart from the knowledge that they had not come for her. Black Jacques himself forbade it.

'Ah, poor Vance, you never bothered to learn of my family history. But why would you? Nothing concerns you except yourself. You see, Jacques Dupont came here long ago in search of treasure, but he found only death. He was murdered by his own crew, betrayed by his so-called friend for his share of the treasure, and the legendary Moonstone Sextant. Only his Warden was loyal, and she attempted to save Jacques' life with her spells, but succeeded only in binding a fragment of Jacques' soul into his signet ring. Jacques and the Warden were murdered.

'The traitor was the only man to escape the dark spirits of these caves. He fled before he could take the sextant, but managed to relieve Jacques of his other treasures, including the ring. He returned home, and led a haunted life, pursued by the curse. Though he was a Heritor, and attracted fortune and fame, he was never at peace. When death came for him, he confessed what he had done, and gave up this ring, which found its way back into the hands of the Dupont family, where it belonged. We have waited a long time to set Jacques' spirit free, and reclaim what is ours.'

Kassandra held aloft the sextant, which shimmered in the shaft of moonlight from the cavern roof.

'As for the traitor… do you know who he was?' Kassandra went on. Vance looked up at her, croaking something unintelligible, the life almost gone from his eyes. 'His name was Glarus Autrus. Your great, great, great grandfather, I believe. He was stronger even than you, and yet the wraiths of the Kraken Caves almost claimed his life. That is how I knew you could not survive this place, Vance. It is why I lured you here. On behalf of my ancestors, I accept your apology, Vance Autrus. Take heart – with your death, the stain upon your family's honour is wiped clean.'

Vance reached up with the last of his strength, as bony fingers dragged him into the black water. 'K… Kass…' he managed, and then he was gone.

'Goodbye, love,' Kassandra whispered.

She held up the sextant once more, and it spun, light radiating from it. One day, perhaps, it would lead her to the Crystal Pool. For now, she needed it only to show her the way home.

* * *

Kor'Thiel's owl swept overhead, signalling Kassandra's return with a hoot, before the crew had even seen her approach.

'Ahoy there!' she called.

The men of the camp stood, and a great cheer went up. 'The Owl! The Owl has returned victorious!'

Kymba was first to greet her, with a bear-hug that lifted Kassandra from her feet. Kor'Thiel bowed, in his usual way, though Kassandra fancied there was the ghost of a smile upon his lips. The others came in turn, with platitudes for their returning captain. And last of all came Konrad, with the broadest grin.

'You played your part magnificently,' Kassandra said.

'I had a good teacher,' Konrad replied. 'Mind you, I was a little too convincing. Kymba here almost pulled my arms off before I could explain the plan. I think I'll leave the acting to the mummers in future.'

'And the *Nightmaiden*?' Kassandra asked with a laugh.

'Anchored off the cove there, and ready to set sail, Captain.'

Kassandra took out the sextant, and let it glow in the moonlight. The men gasped in awe. 'Then what are we waiting for?' Kassandra said. 'Fortune and glory await.'

THE JOURNAL

BY
GAV THORPE

There was a moment – just a moment – when the poisoned darts were whistling past her ear, when the wet leaves slapped her face, when the tangle of roots and sucking mud threatened to trip her, when Marianne Amontill wished she had stayed at home.

The instant of regret, the thought of slinking back to her family begging for them to take her back, set a fire of indignity raging in her chest.

'Keep running!' she shrieked to her companions, ducking beneath a branch as she continued headlong down the winding game track.

Alongside her pounded Gordwyn van der Klyde, curly hair lathered sweatily across his red face, paunch bulging like a sail in a full gale.

'Thanks… For… The… Advice…' the First Mate panted with a scowl. 'I… hadn't…'

'Save ya breath, foe of many pies,' laughed Oata. Her scarlet headscarf and shirt was bright against dark skin, amber pendants and bronze torqs flashed fitfully in the shafts of sun that broke the canopy. Her brow, nose and ears were pierced with small copper bands studded with flint, opal and malachite. The Stone Warden covered the ground with light strides, barely a drop of perspiration on her. She ran with her flint-topped staff strapped across her back, obsidian-edged daggers in hand, eyes scanning the close-growing trees to either side despite her apparent humour.

The three remaining members of Marianne's crew were Gabbri Sala Amaal, sprinting perfectly well despite his traditional dishdasha and veil; Solomon 'the Serpent', his face creased and heavily scarred as evidence of a life spent in the rougher parts of the world and a red-veined nose to indicate much of it passed in the company of a bottle; and Dmitry Freyger, a wiry, pale-skinned deckhand and sometime cook and scribe, whose claim to be fluent in fifteen languages had seemed impressive until it transpired none of them were spoken in the Ghost Archipelago.

'We need to find another boundary marker,' declared Gabbri, who was close on the heel of van der Klyde, almost tripping over the lumbering sailor's feet. 'We'll be off their territory.'

He referred to the waist-high totem poles adorned with skulls and feather fetishes they had blithely ignored earlier. They still had no clue what they signified, nor to whom, for their assailants, from the moment of the first rustle of leaves and whistle of dart in the air, had shown nothing of themselves but for fleeting diminutive shadows and movement in the undergrowth.

Ahead, the path split.

Marianne made a quick decision, drawing again on that part of her that remained of Copernichol's legacy, the part of her that marked her as one of the Heritors. She felt the faintest of sensations through her body, a warmth that was not entirely pleasant. Instinct flashed, bringing formless insight. This was her gift, an intuition beyond reason, the ability to know something before understanding it.

'High ground,' snapped Marianne, flicking a hand towards the left fork, to the volcanic peak that could be seen through the trees.

'Why?' asked the Serpent.

'I'm not sure,' confessed Marianne, taking her own advice as she plunged down the new track, silk scarf and long black hair catching on low-hanging branches. 'I think it's supposed to give us an advantage.'

Her foot caught a root – or perhaps the root snared her foot; nobody that had visited the Ghost Archipelago would be willing to rule out such a thing.

As Marianne fell, her heavy bag came off her shoulder, dropping some of its contents onto the mud and sodden leaves. A small book flapped out, two dozen parchment pages thick at most, and no broader than her palm.

On her knees, she snatched it up and protectively wiped grime from its stained and dog-eared cover. For a moment, she stared at the poorly scrawled script written in faded black ink.

The Journal of Copernichol Amontill.

Fore days after cumming upon the fog bank we thort ourselves completely turnd around. Then Master Blackwicke spyd the orb of the sunne thru the haze an we toke barings an the Captain lookd at hs charts. West, he told us an west we sailed, an mark me words by the following noone we was clear of the fog and sailing prettie.

On the nor-east horizonne we spyd the tip of a fire mountin. Twas reathed in myst and smok, an the seas were a tummult aboute the coste. The cap'n charted afresh an we bore north directly, but the wind backed an we were pushed unto the shore anyways.

We camme upon a cove, golden sand an green trees, gently shoalin into the waters. A perfect harborre, to make repairs after the storm.

'Work harder, you slack dogs,' bellowed Forsca, his knotted rope swinging threateningly in his ham-sized fist. 'The lord ain't payin' us to loiter!'

The four other crewmen of the *Desperado* bent their backs to the labouring, bringing ropes and netting, sacks of dried food and water canteens down from the ship beached in the sandy cove. From the shade of the trees, Amanuel watched his hired team working, while his Storm Warden, Herrick de Gras, paced a short patrol a little further into the treeline, muttering to himself.

The former was a man in late middle age, with a neatly trimmed beard, curled moustaches and greying black hair slicked back with fragrant oil. His broad-brimmed hat sat on the sand by his booted feet. Over simple travelling clothes he wore a breastplate of iron sculpted with the design of his family's crest – a drake's head in profile, upon a stylised sun. A longsword lay in its scabbard across his lap, its unblemished leather hilt testament to lack of use, the curlicue design of its sheath more likely found in a family gallery than a bloody battlefield.

The latter was a short, young man, sturdy of build, with shaven scalp save for a single slender braid that hung to his waist. The Warden's face was inked with dots of red and orange and black, forming swirls of pattern on cheeks and chin. His outfit was a riot of clashing colours, the elbows and cuffs of his green-and-red-checkered leather jacket were adorned with multi-coloured streamers, his leggings beneath the full spectrum of a rainbow. At his waist hung a hand axe, its naked blade inscribed with crossed thunderbolts.

'Anything?' the party master asked, angrily swatting at flies as big as his thumb.

Herrick ceased his pacing and cocked his head, appearing a little like an inquisitive parrot.

'Oh yes, my lord. The wind remembers them well. They are to the north, less than half a day ahead of us.'

'Good. The favourable winds that sped us on their tail were worth alone the coin your services have cost me.'

'And I hope to be of continued service for the remainder of the expedition.' Herrick grinned, revealing a gappy smile and a tongue pierced with a small ruby stud. 'All the way to the Crystal Pool, yes?'

'No,' growled Amanuel. 'I just want my book back. The Heritor's quest is a fool's errand, and if there is a fool greater than Duke Shausa I would be surprised, but his money is as good as any else's.'

'What if the journal is not fake?' suggested the Warden, turning his gaze back to the dense forest. Something screeched in the distance. 'What if Copernichol really did reach the fabled grounds?'

'Copernichol reached that pool, that's for certain. But if that book is several centuries old than I am too. It's goods for sale, nothing else.'

They were interrupted by a call from Forsca. His men had finished their unloading and now approached up the shore. To a man they were clad in black leather armour, bearing short bows, swords and several daggers also. Cut-throats, to be certain, but professional too. The kind of men Amanuel did not like, but also exactly the kind of men he needed at that moment.

He stood up, tied his father's sword on his belt and signalled for Herrick to lead the way.

* * *

The incline grew steeper and the track widened, bringing them under the unrelenting glare of the afternoon sun. Gordwyn was the colour of beetroot, his breaths coming in such stilted, wracking gasps that Marianne could see he would never make it to the top of the hill, never mind any higher up the mountain slope.

She slowed to a walk and then stopped, nursing her aching thighs.

'I think we've lost them,' she said, warily eyeing the trees just half a bowshot away. It was certainly true that it had been a short while since any missiles had come at them from the cover of the foliage. She turned her attention further up the slope, where the trees relinquished even more of their hold on the island, becoming scattered copses against the dark stone of the volcano. The gleam of fire and continuing belch of smoke unnerved her, though they had not felt a ground tremor for over a day now.

Gordwyn flopped down like a sack of wet wool, his sodden clothes clinging to bulbous arms and legs, sweat running rivulets down the hard earth. It looked like he had pulled himself from a pool.

'At least … The mud has… Stopped,' he wheezed, meaning that they had risen clear of the mire that had almost been their downfall.

'Funny thing,' said Dmitry, flicking a finger towards the book still in Marianne's hand. He took a moment to swig from his water bottle, wiping his sleeve across his forehead a moment later. 'Funny thing, old Copernichol, he didn't say anything about swamps and savages with blowpipes on the way to the Golden Caves.'

'Two hundred years is a long time, Dmitry,' she replied. 'A lot can change in two centuries.'

'We knew there were natives,' said Oata. She bent to one knee, staff in hand, and lay her other fingers on the hot rock, a smile creeping over her face at the contact. She stroked the mountainside, lost for a moment, before she looked up, eyes flashing with power for an instant. 'Someone is coming! The rocks feel their feet.'

'From the woods?' asked Gabbri. 'More darts?'

'No.' Oata leaned even lower, her cheek almost upon the warm rock, ear close to the ground.

She closed her eyes. The others waited, immobile, caught entranced by the Warden displaying her stone affinity. After what seemed like the turn of an hourglass she roused.

'Not islanders, not snake-kin. Outsiders. They tread with iron nails in their boots.' The Warden herself was barefoot, though the others had refused her entreaty to proceed likewise, despite her assurances that they would feel 'closer to the islands' if they did so. 'Eight men. Determined.'

'There are many crews searching the Archipelago,' said Marianne. 'I am surprised we have not encountered anyone else yet. Not on land, anyway.'

'I feel their intent, their footsteps echo inside ours.' Oata corrected her, standing up. 'They follow us, for sure.'

Marianne took a breath and looked down to the forest, but she could see nothing. Her skin tingled and her pulse quickened, Heritor blood coursing, bringing a moment of discomfort that flushed her face.

'Are you all right?' asked Gabbri. 'You do not look well.'

'Just the sun,' Marianne said, waving away his concerns. Intuition crackled in her thoughts and she cast her gaze across the mountainside. She spied a crack, the beginnings of a ravine in the shadow of a rock a few dozen paces to her left. 'That way. We'll follow the cleft down.'

'Are you sure?' said Dmitry. He pointed to the right. 'The trees seem thinner that way.'

'Trust me,' said Marianne. She held up the battered journal like a talisman. 'And trust Copernichol.'

Three dayes from the shippe, still we had found no goode timber for the new mast. Fresh water and game aplenty, but not a hard tree in syte. The fyre mountin kept up her growlin and blechin, a furyous fyre on the secondde nite kept us awake with the howl of beast an yammer of byrds. So tire we was and not bidin well, our lookouts dreary in thort.

From the bushes came dreadfull men, the tallist no hier than my chest hares, but all mussle an spere. Blue ink on theyr faces and arms. Black hare streakd red with die, an eyes rimme likewize. Shrill was the yells, lik the catte in a fite or a wild byrd. Darts filld the air. Poizond we latter found. Four of the crew were deade afore their boddys hit the mudde. The cap'n yelld to repel but no sooner had we got steele in our hans than the litle bastids was gone.

The woods resounded with the chop of blades into vines and branches and the continuous stream of curses from Adorl and Belaphus as they hacked their way through the impossible press of foliage, cutting a path for Amanuel and the rest of his crew to follow. Progress had been slow, far too slow, and with a snarl the party leader turned on Herrick.

'We are losing ground, Warden. They did not come this way, obviously. Ask the wind where they went, or whatever it is that you do.'

'The wind does not know,' Herrick said calmly, 'for they moved out of its touch from the mountainside. I told you this but you insisted we continue.'

'It's too late to double-back, it'll be nightfall before we get back to open ground.'

A triumphant shout from Belaphus brought the pair hurrying forward. They pushed through the last crisscross of vines and tangle of undergrowth to find themselves in a clearing no more than fifty paces across, before a high cliff face into which had been carved an immense figure. The woman – a queen or sorceress, or perhaps both judging by the flowing dress, serpentine crown and the egg-like orb set with real diamonds in her hand – stood above a narrow door. Her granite features glowered down at them with disdain.

'Gems,' crooned Adorl. 'Those diamonds be as big as my grandpa's flapping b—'

'Leave them,' snapped Amanuel as the sellsword started towards the cliff face. 'We're here for the book, not a treasure hunt.'

Forsca looked as though he was about to argue but any protest died in his throat as a strange noise issued from the mouth of the stone gateway. It was a susurrant, like the wind in the leaves at first, but quickly growing louder.

The party started to back away as the hissing echoed closer and closer, and two glinting lights appeared in the darkness of the corridor.

A heartbeat later and a massive serpentine head shot from the opening, gaping wide to snap around the head and neck of Belaphus. The snake's body was broad in girth, greater than a man could put his arms around, the scales dark red and patterned with zags of ochre and gold. Its eyes were two multifaceted gems that gleamed with an inner fire.

It reared up, Belaphus's legs still thrashing as it swallowed him further. Adorl and Forsca set upon the creature with their swords, hacking two-handed at the thick scales.

The beast gave up trying to eat its first victim and with a choking convulsion deposited the still form of the pirate into the long grass, blood and venom oozing thickly from two immense wounds just below his shoulder blades, upper body and head slick with saliva.

Amanuel wrestled his longsword free and backed towards the jungle, casting a glance over his shoulder into the shadows. For a moment, he would have sworn something was looking back at him.

Chanting madly, voice now a high-pitched shrieking, Harrick threw up a hand towards the skies, fingers splayed. Clouds writhed above them as the snake turned its attention on another of the crew, the wiry knifeman called Flay. It lunged, but the corsair was ready, leaping aside from the falling maw to land with a roll to his feet.

'Do something!' raged Amanuel. He could feel his Heritor blood starting to race, burning along his limbs, making his heart thunder in his chest. The snake twitched as though scenting something and twisted towards him with a long hiss. 'Kill it!'

With a shout, Harrick brought down his arm and closed his fingers into his fist. A bolt of white lanced down from the sky to strike the head of the serpent. Energy crackled across its scales and fangs, writhing for a moment down its considerable length, charring flesh.

It slumped, oily smoke drifting from its mouth, eye sockets and nostrils blackened. Amanuel felt the blood-heat start to dissipate and approached cautiously, sword stretched before him.

With a last rattle, the serpent flailed towards him, the diamonds of its eyes falling from its face as its jaws widened. Amanuel let out a primeval shout and swung his sword. The blow was devoid of accuracy or elegance but Heritor-born strength propelled it. The blade caught the burnt muzzle of the serpent at an angle and sheared away the top half of its jaw in one blow.

Amanuel spun, the momentum of his attack carrying him three staggering strides away from the snake as it thrashed backwards, its now exposed innards slashed and pierced by the renewed onslaught of the others.

The blood burn raged for several moments, forcing Amanuel to his knees with a groan, his vision swimming, sword falling from spasming fingers. He wanted to be sick, to vomit out the scalding blood that boiled through his body.

With a wordless grunt, he forced back the pain and recovered his sword. He pushed himself unsteadily to his feet and glared at the others.

'I hate having to do that, you cretins.' Amanuel pointed towards the darkness of the cave. 'The guardian is gone, I would say our way through is clear now.'

'I don't like the look of it,' protested Flay.

'Turn back then, and try your luck in the jungles,' snapped Amanuel, remembering the half-seen figure earlier.

'What about him?' asked Adorl, nodding towards the immobile form of Belaphus.

'Dead or dying,' Forsca replied casually, wiping snake blood from his blade. 'No use to us. One less cut of the reward to share.'

* * *

The gulley had led Marianne and her party some distance from the mountain, so far in fact that she began to think they would end up heading back to the coast. However, as the afternoon sun lowered towards the tree-filled mountains, their path turned sharply uphill and it was not long before they were again traversing the lower slopes.

When they came upon a clear stream, Gordwyn suggested a short break to refresh themselves and refill their flasks. While the crew busied themselves with this important chore, Marianne found a large rock beside the brook to use as a seat. The sun was warm still but lacked the strength-sapping intensity of its full glare. She closed her eyes and, for just a few heartbeats, let herself enjoy the warmth on her skin, the smell of the forest, the babbling of the water over rounded stones broken by the splash of fish and amphibians.

The islands of the Ghost Archipelago were beautiful – if one ignored the hostile natives, murderous serpentmen, carnivorous vegetation, predatory fauna and bands of rival Heritors willing to cut the throat of another for the smallest clue to the whereabouts of the fabled Crystal Pool.

Reminded of her purpose, she opened her eyes and brought out the journal of her great-great-great-great-great-

great-great-great-great-grandfather. When she thought of Copernichol like that, it seemed a little more extraordinary that any of his possessions had survived so long. It was hard to not think of the book as her grandfather's rather than Copernichol's, so entwined were the object and her memories of the two.

She found her place marked with a dried oak leaf from the gardens of the ancestral manse set between two slivers of near-transparent bone. Marianne read, occasionally glancing up at the mountains and other features to see if she recognised any landmark from Copernichol's detailed but colourful descriptions.

A shadow passed over the book, causing her to flinch. It was Oata. The Stone Warden jabbed a thumb back towards the others, who were stoppering the last of the water flasks and getting their packs ready.

'Nearly done.'

'Any guidance from Copernichol?' asked Dmitry, coming up behind Oata, his tarred leather bag slung over one skinny shoulder. 'Any great words of advice from the ancestor?'

'Yes, there is,' lied Marianne. Only a little lie, because she was pretty certain that 'the grate parrott of the skyes' referred to a particular outcrop of the mountain some distance to the west, if viewed from a different angle. Her intuition thrummed along her veins and she suppressed a shudder but not the accompanying grunt of discomfort. The parrot rock was definitely the right way to proceed.

'Are you in pain?' Oata asked, regarding her closely. With concern, or was it suspicion?

'Sitting on hard rock for too long,' said Marianne, slipping from the boulder and nursing her backside as she put the book back in her pack. 'And all the walking.'

They found a crossing point and used the water-slicked stepping stones to get to the other side of the stream. The trees were far sparser here, pure grasslands stretched up into the foothills. As they waded into the tall stems, Gabbri indicated the flattened stalks behind.

'Not a hard trail to follow,' he said.

'Nothing we can do about that, we have to go this way,' replied Marianne.

'Because the book says so?' asked Dmitry.

'Yes,' snapped Marianne, a little more harshly than she intended, exasperated by his tone. She turned on him, but softened her voice. 'As far back as I can remember, my grandfather read me the passages from this book and told me about the Heritors. I learned on his knee of how Copernichol Amontill travelled to the Ghost Archipelago, drank from the mystical waters of a crystal-clear pool and returned gifted with extraordinary powers. Generations have passed, each of us a little more declined in our gifts, with no sign that the Ghost Archipelago could be found. My grandfather spent his life looking for these islands, hoping to retrace the steps of his ancestor. Every effort he spent was wasted and it is cruel fate that he died only two years ago, on the cusp of the islands' return. I owe it to him, to his spirit and his memory, to finish the quest he never could.'

She wiped away the tear that had appeared at the thought, the droplet mingling with the sweat that already wetted the cuff of her shirt. Marianne set her shoulders, looked at the others and finished with a meaningful stare at Dmitry.

'You came with me, knowing this is all I have to offer. I promised you all a share of whatever treasures we can find, taking none for myself. I only want to see the Crystal Pool. To fulfil my grandfather's dream. You accepted, spat on your palm and shook hands on it. It is too late for complaint.'

Dmitry shrugged, reluctantly accepting Marianne's acceptance of the situation.

Right, she thought as she started off into the grass once more. *Let's just hope we're not all deluded fools, grandfather included.*

* * *

'I know this place.'

From the ridgeline he looked down into verdant cleft below, a towering waterfall at its head, a treeline rapids running its length.

His heart quickened at the sight, indelibly marked into his memories from seeing it in the book he now sought, rendered in crude ink by the supposed pen of Copernichol Amontill. Somewhere in that valley, according to the journal at least, lay the entrance to the Caves of Gold. He could not remember the accompanying description in detail. Something about an ancient civilisation that had populated the Ghost Archipelago many centuries even before Copernichol's arrival. Long dead, their city remained below the mountains of one of the islands.

'What's that?' asked Forsca, clambering up the last of the incline with his crew close behind.

'Nothing,' Amanuel replied. It was nonsense. The book was a fabrication, his memory playing tricks on him. A waterfall and forest. The islands were littered with such places, he was sure. And it was best not to even suggest to his mercenary companions that there might be any truth in its contents. He could not risk the warband considering the notion that they might earn more by taking the book rather than waiting for the rest of the money he had promised.

He spied colour and movement below and signalled for Herrick to come forward. The heavily tattooed Warden approached.

'Is that them?'

Herrick stepped a small distance away and lifted his hands, eyelids fluttering, lips moving in a whisper as he communed with the winds. It seemed as though a slight fog coalesced about his fingertips despite the strong winds that whipped over the shoulder of the ridge. For a fleeting moment, Amanuel thought he heard words in the sigh of the air, and there was a short outbreak of disconcerted muttering among Forsca's men. Amanuel ignored them. It had to be coming from Herrick.

With a jerk, the Storm Warden opened his eyes. He smiled and nodded.

'Yes, they are the ones we have been following.'

'Good. Now find me a way down there.'

A thirdde our complemente had abandoinned the trek or been killt by serpentes, wildmen, boars and dizzease. The cap'n raged fierce agin that the gold we found in the village twas but a litle of the hord we mite find if we lookd hard still. Such hope was lifid when we found another rivver. Brode but fast, from the peaks.

We follows up the waters for a day more. We came upon a valleye set thick with trees. Fearin more wilduns, we set dubble watch, but a peaseful nite past, an we woke with more strength that morn than for many afore.

After breakin our fast with fresh cort fish and eels, and sum eggs pilferd from nests aboute the water, we headd inland agin. Not long into the morn we saw a bridge of wite, brite in the sunne. We wonderd what hand fashiond such masunry, not a joint to be seen tween the blockes. Sure and hi it past the water. The cap'n left Davies and a quart of the crew to hol the bridg when we crosst. On the other side we found a big gate, marked by deville faces an shokin heathn roons. Some spell, feart the cap'n and we called up G'Nati, the wytchman from Aghad.

Prononucing all safe and sure, G'Nati led the cap'n an a few of us into the cave.

Inside we lit torches and found houses an temples an streets carvd from the rock isself. All stretchd as far as the lite carrid and beyonde.

In the depths of the gorge the sunlight was almost spent. The sky was touched with the red of dusk, the chatter of birds returning to their roosts loud in the trees that flanked the fast-flowing river. Marianne had hoped to find the Caves of Gold before nightfall, if only to have somewhere to shelter for the night. Hope faded as they pressed on, but a call from Dmitry a little way ahead roused their flagging spirits.

'Look,' he cried, pointing up the river. 'Look!'

In the growing gloom it was hard to make out what he had seen at first. Shielding her eyes against the low rays of the sun, Marianne saw better what had excited the crewman. Over the bridge, not more than five hundred paces distant, a bridge of white stone crossed the foaming waters.

Their exclamations of delight and surprise were short-lived, however, as the bushes a short distance ahead rustled with movement. Six men strode onto the bank of the river, blades in hand. Marianne instantly recognised their leader and swallowed a yelp of despair.

Her party drew their weapons, far more awkward in stance and poise than those that approached with grim purpose.

'Oata…' muttered Marianne, drawing the dagger from the sheath at her hip. 'Do something.'

The Warden murmured her assent and broke away. As she did so, two of the opposing group set their weapons back in their scabbards and pulled free bows.

A strange guttural shout emanated from Oata. She threw out her hands, heel of her palms touching, fingers splayed. The ground shook gently, the vibrations building. Stone and sand danced, raced in a zigzag towards the oncoming brigands. The Stone Warden's bass growling continued, like the sound of a rockfall echoing from a distant cave. The ripple became a crack, which became a broadening ravine as Oata dragged her hands apart, teeth gritted, eyes scrunched with effort as though she physically pulled the gap wider.

The slap of bowstrings was lost in the crash of breaking rock and thunder of the water. A moment later Oata staggered back, a more human cry wrenched from her lips. One shaft had missed, but the other jutted from her left arm, just above the elbow. Her incantation broken, the earth-tumult subsided, leaving the ground broken.

A chill gloom swept the valley. Marianne looked up to see swiftly gathering storm clouds above. Only then did she see the figure hanging back from the others, a seventh man in bright clothes gesturing in exaggerated fashion at the sky. A Storm Warden.

Gordwyn had seen enough and broke into a run, bellowing for his crew to follow. Their opponents countered, nimbly leaping over the scattered rocks and debris left from Oata's spell to fall upon the crew with clashing blades. The ring of fighting seemed harsh and loud, accompanied by the panicked squawk of birds taking flight into the darkening air. Lightning flickered, its gleam reflected in the blades of the combatants below.

Marianne's faithful followers tried their best. Dmitry was a swift target, always moving, but though he parried and wove with studied practice, his opponent laid his blade repeatedly against the crewman's own, forcing him back step by step. Gordwyn moved well for his bulk, roaring and shouting as he laid about with passion rather than skill. He shouldered a knife-wielding foe to the floor and stepped on the man's leg, eliciting howls of agony as bones broke under the pressure of his considerable weight.

Through the melee advanced the other party leader. He barely paid any attention to the hacking and ripostes around him, eyes fixed on Marianne.

Despite their enthusiasm, her crew were no match for the professional warriors. One by one they were beaten down and disarmed, so that when all was done they knelt in a scattered group, blades at their throats, arrows from the two bowmen directed towards Marianne. She broke her gaze long enough to check on Oata. The Warden was sitting down, teeth bared in pain, but she nodded at the unspoken question in Marianne's gaze. She'd live.

'Give me the book, Marianne,' snarled the bearded man, thrusting out his hand in demand.

She looked at him, fear, revulsion and shame all vying in her gut to make her dizzy and sick. She met his glare with defiance.

'It belongs to me, father.'

* * *

'Father?' The big one's incredulity almost made Amanuel laugh. He slid his sword – unused – back into the scabbard and turned a disparaging look on the motley assortment of outcasts his daughter had scraped into the semblance of a crew.

'Yes, she's my daughter, you artless, rump-fed bugbear. Who else do you think would chase your sorry little expedition across the sea and through these cursed jungles?'

'Father…' Marianne had tears in her eyes. She couldn't look at him, her concerned gaze returning again and again to her companions.

'Stop fretting, I'm not going to hurt anyone.'

'Tell that to her,' said Dmitry, jerking his head to where Oata was bandaging her arm with a strip torn from her clothes.

'The fat one broke my leg!' whined Flay in protest. He sat with his back to a rock clutching the damaged limb. 'I want to cut him!'

'Enough.' Amanuel's curt command silenced everybody. He twitched the fingers of his outstretched hand. 'The book, Marianne.'

'But we could do it together,' she pleaded, eyes wide. 'We can find the pool together. Grandfather would have l—'

'My father wasted his life and the fortunes of my family chasing this nonsense. I'll not see my kin homeless and bereft on this fancy. Give me the book.'

'It's worth more than whatever the duke is offering.' She pointed up the river. 'Look, that's the bridge before the Caves of Gold. Just like the entry says. It's true. Father, listen to me. My talent is never wrong. It's all true.'

His hand did not waver.

'I will take the book and get back the money your grandfather squandered. If you want a home to return to, child, then you will come with me.'

Reluctantly she pulled off her pack and brought forth the journal. She hesitantly offered it forward and Amanuel grabbed it from her grasp.

'Thank you.'

'What now?' she asked with quivering lip.

'We go back home. If you want to sail with these rejects of the dock beer houses feel free, but I think you would be better off staying with me.'

He signalled to Forsca, who nodded to his men to raise their weapons. Two of them moved to help Flay to his feet, pulling him up between them. Amanuel gestured for Forsca to approach and pulled ointment and proper bandages from the Captain's waistbag. He tossed it to the ground in front of Marianne's Stone Warden.

'You're the only one here worth a damn,' he told her. 'I can't for the life of me think why you would accompany such a ragtag of uselessness.'

'No, you can't,' she sneered in return.

Shrugging, Amanuel turned away, back to his daughter.

'I'll make camp further down the river and then we'll move along the coast back to the ship,' he told her, not looking back. 'I suggest you join us by nightfall.'

And, with that, Amanuel stuffed the old book into his belt and walked away.

Twas axidente that Markus nocked the dark stone plinthe of the large idol in the central plazza. The surfiss crakd, becoming dust like plasster. In the lite of the brandes reflctd from the large bronz mirrores abuv, we saw a glint. Excitd, the cap'n took his pommell to the stone an sure enuff it flakd away. Benith we found gold.

188

We set to explorin wit more viggor, testin every statue an even the walles. Sure enuff, as much was gold as was stone. Enuff for each manne presente to buy hisself a citie.

An then it was that the cap'n came over kweer and tol us that if this was jus a one city, wot mite the hart of the iland hide.

Tears streaming, Marianne watched her father and his cut-throats depart, heading down the river to the sea. She shook her head, unable to believe that the adventure had been ended even as it had begun.

She looked at her companions and her tears became sobs at the sight of their incredulity and hurt.

'I'm sorry,' she started, but no more words came. She fell to her knees, vision misted with tears.

Figures approached, she was not sure who in the dying light.

'I'm sorry,' she said again, sniffing loudly. 'The book… Without the book I have nothing to offer you.'

There was a short pause and then Dmitry crouched beside her, a hand on her shoulder.

'We didn't follow a book,' he said quietly.

'What do you mean?' She stifled another sob and wiped her face.

'Your father was right,' said Oata, coming up behind the crewman, the bandage on her arm stained red. She gestured to Gordwyn and the others, pain causing her to wince before she continued. 'Nobody else would hire a group like this. And no crew worth the salt in the water would have agreed to sail on a promise and prayer. We *are*

189

the dregs of the waterfront. The flotsam of the surge to find these islands. Gordwyn will be lucky if his heart lasts until we get back. Dmitry can barely string a sentence together in his own tongue, never mind any others. If you think 'Gabbri' is actually a man behind that veil...'

A feminine laugh betrayed the truth of this.

'Solomon's one drink away from a coma at any given moment. And everyone knows about your lotus addiction,' rumbled Gordwyn, looking at Oata. 'The stains on your tongue, the vague look first thing in the morning?'

The Stone Warden looked as though she might dispute this. Her angry glare became an expression of shame and she looked away, nursing her wounded arm.

'I still don't understand,' confessed Marianne as Dmitry helped her to get up.

'I never thought the book was real,' said the deck hand.

'I did,' said Gordwyn with a smile. 'But that isn't the point.'

'We followed *you*, Marianne,' said Solomon, a rare declaration from the taciturn swordsman.

'Don't go back with your father,' said Oata, turning around. 'If you give up, then we all have to. I still dream that we might find the Crystal Pool.'

'And if we don't, it doesn't matter,' declared Gordwyn. 'We came for the adventure, for the chance to be someone, to do something!'

'This is...' Marianne could not find the words. She smiled at each of them, wondering how she might have been so blessed in such desperate times. Then it occurred to her. Her Heritor-gifted intuition. She had been drawn to these people, not simply by chance but her own instinct.

'Then let us carry on,' she announced, straightening her clothes and pushing wisps of hair from her tear-streaked face.

She strode with determination along the river path until they reached the bridge. She paused, shared a glance with the others at the seemingly timeless stone crossing, and then set over the span. When they reached the crest of the bridge, a grand gateway came into view, carved into the rock of the gorge wall. It looked like a totem pole of the natives, with two dozen square blocks set upon each other, each a different, bizarre face with bulging eyes, beaks, leering tongues, and other grotesque features.

Steps, untouched by the many passing seasons, wound down from the bridge to the dark opening.

'Copernichol was right,' whispered Dmitry. 'There is a city here.'

'And gold?' ventured Gordwyn. 'Maybe the gold?'

'More than that,' said Oata. She gave Marianne a look, her meaning clear.

'Yes. Copernichol Amontill made it all the way to the Crystal Pool.' She turned and looked down the river, determination steeling her resolve, her heart fluttering with excitement rather than fright. 'The journal isn't fake. I don't know how, but we are going to get *my* book back.'

THE CLOCKWORK
CHART

BY
M. HAROLD PAGE

Ulrich awoke from dreams of drowning. His eyes opened on the darkness of his deck tent. Beyond the canvas, the waters of the Ghost Sea slapped the hull of his pinnace.

Somebody shook his shoulder. Whiskers tickled his ear. A voice hissed in his ear, 'Wake up, Heritor, you are being robbed!'

The Heritor curse crackled through Ulrich's skull. It drew little lightnings on his night vision, sent his body into motion. His arm snaked out, tangled a plump limb. He rolled and pulled.

The intruder tumbled over him; a bundle of flapping streamers and feathers in the gloom of the canvas tent.

A Storm Warden, then.

Ulrich rolled further, ended on top, his knee in the stranger's pudgy back. His left hand found a mane of dry scraggly hair and grabbed it. His right got his dagger – when had he drawn that? – at the other man's soft throat.

The Storm Warden chuckled. 'No thief I, Heritor. I came to serve you. And my first service is to warn you that you are being robbed.'

Ulrich strained his ears. His curse jolted his awareness into expanding.

On the Torraga dockside, a man joked and a woman laughed falsely. A tavern rumbled with talk. Several drunks bawled out a sea shanty with lengthy pauses to recall the words. A barmaid whispered in a patron's ear. A tapster broke wind. A cat stalked a rat. Fleas…

Too much! His headache would be bad enough as it was.

Ulrich furled in his perceptions, attuned himself to his pinnace, the *Redeemer*; the slap of water, yes, but also the creak of tarred ropes, the slight pitch and roll as a gentle swell ebbed and flowed through the harbour.

Nearby, somebody snored. Further off, bare feet pattered over the planking. Metal scraped. Somebody was picking the lock of one of the chests stowed near the mast. Ulrich could guess which one.

But how was it thieves moved around unchallenged?

A cold hand clutched his heart. 'My people!'

'Asleep,' hissed the Storm Warden. 'Ensorcelled. Get off me and I shall dispel the magic.'

But Ulrich was already sheathing his dagger and rising, hands lightly clutching Guiltbringer.

He shuddered. He had no memory of scooping up the long-bladed greatsword from where it lay by his side. Once again, his curse had reduced him to a mere puppet. How dare the intruders do this to him!

'Heritor, wait!' hissed the Storm Warden. 'The odds! It won't be a fair fight.'

'Since the ethics concern you, I'll challenge them first,' said Ulrich. He pushed out of his tent and crouched by the wheel.

The full moon painted the pinnace's deck in ghostly colours. The thieves hunkered by the mast, shadowy figures fumbling with the sea chests. They had a little rowing boat tied up amidships.

Ulrich's limbs twitched. His curse wanted him to plunge in among the intruders. Instead, he checked on his crew.

The six men and women lay beyond the mast on the foredeck where they had bedded down, all except portly Ayesha, the sailing mistress. She should have been on watch, but instead she sat slumped against the rail, snoring, her club on the deck by her side.

Ulrich exhaled. Just as the Storm Warden had said, they really were safe… for now. He stalked forward, untied the thieves' rowing boat and cast it off.

The thieves didn't seem to notice. Lock-picks clicked and scraped. Hinges creaked.

The pinnace's sail was furled out of the way, so Ulrich raised Guiltbringer above his head – a nice, intimidating guard that would let him strike to right and left – and stepped out from behind the slender mast.

He could.

He could just cut them down.

But that was what the curse wanted.

'Get off my ship, scum!' he growled.

The thieves whirled, drew weapons: nasty long knives, a length of chain. A chest gaped open. Already, a thief was stuffing the Pilgrim Banner into his coat.

Moving like a dancer, Ulrich glided closer. 'Give me back my banner,' he said. 'Last warning.'

The chain wielder whirled his weapon so that the links made a whirring hornet sound. 'Get out of the way, northman. There are six of us and one of you.'

Ulrich cocked his greatsword just a little bit higher.

'Hah,' said the chain wielder. 'You won't have room for fancy footwork here. Be reasonable—'

Guiltbringer split his skull as far as his teeth. The corpse slammed to the deck.

Two thieves sprang, tried to get Ulrich from left and right before he could pull back for a second strike. *Professionals!*

He pivoted back, brought the point around, plunged it into the leftmost man's chest. The blade sheared bone, found softer tissue.

The other man tried to slash his face.

Ulrich blocked against the unarmoured wrist. He flicked the sword up and over, cutting around the limb.

The man screamed, sprayed blood.

Ulrich sprang in amongst the survivors.

One threw himself overboard.

Ulrich's blade whirled into the other two: left, right, right, left, down…

Bits of corpse rained on the deck.

Ulrich's gorge rose. His limbs shook. A vice seemed to clamp around his temples. He lowered Guiltbringer until the blade trailed against the blood-spattered deck.

'Fine swordsmanship!' exclaimed the Storm Warden.

'Don't praise him!' cried Ayesha, now on her feet.

The sword clanged to the deck. The blade sang as if satisfied by its feast.

The crew struggled out of their bedding.

The Storm Warden stood in their midst, a shaggy little ball of feathers and streamers.

'No, Storm Warden,' said Ulrich, 'it was my curse doing the fighting. I take no joy of it.' He cocked his head at his crew. 'Hurry. Before the sun rises and the good citizens of Torraga notice the mess.'

Ayesha sent a couple of deckhands scurrying for buckets and mops. She eyed the intruder suspiciously.

'I am Stochastus,' said the Storm Warden, with a half bow to Ulrich and a polite nod to Ayesha, his sailing mistress.

'Check the banner,' ordered Ulrich. He beckoned and led the Storm Warden off to the stern so they were not overheard. 'I am grateful for the warning, sir, but why?'

'A kestrel whispered to me that you are my Eye of the Storm.'

'What? Me?' Ulrich let out a bark of laughter that hurt his head. He massaged his temples, realised his hands were sticky with other men's blood. 'When I am done with my quest, there will be no more Heritors, no more "eyes of the storm". Is that what you want, Stochastus?'

Stochastus grinned. The skin around his eyes crinkled into fleshy folds. 'I can only trust the kestrel and serve you.'

'*You* may trust a random bird, but I do not trust random strangers,' said Ulrich.

'Ulrich!' said Ayesha, hurrying up. 'The Pilgrim Banner is gone. Perhaps it's for the best.'

Ulrich smiled sadly. His sailing mistress had known him since he was a child. She must suspect that the price of concluding his quest would be his own death.

After the… the *incident*, Ulrich had thrown himself into discovering everything he could about his curse. He had unearthed his ancestor's journal in a cobwebbed attic. The legend really was true: She, along with a few score other explorers, had gained her murderous powers by drinking from the Crystal Pool during an ill-fated expedition to the Ghost Archipelago. Two hundred years later, and her blood-borne curse had surfaced in Ulrich.

He defied his family by writing to his disgraced cousin Linnet, a sorceress who spent her days wresting antiquities from an ancient frozen city people called 'Frostgrave'. In reply, she sent him a long letter about her adventures, plus an ancient leather-bound tome written in a dead language.

It took him months to translate the book. The labour had been a welcome distraction from his guilt and self-loathing. His conclusions had brought him a certain bleak satisfaction: in order to take the powers from all the Heritors, he must find the Crystal Pool and drown himself in it.

In one stroke, he would end his own torment, redeem himself, *and* rid the world of a malign influence.

Unfortunately, nobody knew how to find the Isle of the Crystal Pool in the ever-shifting maze that was the Ghost Archipelago, hence his need to consult the Clockwork Chart… and hence the need for the Pilgrim Banner.

'It's just a flag,' he said. 'We can get another one made up as soon as Tailor's Lane wakes up.'

'But whoever stole the banner will already be underway,' said Ayesha. 'We'll never catch up.'

'If only,' said Stochastus, 'you had assurance of a friendly wind to propel you all the way to the Isle of Farsight.'

Ulrich considered the Storm Warden. With his twinkly eyes and the bows tied into the braids of his beard, he looked like the favourite funny uncle everybody wished they remembered from childhood. Even so, he would have his own agenda – they always did. 'How do you know the object of my voyage, sir?'

Stochastus laughed. 'Why a zephyr fresh off the Northern Sea sang me ballads of adventure past and future, and one of them told of your quest for the fabled Clockwork Chart.'

'Welcome aboard the *Redeemer*, Stochastus,' said Ulrich.

* * *

For twelve days, the unnatural wind made a balloon of the spinnaker sail. The pinnace *Redeemer* skipped across the warm ocean like a happy porpoise. The plump little Storm Warden moved among the crew, swapping tall stories while Ulrich brooded and scanned the horizon.

On the morning of the thirteenth day, they sighted a plume of smoke. Slowly, the Ghost Archipelago heaved itself over the horizon; first, the black peak of the smoldering volcano, then mountains of lush green.

Ulrich roused himself from his dark thoughts and raised his spyglass.

It didn't take long to spot the jagged profile of the Isle of Farsight. It was exactly where the reports had sighted it – not guaranteed in the Ghost Archipelago, where islands jostled around like revellers at a midwinter festival. He gave orders and Ayesha wove the pinnace through shoals and around rocky headlands. Finally, their destination lay before them across a wide blue channel.

The spinnaker sail flapped and billowed backwards. The ship lost headway.

Ulrich gave Stochastus a questioning look.

The little Storm Warden shrugged expansively, making his feathers and streamers rustle. 'I am a better surprise than a threat.'

Ulrich nodded. 'Open the hold for the Storm Warden. Quickly.'

The hold wasn't much, just a damp space for stashing sealed barrels of supplies and weapons.

Stochastus contemplated it and, for the first time, frowned. 'I have no love of confined places.'

'Nor I,' said Ulrich, gently pushing his shoulders.

The crew stowed the spinnaker sail and worked the sheets. Ayesha hauled on the wheel and brought the pinnace out of irons. Now close hauled, she sailed at an angle into the wind while the crew leaned out to stop her from keeling over.

They entered a swarm of small fishing boats that raised sails and scattered. A sleek galley splashed to intercept them.

'A Drichean pentaconter with its mast down,' said Ulrich.

'Buccaneers,' said Ayesha.

'But still Dricheans,' said Ulrich. 'Hoist the Pilgrim Banner. Drop sail.'

As the pentaconter swept closer, the figures of bowmen became visible on its low forecastle.

'This had better work, Ulrich,' said Ayesha.

They came to a standstill. The pilgrim banner fluttered and snapped overhead. Ulrich glanced up at it and tried to look confident.

The original banner had been properly embroidered with gold thread and a fringe of little bells. This one, run up over a day by a gang of Torraga seamstresses, was just a yellow albatross stitched onto a blue cloth.

It did the trick though. Just within hailing distance, the galley rested oars. A big man leaned out from the prow. The streaks of white in his bushy black beard told of advanced years. However, his voice rang out deep and clear. 'Who dares violate the home waters of the Isle of Farsight?'

'Humble pilgrims,' replied Ulrich. 'We travel under the protection of the Holy Albatross.'

The man didn't respond. However, the oars splashed. The galley went about and sped off back towards land.

'They believed you!' exclaimed Ayesha.

'I told the truth,' said Ulrich.

The *Redeemer* sailed on into the wide bay. To starboard, a walled citadel rose up from a rocky headland. Ahead, sleek ships lay drawn up on the sandy beach, to which the first galley was headed.

Ulrich panned his spyglass over the strand.

He counted four fifty-oared galleys, each with a single mast. 'More Drichean pentaconters,' he said.

'This is a den of buccaneers,' said Ayesha. 'But why aren't they out raiding?'

'Not our problem,' said Ulrich. He panned over the headland until he picked out a small harbour, really just two moles embracing a rocky bay beneath the citadel walls. Carved albatrosses bracketed the harbour entrance. More stone albatrosses adorned a gate tower which guarded the foot of a long flight of steps. These zigzagged up the cliff face, connecting the harbour to the fortified enclosure far above on the summit.

A single pinnace lay tied up at the quayside. Ulrich's stolen – and much more expensive – Pilgrim Banner drooped from its mast. The sun flashed on a lens: somebody was looking back their way.

Ulrich pointed without lowering his glass.

Ayesha changed course, zigzagging them across the bay towards the little harbour.

Drichean soldiers patrolled the battlements of the gate tower. Their bronze armour was the kind of relic that cousin Linet sketched in her letter home: war gear to be fished out of the tombs of Frostgrave, not to be worn by living people. However, their recurved whalebone bows looked horribly functional.

As the *Redeemer* drew towards the harbour, Ayesha saw them too. 'Don't screw this up,' she said.

Ulrich nodded as he folded away his spyglass.

Ayesha gave the order to man the sweeps, and the *Redeemer* crept the last few yards up to the dockside. Meanwhile, Ulrich strapped on his sword belt.

The crew of the other pinnace left off games of dice, drew themselves up.

The *Redeemer* bumped the plaited rope buffers.

Ulrich leapt ashore and strode towards the other vessel. After three days at sea, the land seemed to tilt as he walked, but it wouldn't matter if it came to a fight – his curse could be relied on to seize each and every opportunity to take control of his mind.

A big man strode to meet him. His left hand casually steadied the hilt of a greatsword that rode at his hip. He moved just a little too quickly, too smoothly.

A knot formed in Ulrich's stomach. This was his mirror image: another Heritor swordsman who could match him blade for blade. Somebody who shared his curse, but relished its murderous power.

They met halfway between the vessels.

As the newcomer, Ulrich bowed first. 'Santino. So nice to see a friend from home.'

Santino bowed just deeply enough to avoid giving obvious offence, but not deeply enough to show proper respect. Close to, rust marks were visible on his doublet. Evidently, the big man usually wore a breastplate over that garment. 'Ulrich,' he boomed. 'I have heard that being your friend is dangerous.'

Ulrich ignored the barb. 'Nice banner,' he said. 'I used to have one just like it.'

'Amazing what you can buy in the night markets,' said Santino.

'Indeed,' said Ulrich. 'And apparently you can hire thieves as well.'

Santino's crew gathered in behind their captain: tough men and women, some sporting battle scars. They bore only daggers and long knives, but their belts boasted hangers crafted to hold axes and swords.

Ulrich looked past them to the other vessel. It was a single-masted pinnace like his. The hatch was open, but the sails were all neatly stowed, the ropes coiled. He considered the dice, the state of the ship, the twitchy aspect of the crew. 'I see the banner did not take you further than this dockside.'

Santino shrugged his broad shoulders. 'There is nothing for you here.' He waved meaty fingers as if dispelling a stench. 'If you turn around now, I might just let your family keep their house when I am king of Markibec.'

Ulrich blinked. Just like Ulrich, Santino could trace his line back to the old dynasty. 'Let me know when you make your attempt so I can return home to attend your execution.'

The big man laughed. 'The people tire of faction fights. The Grand Council is easily bribable. The city belongs to the first strong man armed with a few sacks of gold.'

'If you had even one sack of gold, you would not be here, hoping that the Clockwork Chart will show you where to find some,' said Ulrich.

Footfalls sounded from behind. He sensed his crew moving up to support him. He frowned. If things came to a fight, he would have his hands full with Santino. His crew would have to face the hard-bitten fighters of the rival expedition.

Santino shifted his left hand to his scabbard, ready for a fast draw.

'If you draw steel,' said Ulrich, 'then you will have broken the taboos that protect pilgrims. The Drichean bowmen will shoot us all down like dogs.'

Santino glanced up at the guards on the gate tower, who were indeed watching with interest. 'Hah!' he boomed. 'Stay if you like, little man. Your presence won't change anything.'

'Similarly,' said Ulrich, 'if you try to fight your way in, you will doom both our crews.'

'Taboo or not, do not insult one who could swat you like a bug,' said Santino. 'I am no fool.'

'And yet here you are, becalmed on the dockside,' said Ulrich.

'And you think you will fare better?'

'As a result of my close study of Drichean customs? Why, yes,' said Ulrich. 'That is as long as your rashness does not foul up my efforts.' He made a conscious effort to lighten his tone. 'Look, we both want to consult the Clockwork Chart, but for different purposes. I dislike you, but I can see the merit in a strong hand bringing peace to Markibec's streets. Why don't you stand down and let me negotiate for both of us? Give me seven days.'

'Seven years, more like!' Santino slapped his thigh and laughed. His crew laughed with him.

Santino was worse than a bully, realised Ulrich, he was a fool. Better the faction fighting should continue, than this oaf's posturing bring disaster to his home city.

Ulrich bowed shallowly. 'Good day, sir.' He turned away. Then, to his own crew, 'Come my friends.'

As they reached the *Redeemer*, Ulrich unbuckled his sword and handed it to Ayesha. 'I have to move fast, before Santino does something stupid. Break out my pilgrim robes.'

* * *

An hour later, Ulrich stood in the scant shade of the rock walls of the little bay. He mopped his brow and wished that the Drichean pilgrim robes were more convenient to get into and more comfortable to wear.

The too-tight headdress – the 'Crown of Known Unknowns'– squeezed his temples, giving him a headache. The thick weave of the tunic –'the Shirt of Potential Repentance'– soaked up perspiration as quickly as it generated it. The overall weight dragged on his shoulders, making him want to just sit down and snooze.

'Your arm?' prompted Ayesha.

He held out the limb so she could fasten on the nine bangles –'the Holes in Knowledge', apparently, though he was not certain of the translation.

'You look like a drowned dog, Ulrich!' said Ayesha. 'Or a thirsty one.' She handed him a water skin.

'I would go on all fours and bark like a dog,' said Ulrich. He gulped the lukewarm liquid. '…if only it would get me through that gate.'

On cue, the gate opened. A pair of Drichean sailors stepped through and made for Santino's pinnace. Though they sported bronze armbands and torques, on their hips hung steel swords of northern origin – looted no doubt.

'Drichean buccaneers,' said Ulrich.

The buccaneers sat cross-legged on the dockside. The big blond captain awkwardly folded his legs to join them.

'Faster, Ayesha,' ordered Ulrich. 'Santino's scheme seems to be taking shape, whatever it is…' He sighed.

It would cost him a headache, but he had no choice but to unleash his perceptions so he could hear them talk.

'*So we are friends now?*' That was Santino, using the old trade language.

'*Do friends help each other?*'

This was a second voice, deep and accented. Ulrich glanced down the wharf and saw that the older of the two buccaneers seemed to be doing the talking – big and with a grey-streaked beard, this was the Captain who had challenged them in the bay.

'*Of course,*' said Santino.

'*Then we are indeed friends,*' concluded the buccaneer, rising. Moments later and he and his companion passed back through the gate.

'I was right about urgent,' said Ulrich as Ayesha fastened the last of the little bells on the sleeve of his left arm.

* * *

Ulrich knocked on the bronze gate nine times, alternating between left and right hand. The metal had soaked up the heat of the morning so that each contact stung his skin. The jangly little bells on his sleeves did not improve his mood.

Bows creaked from within. One slip of a finger and a bronze-tipped shaft would skewer his body.

Sweat trickled into Ulrich's eyes. He schooled his breathing and told himself firmly that he could die here or he could die later – it was all one.

A hatch opened in the gate. The unseen guard spoke the ritual challenge.

Ulrich answered by loudly declaring his ignorance.

There was a pause and what could have been the rustle of parchment. The guard coughed and read out a stanza of poetry.

Ulrich responded by reciting the entire verse.

The guard read out a second stanza from a different poem, then several more. Each time Ulrich supplied the matching verse.

Ulrich mopped his brow.

The archers must be getting tired arms by now. There was nothing to stop them from just shooting him then claiming he had misspoken.

Metal clanged.

Ulrich jumped back. His right hand went to his hip where Guiltbringer should have hung.

It was only the bar being drawn back. The bronze door swung inward.

'Come,' said the guard.

Ahead lay the staircase that wove up the cliff face. One armoured warrior led the way. A second brought up the rear.

Sweltering in his pilgrim's garb, Ulrich trudged upwards. Each step became a battle. Halfway up, he swayed and rested his back against the rock wall. It would be a long drop to the stone quayside.

One of the guards motioned with his spear and flashed his teeth. 'Not far now, pilgrim.'

The steps ended, not at a gate in the citadel's ramparts, but at an open-sided pavilion perched on the cliff edge.

Ulrich gratefully stood in its shade and took a good look at the defences.

The citadel took up about the same space as a middle-sized castle. Where the walls weren't flush with the clifftops, a deep moat had been cut into the rock. He could spot only one entrance: a gate on the landward side, accessible via a drawbridge.

A woman said, 'Will you not join us, pilgrim?'

Ulrich turned and moved further into the pavilion. His eyes grew used to the shadows. He found himself facing a tall blue-clad woman. Behind her, attendants heated pots on charcoal tubs.

'I am Lady Brightfeather,' said the woman, 'High Priestess of the Holy Albatross.'

Ulrich genuflected. Voice croaking, he began the ritual greetings he'd memorised.

The priestess waved them aside. 'I think, sir, we have established that you have studied our customs. We should like to know whence came such knowledge. Sit.'

As bidden, Ulrich took his seat on the cool stone floor.

Lady Brightfeather descended to sit cross-legged in front of him. She was a striking woman; sharp eyes and a hawk nose, with braided black hair that made it difficult to judge her age. 'Well?' she prompted.

'The writings of Sir John Mandeville, my lady,' said Ulrich.

'Ah,' said the high priestess. 'I shall have the records searched.' She motioned to the servants, who brought steaming cups of coffee.

The drink was sweet and aromatic.

Ulrich sipped appreciatively and contemplated the Ghost Archipelago running off to the south. There was no order to the islands and coral reefs. Jungled mounds jostled rocky peaks. Nearby, horseshoes of sand framed placid lagoons. In the distance, a column of black smoke marked a volcano's position. White sails speckled the sea like scraps of windblown paper: explorers and adventurers seeking fortune or enlightenment.

'What are you thinking?' asked the priestess.

'That somewhere out there lies the Isle of the Crystal Pool,' said Ulrich. He frowned. Something about the priestess commanded his honesty. The worst of it was that, though he was sure magic was at work, he had no will to resist.

'Just another seeker after power,' said the priestess. 'You disappoint me.'

'I seek the opposite of power.' Ulrich set his coffee down on the flagstones. 'The Crystal Pool's powers have cursed my family, made its sons and daughters into killers. Not just my family. It has turned honourable lines into dynasties of cruel tyrants, merchant houses into pirate clans, and dissolved whole generations into scatterings of rogues.'

'They all had choices,' said the priestess. 'Just as you did when you killed your friend.'

Ulrich rose. 'Now you are reading my memories. That is one intrusion too many...' His voice trailed off as his mind whirled back to a faction fight in a narrow Markibec street... to the elation of suddenly *really* understanding how to use a sword... the bliss of flowing through the spaces in the whirl of blades... then the shock in the faces of both sides as they drew apart, dragging their dead with them... Finally, Hans's maimed corpse and the knowledge that his curse had driven him to cut down his childhood friend.

Ulrich steadied himself against a column. 'That was uncalled for.'

Lady Brightfeather shook her head. 'Choices,' she repeated, now standing eye to eye with him.

'My curse gave me none,' said Ulrich. 'But I have the choice to end the curse for everybody. As a pilgrim I have a right to know the position of the Isle of the Crystal Pool.'

Lady Brightfeather motioned to a servant who handed Ulrich a sheet of parchment bearing sailing directions. 'Your request was anticipated.'

Ulrich glanced at the chart, laughed and handed it back. 'And your response was disingenuous. The elusive Isle will have gone before I can reach it.'

Lady Brightfeather made an open-handed gesture. 'Alas, the Clockwork Chart informs but does not predict.'

'So let me examine it!' said Ulrich. 'I am a scholar of all things mathematical. If there are cogs and gears, then predictive formulae can be derived. Think of the...'

She held up her hand to cut off his words. 'By custom, only the pure may enter the citadel. The priestesses draw up charts and convey them to the supplicants.'

'That may change,' said Ulrich, 'despite your custom. My countryman in the other pinnace conspires with your buccaneers.'

'They are not *my* buccaneers,' she said. 'They are renegades who exploit this island's path through the Archipelago.'

'Whether they are yours or not, they threaten your safety,' said Ulrich.

'If they attack the temple, then the Holy Albatross will unleash her wrath on them.'

'Meaning *you* will unleash *your* wrath on them.'

The high priestess tilted her head but said nothing.

'That explains why they respected the Pilgrim Banner when we sailed in…' mused Ulrich. Sweat trickled into his eyes. He blinked and mopped his brow. 'But if Santino is involved, he will have some scheme to win. Do not underestimate him.'

'Do not underestimate *me*,' said Lady Brightfeather.

Some preternatural quality in her voice made the hair stand up on the back of Ulrich's neck. No, he should not underestimate her. But nor should he and his crew become swept up in the impending storm.

'I wish you well,' said Ulrich. He pulled off the pilgrim headdress and placed it carefully on the flagstones. He took the opportunity to pick up the half-empty coffee cup and gulp it down. Then he shed the pilgrim robe and twisted off the armlets. 'Give these to somebody who needs them.' He straightened. 'I will find the Crystal Pool without the Clockwork Chart.'

Ulrich's headache came on as he descended the steps.

* * *

The gate guards looked at him oddly, but let him back through into the Pilgrim's Harbour.

Santino blocked his path. The big Heritor sneered down at him. 'I see your knowledge of Drichean custom did not help you.'

Ulrich's fingers tensed, longing for his sword. 'You were right,' he said, 'there is nothing for me here.'

Santino smirked, but he also bowed and stepped aside.

Ulrich's crew awaited him on the *Redeemer*. 'Cast off,' he ordered. 'Get us away from here.'

They shoved off and used the long-handled sweeps to nudge the boat out of the harbour, all the while putting up with jeers and catcalls from Santino's crew.

In the bay, the wind was against them, but the light pinnace easily zigzagged across the wide blue waters. They made good headway towards the ocean.

'Where to?' asked Ayesha.

'I need to find some other way to locate the Isle of the Crystal Pool,' said Ulrich.

'Back to Markibec, then?' she asked. 'We could break the voyage at...'

Ulrich shook his head. 'I cannot face going home.'

'Your friend Hans came to a faction fight with a sword in his hand,' said Ayesha. 'It wasn't your fault you killed him.'

'Wasn't it?' He raised his spyglass and trained it on the harbour. Santino's men loitered on their pinnace. There was an unfamiliar figure in their midst – a mountain of a man in a shaggy coat with red and white toadstools growing out of its shoulders. Santino had *also* been hiding his own mystic, though this one was an Earth Warden.

'You were in the grip of your Heritor powers,' said Ayesha.

'I didn't have to be. I had a choice,' said Ulrich.

'You were young!'

'Young and a bad person, apparently,' said Ulrich.

Now Santino gave an order. His crew cast off and manned the sweeps. The pinnace pulled out from the dockside and headed for the harbour mouth.

Meanwhile, the Earth Warden made more subtle arm gestures.

'Nobody prepared you,' said Ayesha.

'Isn't that how life works?' said Ulrich. 'Damn!'

A house-sized chunk of rock detached from the cliff face. It fell oh-so-very-slowly, taking with it a cloud of pebbles. It crunched into the gatehouse, utterly erasing it, then splashed into the harbour – all eerily soundless thanks to the distance.

Some of the crew pointed and shouted.

The rumble-crash of falling stone finally reached them over the water.

Ayesha looked over her shoulder and cursed. 'We're well out of it.'

'Yes,' said Ulrich.

Santino's pinnace was already heading back for the quayside. The men on the deck threw off their cloaks. Breastplates and ringmail sleeves flashed in the sun. As the vessel touched, they leapt off and headed for the now-unguarded steps, the Earth Warden striding along in their midst.

Ulrich recalled how the landward section of the citadel walls sat above a deep rock-cut moat. It should have vouchsafed them extra protection. Now, at the hands of the Earth Warden, that moat would become a liability.

He panned the telescope over the harbour beach. The little fishing boats had upped anchors and were making for shore as if a storm were coming.

The five beached buccaneer ships, however, were deserted. Ulrich did not need his curse to tell him exactly where their crew had gone.

'Turn about,' he said. 'If Santino succeeds in his scheme, then he will make himself King of Markibec. This is my fault. I have to stop him.'

Ayesha bellowed orders.

They came about. The sail billowed. The wind behind them, they skipped back the way they had come.

Ulrich called for his armour. First came the brigandine – a leather waistcoat of which a lining of metal plates held in place by brass studs. As a crewman buckled it on, Ulrich said, 'You can put me off at the harbour.'

'No,' said Ayesha. 'We'll come with you.'

Ulrich circled his shoulders, checking he could move in the armour. 'This is not your fight,' he said.

Next came the bascinet, an open-faced helm that gave him good visibility. He flipped down the hinged nose piece.

'But we are all citizens of Markibec,' said Ayesha. She raised her voice. 'What say you, friends? Shall we flee while Santino loots enough wealth to buy the crown of Markibec?'

The crew chorused, 'No!' and 'Fight!'

The hatch flipped open and Stochastus clambered out.

'What about you Storm Warden?' asked Ulrich.

Stochastus grinned. 'I will follow the Eye of the Storm.'

* * *

The *Redeemer* swept unchallenged into the Pilgrim Harbour.

The dockside was empty except for some bronze-armoured corpses scattered over the rubble of the guard tower. A bell clanged faintly. Overhead, a whorl of dark clouds coiled like a great spring.

Ulrich jumped ashore. 'Come on, my friends, we have some climbing to do.'

The brigandine was heavy, but less cumbersome than the pilgrim robes had been. The air was so thick it was like wading through water. Ulrich didn't care. He took the steps two at a time while his people struggled to keep up.

From above, stone crashed. Men roared. Weapons clashed.

So much for the priestess's strong-walled citadel.

Ulrich realised he was taking the steps in long bounds – a moment of distraction and his curse had snared him. He slacked off a little, but still reached the top ahead of his people.

He halted in the cover of the little pavilion where he had taken coffee with Lady Brightfeather only that morning.

A chunk of the landward section of the citadel walls had collapsed into the moat, forming a causeway. Santino and his heavily armoured crew formed the tip of a wedge of buccaneers who strove to force their way inside. More milled around outside, trading arrows with the defenders or just yelling encouragement.

Ulrich's crew arrived; panting, red-faced, clutching spears with sweaty hands.

The dark clouds now spread across the sky, bringing an early twilight.

Ayesha squinted into the gathering gloom. 'What now?'

Ulrich turned to the Storm Warden, who seemed none the worse for his climb. 'Can you get us over the wall to join the defenders?'

'I've no idea!' said Stochastus. 'I could certainly hurl you over, but the citadel has magical defences.'

'They didn't stop the wall from coming down,' said Ayesha.

'No, they didn't, did they?'

'Hey, northmen!' The grey-bearded buccaneer was shouting at them in the trade language. 'Come on! No hiding in the shadows. You all fight or no deal. Even the crazy little fat guy.'

'Who can he mean?' asked Stochastus.

Ulrich raised his voice, 'Just coming!' He turned to his crew. 'Right. It seems we all look the same to them... Let's get close and let them have it. That should turn the tide.'

He led his people through the milling crowd of buccaneers – most of them more lightly armoured than the storming party – and made for the breach. 'Hold steady, my friends,' he said. 'Nearly there...'

Another moment and their surprise attack would let the defenders sally out and rout the buccaneers. Hopefully, they would realise his crew was fighting on Lady Brightfeather's side.

Forked lightning connected sky and ground. Two buccaneers simply exploded. Several more fell prone. One ran in circles with his hair on fire.

Ulrich's ears rang but he grinned. Lady Brightfeather was certainly bringing down the wrath of her god as she had promised.

The surviving throngs of buccaneers yelled and went for the only cover they could find, pushing in towards the breach. The extra weight of numbers drove the head of the wedge inside. The defenders broke. The buccaneers streamed across the moat.

'What now?' asked Ayesha.

But Ulrich was already striding towards the breach.

They picked their way over the rubble and into the precinct of the citadel where even Sir John Mandeville had not managed to penetrate.

Inside, a wild melee surged around a jumble of buildings. There was more yelling than killing. Though the buccaneers had steel weapons, the temple guards plied their bronze-tipped spears with gusto, keeping the other fighters at bay.

Ulrich sensed Santino moving deeper into the warren. Avoiding the knots of combat, he led his people after his adversary.

The way opened into a small plaza in front of an octagonal temple.

Red plumes waved over a mass of buccaneers – the temple guards were holding the entrance. Lady Brightfeather and her attendants stood on a balcony overlooking the fighting. She raised her arms. Lightning cracked down into the plaza.

It haloed the mighty figure of the Earth Warden who stood further back, in the middle of a loose circle of Santino's crew. The thunderclap was like a slap in the ears.

Ulrich flinched. His crew back stepped, reeled.

Unperturbed, undamaged, Santino's Earth Warden struck the paving slabs with his staff. Shards of stone flew off in the direction of the high priestess.

She held out her hands, pushing the air.

The stones seemed to hit an invisible wall. They stopped dead, then dropped into the melee on the temple threshold.

Lady Brightfeather staggered. Her attendants set her back on her feet. Again, she raised her arms. Lightning webbed the clouds, but no bolts struck the plaza. She sagged against her companions.

Santino's Earth Warden slammed his staff into the ground. His deep-throated chant reverberated below the sound of the melee. The earth rumbled.

Stochastus the Storm Warden broke into song; something between a shanty and an ululating prayer. He went up on his toes and, despite his rotund figure, performed a nimble-footed dance. Little dust devils whirled across the darkened plaza and converged on the Earth Warden.

The big man flailed his arms as if mobbed by a swarm of hornets.

Stochastus laughed as he pranced and pirouetted. 'That should give the lady some breathing space.'

Santino's head whipped around. He pointed his sword at Ulrich's crew. His men formed up around him and began to advance on them.

Ulrich drew Guiltbringer and strode to meet his adversary.

* * *

Santino, extending his sword like a lance, roared and charged.

'Split and flank,' ordered Ulrich. 'I'll deal with the buffalo.'

As his crew ran off to the left and right, Ulrich dropped into a fighting stance – bent legs, left foot forward – and cocked Guiltbringer over his rear shoulder. His opponent obviously planned to use bulk and better armour to intimidate then overwhelm him.

Still roaring, Santino bounded closer, long legs devouring the distance between them, driving the lethal point of his sword towards Ulrich's face.

The timing had to be just right.

The blood rushed in Ulrich's ears. His breathing quickened. He tried to relax, tried to focus, but not on the image of the sword driving through his cheek, smashing his teeth…

Santino was nearly on him now, whites of his eyes wide, lips distended in a berserker grin.

Any moment…

Any moment…

NOW!

Ulrich's curse blazed through his limbs, setting his veins on fire.

He twitched his sword across and down, pivoting to the side as he cut.

Guiltbringer whistled down on top of Santino's sword and forearms. The crossguard deflected the wild thrust. The blade slammed uselessly into his enemy's mail. The point, however, split the rings and skewered the meat of the bicep.

That wasn't enough to stop the big Heritor.

Santino kept coming. He took his left hand off his sword, and pivoting forward, reached for Ulrich's neck. Meanwhile, he raised his right hand into a hanging parry, shoving Guiltbringer aside.

Ulrich did not resist the push on his sword. His blade swung behind him, bringing forward the pommel: the solid iron counterbalance.

He slammed it into Santino's face.

Crimson splashed.

The big man staggered back. Blood streamed from his wrecked nose.

Ulrich whipped his sword back around. The blade clanged off Santino's helmet.

Santino roared and threw a wild blow at Ulrich's head.

Ulrich sprang out of the way. He cut to the other side, slightly lower.

This time Guiltbringer struck home below his helmet. The keen-edged blade sheared flesh and bone. Head and helmet clanged to the flagstones.

The corpse stumbled past, fountaining blood.

Now Ulrich could take in the situation.

Stochastus and Santino's Earth Warden wrestled on the ground, the larger mystic somehow failing to pin down the plump little Storm Warden. Two of the *Redeemer*'s crew were obviously dead. Ayesha was also down, but clutching her leg and cursing loudly. The three survivors stood over her, using their spears to fend off twice their number of hardened mercenaries.

Ulrich ran over, dropped back into a fighting stance.

One of the mercenaries saw him, turned.

Ulrich cut him down. And the next man. And the next.

He passed through the professional soldiers like a dancer making his way down the line at a wedding.

The last man stumbled away clutching the stump of his wrist.

Ulrich tensed to spring after him, finish the job. Instead he forced himself to stop and check his sailing mistress.

'Go,' said Ayesha. She bit back a groan. 'Save the Storm Warden.'

Santino's Earth Warden now sat astride Stochastus, trying to punch him in the face while the latter squirmed and wriggled.

Ulrich ran the Earth Warden through the back and kicked the dying man off his friend.

A female scream cut through the sound; not so much a scream as a great bird of prey roaring a challenge. Lady Brightfeather stood on the balustrade of her balcony, arms and legs spread, head thrown back, tendrils of lightning writhing across her body. The scream mingled with the howl of a rising wind.

The world tilted... or rather the clouds raced past overhead.

Air currents roared between the buildings, plucked at roof tiles, buffeted Ulrich and his crew.

The buccaneers battling at the temple entrance faltered. A couple of men turned and ran. Then a half-dozen. Then a score, until only the temple guards remained: twelve warriors standing shoulder to shoulder, big shields locked, war gear splintered and dented and notched, mounds of corpses at their feet.

Stochastus nudged Ulrich. 'We're being summoned, Heritor.'

Lady Brightfeather now stood more demurely behind the balustrade, her headdress snaking in the wind she had called up. One arm rested on the shoulders of a supporting attendant, the other waved in invitation.

Two of the crew picked up Ayesha. 'We won!' she shouted above the rising storm. 'Now let's get inside.'

* * *

The wind pushed at Ulrich. It whistled against the edge of his helmet, chilled the exposed skin of his face and hands. Beside him, the crew weaved and stumbled like drunks. The plump Storm Warden danced, braids and streams alive in the air currents.

They made it to the colonnade, then through the doorway to stand in the antechamber amongst dead and wounded temple guards.

The door to the Sanctuary of the Holy Albatross lay open. At the far end, flickering lamplight played across a giant figurine of the goddess, whose golden wings stretched across the entire vault.

A couple of unwounded guards shoved on the doors: great bronze disks rolled in grooves to close the curved-sided entrance. The wind shrilled through the narrowing gap. Finally, the doors thudded into place.

Strong enough to withstand the storm, judged Ulrich, but not an armed attack.

An eerie silence descended, broken only by the whine and hiss of the wild weather beyond the temple's threshold.

'I don't understand,' said Ulrich. 'The storm is impressive, but hardly lethal. Why did the buccaneers flee? They were winning.'

'Buccaneers cannot go buccaneering without their ships,' said Ayesha. His sailing mistress was seated on the floor while a temple guard bound her injured leg.

Ulrich imagined the storm thundering into the great bay. The fisherfolk must have known it was coming, which is why they fled inland. He shuddered. 'Is the *Redeemer* in peril?'

'No,' said Lady Brightfeather, emerging from a side room at the head of her attendants. She smiled tightly. 'Oddly, the Holy Albatross will leave the Pilgrim Harbour unscathed.'

Ulrich shuddered again. A tremor went through his limbs. His helmet seemed to have tightened. The first claws of his headache sank into his temples. 'How long before we can take our leave?' he asked, unbuckling his chinstrap.

'A while. Long enough for you to view the Clockwork Chart.'

'What?' Ulrich half-lifted Guiltbringer. He gestured with his left hand, indicating the blood on the blade, the splatter on his arm and chest. 'If I was impure earlier, how much more impure must I be now?'

Lady Brightfeather made her open-handed gesture. 'You will understand. Come.'

Ulrich left his sword and helm and followed the high priestess into the side room, then down a narrow staircase.

Cool, still air soothed his head but the metal-plated brigandine grew heavier with each step. His shoulders were sagging by the time they reached the bottom.

The staircase opened out onto a raised wooden walkway that ran around the side of a torch-lit cavern.

'The Clockwork Chart,' declared Lady Brightfeather.

Weights and pulleys decked the walls. What looked like four massive orreries filled the cavern floor. Instead of the Sun and planets, the brass arms bore little model islands. Each orbited around yet another island placed over the spindle. The nearest of these was clearly a detailed model of the Isle of Farsight.

Ulrich leaned against the rail and recalled the chart Lady Brightfeather had given him. Using the Isle of Farsight as a fixed point, he cast about.

There! On the other side of the cavern hung a little island with a cup on its summit – the Isle of the Crystal Pool.

'I knew it!' cried Ulrich. He winced, clutched his temple. He continued in softer tones. 'There *is* a pattern. I can work out the formula... let me fetch measuring tools.'

Lady Brightfeather laughed. She pulled a lever. 'Watch.'

Gears creaked. Weights dropped. Metal clunked. The sound reverberated in Ulrich's skull. He flinched, gritted his teeth.

With a metallic squeal, extra empty arms lifted into position, giving each orrery the look of a dandelion seed.

A spring boinged. With a painful clattering, everything began to move. The islands turned around the spindles, some clockwise, some anticlockwise. As they rotated, the arms rippled, shortening and lengthening in waves. Every so often, there was a collision and an island attached itself to the tip, an empty arm belonging to one of the other orreries.

Ulrich stared, jaw open. After a while he cried, 'It's utterly random! There's no damned pattern.'

Lady Brightfeather yelled over the noise. 'It's a divination tool, like casting the bones or shuffling the cards.'

The clatter died away. The movement ebbed. Now almost all the islands were back where they had started.

'Each island incorporates a stone from the real island,' said the high priestess.

Ulrich leaned further out. 'Sympathetic magic…'

One particular island had moved. The Isle of the Crystal Pool now sat very close to the Isle of Farsight… perhaps just a morning's voyage away. Were things to end so abruptly?

'How long…' Ulrich realised he was shouting. He lowered his voice. '…will it stay there?'

'A few days, perhaps,' said the high priestess.

Ulrich averted his eyes from the place where he would die.

Other islands had also shifted location.

He pointed to one that bore what looked like a broken tower. 'What's that one?'

'Oh,' said Lady Brightfeather. 'The Tower of the Sanguine Topiarists. Long abandoned, but said to be dangerous and full of riches.'

'And that one?'

'The Tombs of the Skyborn… no I don't know what that means. Again, reputed to be full of treasure.'

'Santino could have done it, then. Gathered enough wealth to make himself king of Markibec,' said Ulrich.

'There will be others like him,' said Lady Brightfeather. 'Patient enough not to need the Clockwork Chart.'

Ulrich stared at the little model islands. Even if he did away with the Heritors, the Ghost Isles would remain. Their real curse was that they offered easy wealth to the ruthless and the ambitious, who could then return to wreak havoc in their own societies.

And with that realisation came the understanding that it wasn't Ulrich's Heritor curse that killed Hans. Nor even were Ulrich's own moral failings really to blame. Hans was just another victim of the senseless faction fighting that wracked Markibec, faction fighting that put childhood friends on opposite sides.

Perhaps Santino was right and the crown of Markibec was ripe for the plucking. If so, why shouldn't Ulrich be the one to make himself king? To end the faction fights and hold the throne against all comers?

His mind raced. Once he had established order in the city, he could deal with all the robber barons that beset the trade routes, and then perhaps extend his peace to the other neighbouring cities…

'When we first talked,' said Lady Brightfeather, 'you were divided against yourself and impurity festered in that division. Now you are pure and whole.'

'Pure *what*, though?' asked Ulrich. 'I don't feel I have become a better person.'

'Perhaps not,' said Lady Brightfeather. She offered him her arm. 'Come. Your Storm Warden awaits you, Eye of the Storm.'

THE PRICE YOU PAY

BY
PETER MCLEAN

I almost died in Southport.

I stood at the prow of *Dancing Girl* with the salt wind blowing in my hair and the spray in my face as the ship wallowed across the waves, and fought back the tears of shame. I had been so godsdamned scared.

There were four of them, from the Guild of Mercers. Mercers, for the love of the gods. Cloth merchants. Hardly known for their murderous reputation, but they'd had an axe to grind about those bolts of silk I had sold them the previous day. They had brought that axe to the harbourside tavern with them, and some knives too.

I was drinking with Jondan while the rest of my crew were off entertaining themselves with whatever they did when I wasn't looking. I dread to think, really. The mercers cornered us in the tavern, their blades glinting in the lantern light, and put their case to me.

Perhaps those bolts hadn't been silk all the way through, I'll admit that. Perhaps I had padded them a little with roughspun cloth. Perhaps I had padded them a lot.

If we had sailed with the dawn tide like Jondan had urged then I would have got away with it too, but no. I'd had to stay in Southport one more day, chasing rumours. That decision almost cost me my life.

'Well?' the lead mercer demanded. 'What do you have to say for yourself, Marek Price?'

He was a swarthy fellow with an angry look on his face and that axe in his hand, only half-concealed under his loose robe.

I swallowed. I could have taken him, axe or no axe, I knew that. Was I not the last living descendant of the great Marta Price, founder of Price Shipping and oh-so much more? Marta Price, who, seven generations ago, had journeyed to the fabled Ghost Archipelago and there drunk the waters of the legendary Crystal Pool.

Marta Price, who had made herself invincible.

I was that indeed, not that my crew knew anything of it. Even Jondan didn't know about Marta's legacy. I may have inherited some of Marta's powers but not, I'm afraid, her bravery. By my own admission, I am a coward.

I wore a sword at my hip but that was more for show than anything else, nothing more than was expected of a ship's captain. With the blade alone I'm no better than any other man, if even that good. Only if I use the legacy of Marta Price do I become unstoppable, and this is the very thing I fear. I could feel my heart pounding in my chest just thinking of it. Jondan is even less use in a straight fight than I am, and the only things that hung at his tattered belt were a trowel with a clod of earth still stuck to it, and two small bags of what he called 'interesting stones'. Right then I was more interested in the mercer's axe than Jondan's bags of dirt. I took a deep breath to steady my nerves, and forced myself into action.

'I say this!' I yelled, and flipped over the table so that our tankards of ale flew up into the faces of the armed men in front of us.

A choice between fight or flight is one that makes itself, in my opinion.

I grabbed Jondan's arm and half-dragged him after me as I sprinted for the back door of the tavern and out into the heat of the yard. Even in the evening darkness the air sweltered, and there was not so much as a breath of wind from the sea.

'You're going to get me killed one of these days,' Jondan panted as he ran at my side.

The back door of the tavern crashed open again as the mercers charged after us. I could almost feel the wicked blade of that axe slamming between my shoulder blades.

Don't make me do it, don't make me…

'Do something!' I gasped at my friend.

Jondan cursed under his breath and stabbed out a hand towards the crumbling stone wall that edged the yard. There was a grinding noise as four hefty rocks pulled themselves free of the wall and shot through the air, striking down our pursuers with satisfying thuds.

I kept running, out through the back gate of the yard and into an alley that ran behind the tavern, the breath coming hard through my mouth until I realised Jondan was no longer at my side. I stopped halfway down the alley and leaned against a rotting wooden fence for a moment, gasping.

My friend strolled out of the tavern yard a moment later with a small stone in his hand, studying it closely as he walked. I shook my head at the state of him, his frayed and patched clothes and the deeply ingrained dirt on his hands. Jondan was an Earth Warden, of course, one of those peculiar fellows who believe that the land is sacred and connects all living things in some strange, mystical web of nature magic. I didn't understand anything of it, but at least his brand of magic didn't seem to hurt him when he used it. There he had me at a great disadvantage, I had to admit.

'Will you hurry up?' I hissed at him. 'I don't want to finish the evening dead.'

'Hmm? Oh, they're all out cold,' he said. 'When I move a rock, it goes where I put it.'

I nodded and heaved a great sigh of relief.

I hadn't had to do it. Marta's legacy was untapped, thank the gods.

Marta's legacy was my inheritance from the Price dynasty, that and one lone, leaky single-masted ship with the unlikely name of *Dancing Girl*.

That legacy was my blessing and my utmost curse. What is the point of superhuman powers if you don't dare use them?

* * *

A great wash of spray burst across the prow of *Dancing Girl*, soaking my thin linen shirt to my chest and jolting me out of my thoughts. I was glad of the momentary coolness the water brought me. Here in the Southern Ocean the heat was like a living thing, even out on the open sea. I pushed my wide-brimmed hat back from my eyes and wiped sweat and salt water from my forehead with the back of my hand, and squinted into the distance.

Leaving the whole 'nearly dying' thing aside, our stopover in Southport had been a success. There was coin in my purse again at last, and more importantly there was news. Rumours, yes, but believable ones. The word on the docks and in the taverns was that the Ghost Archipelago had finally reappeared, after seven long generations.

Two hundred years of nothing, and now… now, if the rumours were to be believed, it had returned. Two hundred years ago Marta Price had walked those islands, drank the waters of the Crystal Pool and plundered the untold treasures of lost civilisations. She had returned both magically invincible and fabulously wealthy, and had founded the Price Shipping dynasty that six successive generations of Prices had run into the ground and virtually bankrupted. If only she had come back immortal as well we might still be rich, but alas that was not the case. My father, alas again, was probably the worst of the Prices. In the thirty years it had taken him to drink himself to death, the Price line had reduced from nine ships to one, and I suspected *Dancing Girl* was only left for me into inherit because no one had wanted to buy her.

Truth be told she was an ugly ship, and she leaked badly enough to keep my six-strong crew busy with the bilge pumps in anything but the calmest sea. Ah well, a leaky ship was better than no ship, and being a ship's captain was considerably better than actually working for a living.

'Land ho!'

The cry came from Melissa in the crow's nest, and I craned my neck to see her leaning from her precarious perch with one thin arm pointing ahead and slightly to the east. I lowered my hat to shade my eyes and squinted into the distance, wincing as the bright sunlight flashed from the shining blue waves.

I could see it now, a distant shape and a thin column of smoke on the horizon. The fire mountain!

The rumours had been true, I realised. When the far-ranging fishermen of Southport had first brought back tales of a fire mountain seen where no land should be, the port had suddenly become a bustle of seafarers out to seek their fortunes. The Ghost Archipelago might be little more than legend these days, but it was a legend built on the promise of gold. Gold for the taking, for those brave enough to seek it out.

Now I may be a coward where Marta's legacy is concerned, but if there is one thing that can drive me to flights of reckless bravery it is money. Saddled as I was with the name of Price, with the weight of all that family history around my neck and barely enough coin in my purse to pay my crew, the lure of easy plunder was strong indeed. The Archipelago was virtually made of gold, to hear the tales. Nuggets of it lying on the beaches, so men said, ripe for plucking by any man prepared to make the voyage.

I grinned and turned to Erik at the wheel.

'Three points sou-south east,' I told him. 'Make for the smoke.'

'Aye, cap'n,' he said, grinning back at me through his unkempt grey beard, and the great wheel turned in his skilful hands.

Dancing Girl creaked alarmingly as she leaned into the turn, and I saw Francis and Headhunter swarm up the rigging like monkeys to do whatever it was they did with the sails. I'm more of a businessman than a seafarer, truth be told, and the actual working of the ship was something of a mystery to me. Erik was my first mate, which made him the Captain in all but name. I owned the godsdamned ship, but I have to confess I had no idea how to sail her.

Jondan joined me at the prow a moment later, an excited gleam in his eye.

'Think of it, Marek,' he said. 'A lost land, untouched for two hundred years. Where has that soil been? What stones might I find upon those shores?'

'Gold ones, with any luck,' I said. 'You heard what they were saying in Southport, Jon. Gold lying on the beaches! Think of it, man!'

I wanted that gold, of course I did, but there was more to this mad voyage than simple plunder. Marta Price had found the Crystal Pool somewhere amongst these islands, and drank its sorcerous waters. If I could do that, then might not the curse of Marta's legacy be lifted from me? Family legend spoke at length about her powers, and never a word of them bringing her crippling pain. I thought that was a corruption in the bloodline, something that seven generations of dilution might have brought. If I could find the Crystal Pool for myself, if I could make myself great as Marta had been great...

Jondan slapped me on the back and laughed, bringing me sharply back from my dreams and into the here and now.

'Gold,' he said, and shook his head. 'Dead metal is nothing next to living soil, my friend. Nothing lives in metal. Metal makes nothing grow.'

'Gold would make my fortunes grow quite impressively,' I snapped at him.

Even after a week at sea Jondan was somehow still filthy, with black crescents of soil under his nails and dirt ground hopelessly deep into the lines of his knuckles and palms. His threadbare shirt was half unbuttoned over his sweaty chest and I saw now that he wore a stone around his neck on a leather thong, one of his 'interesting' ones with a natural hole in it.

'What's that around your neck?' I asked him.

'A piece of home,' he said. 'I carry it with me always, so that I am always connected to the land that birthed me.'

The whitecaps were higher now as we neared land, and seabirds wheeled and called overhead. In the distance, I could see a wide green line of dense jungle with a short beach where breakers rolled against the shore. The fire mountain was still distant, perhaps on a different island entirely. The Ghost Archipelago was rumoured to be huge and widely spread out, island after island in a long, confusing chain that seemed never to stay entirely still.

'This place cannot be natural,' I mused. 'No normal islands disappear for hundreds of years, or move about by themselves. Doesn't that bother you?'

Jondan just smiled at me.

'Not all of nature is understood,' he said, 'but it is all wondrous.'

I shrugged. He could have it his own way, but I wasn't convinced. Magic worried me, and for a very good reason. Marta's legacy had given me a healthy distrust of it since the very first time I had tried to use my inherited powers, and had ended up screaming on the floor for an hour afterwards.

'Hallan, sound the depth,' I heard Erik order.

A moment later we had to move back to admit Hallan to the space at the prow of the ship, with her long-weighted rope in her hand. She was a big, burly woman, with more years at sea than I had been alive. She threw out the rope and hauled it back, and called out numbers to Erik that meant nothing to me. He nodded and barked orders, and in the rigging Headhunter and Francis pulled ropes and furled the sail.

Dancing Girl slowed, and again Erik turned the wheel and called for the depth. This mysterious dance of ship husbandry continued for some time, until I was bored and the shoreline was less than a hundred yards from starboard.

'Drop anchor,' Erik said, and it was done.

I leaned on the rail and looked at the beach. The sand was pale, almost white, and beyond it the jungle rose up in a wall of impenetrable vegetation of so dark a green it was close to black. Ropes creaked and boards flexed underfoot, and the breakers washed against the shore with a steady rhythm. It was hotter than ever now, the beating sun making sweat course down my face as I stared at the beach. One thing I couldn't see was gold glinting on the sand.

'Lower the boat,' I ordered, and Francis and Hallan set to it while Headhunter stayed in the rigging, making things fast I could only assume. I know little of seamanship, as I said.

Eventually he dropped down to the deck as the boat was settling into the swell beside *Dancing Girl*.

'Done, boss,' he said.

I nodded as though I knew what had been done, and why. I would have hated to shatter anyone's illusions of my competence, after all.

'Where's Iain?' I asked.

'Bilges,' Erik said. 'It's calm enough here, but he'll be on the pump for a while before we're dry again.'

'Aye,' I said, pulling a face.

If I came home with enough gold, I promised myself, the first thing I would do was buy a ship that didn't leak. Well, perhaps the second thing.

'He can hold the ship while we're ashore,' Erik suggested, and I nodded.

He was a good man, was Erik, and a better first mate. He had the knack of telling me what needed to be done in a way that sounded like he was simply echoing thoughts I had already had.

'Exactly,' I said. 'The rest of you in that boat, before anyone else turns up and beats us to it.'

The men and women of my crew swarmed down the rope into the boat, and I followed with somewhat less skill but a great deal of enthusiasm. Gold, just lying on the sand!

Francis and Headhunter put their backs to the oars and the boat pulled away from *Dancing Girl*, bouncing over the waves in a way that made me regret the salt fish I'd eaten for lunch that day. When the shallow keel scraped on sand at last we jumped out into the surf and hauled the boat up the beach, above the seaweed-marked line of the high tide.

I stretched my back and looked around me, feeling fresh sweat break out on my face. The heat was suffocating even at the shore, seeming to roll down the beach from the dark line of jungle. I wiped my sweating hands on my britches and looked around me. My five companions looked similarly uncomfortable, all except Jondan, who was already digging enthusiastically in the sand with the trowel that was always at his belt.

'Found any gold yet?' Melissa asked him, her keen eyes bright with greed in her dark face.

'The pattern of the mica is interesting,' Jondan said, more to himself than her, and bent over his growing hole with obvious fascination.

Melissa had already lost interest, and went to stand beside Erik on the shoreline.

'Now what?' Headhunter asked.

He was a huge man, his arms rippling with muscle as he lifted them to shade his eyes with both hands.

'Now we explore,' I said.

The beach itself was featureless and sadly devoid of nuggets of gold, but then rumours always exaggerate.

'Do you hear something?' Hallan asked suddenly. The big woman was staring intently at the dark line of the jungle, a frown on her sour face. 'Sounds like drums.'

'Drums?' I asked her. 'Why would there be…'

The words died in my throat as I realised I could hear it too. It was definitely drums, and it was getting nearer and louder by the moment.

Erik swore and unsheathed his shortsword, and a moment later the rest of my crew had their blades in their hands too. Except for Jondan, who was still busy digging, and me, who was almost paralysed with fear.

Maybe they're friendly, I told myself as they burst out of the green.

They weren't friendly.

One look at them was enough to tell me that. A second look told me just how many of them there were.

They were human, or thereabouts, but that's where their similarity with us ended. They were almost naked, the lot of them, and brandishing a wide variety of sharp things. Their weapons ranged from what looked like wooden paddles edged with sharks' teeth to wickedly cut flints lashed to branches. No match for our good steel swords, of course, but then there were only seven of us and that was if you counted Jondan. There were at least forty of them and they were coming on at a dead run, whooping and snarling like animals.

Oh gods.

'Brace for attack!' Erik roared, lifting his sword high.

All the hells let loose at once.

The tribal warriors were on us in seconds, screaming for blood with their primitive weapons crashing against my crew's blades. These were sailors not knights, more used to tavern brawls than facing a mass charge of armed men. Francis went down almost at once, his head split open by a crude flint axe.

Jondan was on his feet now and hurling rocks out of the ground at the tribesmen, but it wasn't enough. Headhunter roared and swung his blade, decapitating one tribesman and taking another's arm off on the backswing, but it was no good. There were too many of them. Melissa was falling back already, blood streaming from a long cut on her arm, and Erik was trying to fight off three men at once while Hallan fought like a woman possessed and hopelessly outnumbered. Only a miracle could save us now.

A miracle, or a superhuman.

A Heritor.

Oh gods, oh gods, oh gods…

There was simply no other way, was there? I took a deep, deep breath, and called on my inheritance.

Power roared through my body like a summer storm at sea.

My muscles swelled, bursting the seams of my thin linen shirt. I felt my eyesight become keener, my senses come alive with an almost feral awareness. I could smell the salt tang of the sea, the stink of unwashed bodies and the steaming rot of the jungle. Time seemed to slow, the tribesmen now appearing to move as though wading through molasses. The power was like a drug, singing in my blood.

With it came the pain, but that was nothing compared to the hatred that washed over me. The ferocity, the desire… no, the need to kill.

The world washed red.

I unsheathed my blade and severed a head in the same movement, ran one man through and kicked another hard enough to break his spine. I roared.

This was Marta's legacy.

* * *

I was lying on the shoreline, screaming.

The pain!

They call it blood burn, those who have never experienced it. Heritors have been studied by physicians, of course, those of us who carry the cursed blessing of our inheritance from the original few who drank from the Crystal Pool. I read once, in a medical text, a description of how the sensation is akin to one's blood growing hot within the veins. If only that were all!

My body was wracked with agony, every vein bulging through my skin and feeling as though it were filled with liquid fire.

'Shhhhh now, it's done,' Jondan said, and I felt him mop my fevered brow with a cloth that was wet with seawater.

Whether his earth magic had some unknown healing powers or if the fit had simply burned itself out I didn't know, but I felt myself beginning to recover. I looked up at the sky and saw that the sun was setting. Some three hours must have passed since we had landed on this island of the Ghost Archipelago.

I forced myself up into a sitting position and stared at the carnage I had wrought. The white sand was black with blood and littered with corpses.

'Twenty-two,' Jondan said quietly, saving me the effort of counting. 'Twenty-two tribesmen, dead at your hand. I got a couple with my rocks, and Erik and Hallan and Headhunter gave good account of themselves, but the butcher's bill is yours to pay.'

'What of Melissa?' I asked. 'Francis?'

'Francis is dead,' he said. 'Melissa is wounded, but I've patched her up as best I can. She'll live.'

I nodded, and blew a sigh out through my cheeks.

'And who are they?'

'Ah,' Jondan said. 'Yes.'

'What in the hells does "yes" mean?'

There was a group of figures standing in the shadow of the jungle, watching us. They were men, dark-skinned and dressed in leather. Each had a bronze-headed axe at his hip, but none were drawn against us. Yet.

'I don't know,' Jondan admitted. 'They came while you were... were in your other aspect. Seven hells Marek, three years I've known you and you didn't tell me you were a Heritor?'

'It's not something I'm proud of,' I muttered. 'What do they want?'

'Erik spoke with them,' he said. 'Apparently they saw you fight, and now they want to show us the way to their city of gold.'

'Gold?' I sat up sharply, and instantly regretted it as a fresh wave of pain battered my head. 'A city of gold?'

'Hmmm,' Jondan said. 'So they say. Do they look trustworthy, to you?'

I shrugged. This was a strange land, one that vanished for centuries at a time and returned on a whim, a land made of islands that didn't even stay in the same place from one day to the next. Who was to say what an honest face looked like, in a place like this?

'Perhaps,' I said. 'Help me up.'

Jondan put an arm under my shoulders and heaved me to my feet, and I retrieved my fallen sword and sheathed it at my hip. I spared a look for Francis' body, but there was little enough to be done for him now.

'Right,' I said. 'Come on then.'

The dark men led us into the jungle while dusk gathered around us. The heat was so oppressive that my entire body felt slick with sweat, a thick liquid coating on my skin that made my clothes stick to my back and chafe under my arms. I could hear monkeys chattering somewhere in the canopy above.

I was aware of my crew hanging back from me, of the nervous glances they passed between them. None of them had known, of course. None of them had known what I was, what I could do. I sensed a new-found respect for me amongst them, and something else too.

A fear.

Everyone knows that Heritors exist, of course, but no one expected to ever meet one. Much less be led by one, on an adventure such as this.

Only one of the natives appeared to be able to speak the trade tongue, albeit haltingly, but he seemed happy to talk with me while we waded through the steaming, swampy terrain. Great ropes of plant life hung from the twisted boughs of the trees, alive with huge, pale spiders. In the thick, greenish waters around our ankles worse things moved, always just out of sight.

'We are Dricheans,' he told me, and his dark eyes looked at me as though that word should mean something to me. 'Javan will welcome you, man from ship.'

'What are Dricheans?' I was forced to ask.

He made a noise somewhere between a laugh and a snarl. I swiped at a dragonfly as big as my palm, sending it coruscating into the steaming undergrowth.

'Warriors,' he said. 'Overlords. Stone city men. We are their rangers.'

'And you're… friendly?'

'Warriors,' he said again, and nodded. 'You great warrior, we see. We watch. You kill many Tribals. We respect that.'

'There is a city of gold, you told my man?'

'We have great gold,' he said proudly, nodding his head as he spoke. 'Much gold. Much weapons. Great warriors.'

'And you don't like the tribesmen?'

'No one likes them,' the man said. 'They are savages. Cannibals. No one like. Drichean make war, but Tribals are many, and hidden. You kill many Tribals. Dricheans respect you.'

There was that, I supposed. I'd rather have their gold than their respect, but it was a good start. This talk of a stone city resonated with family legend. Marta Price had found the Crystal Pool in a lost city of stone, I remembered. Uninhabited then, to be sure, but a lot could change in two hundred years.

'Where is this stone city?' I asked him.

'Not far, not far,' he said. 'Close now. We scout, we show the way.'

Scouts…

'Say,' I said, as though it was an afterthought, 'you rangers must have been all over these islands. Have you ever heard of a Crystal Pool?'

The Drichean stopped in his tracks. The look he turned on me was like razors.

'No.'

I swallowed. My question had angered him, that much was plain, and I didn't want to make an enemy of these men. Not now they had led us deep into their own country.

'It's nothing, really, I'm sure,' I said. 'Just something I heard about back home, that's all.'

'Forget about that,' he said. 'You forget all about that, man from ship. That knowledge is not for you.'

I frowned, but had little choice other than to accept his words.

'So, where's this city then?'

'Too late, too late now,' he said. 'Camp for night. Find dry ground. Light fire, sentries find us.'

* * *

They came at dawn.

I woke to see twenty warriors arrayed at the perimeter of the rangers' primitive camp. They were tall and dark-skinned like the rangers, but these were dressed in leather armour studded with bronze, with bronze-tipped spears in their hands. Each carried a great shield of beaten bronze, embossed with a seahorse motif, and wore a short-hafted bronze axe at his belt.

'Warriors,' the ranger told me, but by then I had worked that out for myself.

I got to my feet and brushed the worst of the spiders off my clothes and out of my hair, and raised my hand in greeting to the one I took to be in charge. He was the only one wearing a helmet anyway, a great bronze helm topped with the figure of a leaping fish.

'My name is Marek Price,' I said, slowly and clearly.

'We know,' the man said.

His dark face was impassive in the open front of his helmet, giving nothing away. I was at a loss for anything else to say, so I resorted to the sort of rubbish one says to foreigners.

'I come in peace.'

The man threw back his head and laughed.

'You jest well, Marek Price,' he said. At least this one spoke the trade tongue properly. 'The rangers have told us of the bloody slaughter you wrought upon the beaches. You are a warrior born, and you came in blood.'

'Yes, well,' I said, feeling somehow slightly embarrassed.

I was aware of Jondan and the four surviving members of my crew standing behind me, watching me face down this bronze-clad avatar of war. Truth be told I was feeling rather like I was swimming out of my depth, and it's widely known that most sailors don't swim well.

'My name is Javan. You will come with us, to the city,' he said. 'We will show you true Drichean hospitality.'

'Thank you,' I said, although I had a feeling that his words had been more of a statement than an invitation.

We left the rangers there in the jungle, their work done, and followed the Dricheans through the suffocating weight of the green. I could feel my boots starting to rot around my feet as I waded through the stinking mire, the sweat rolling down my face in the oppressive heat. The Drichean warriors showed no sign of discomfort though, and set a punishing pace.

At last we came out from under the darkness of the canopy into a shaft of searing bright sunlight, and there before us was the Drichean city. Long ages had passed since it had been built, I could see that much. The city was made of great blocks of grey stone piled one upon another, moss-covered and heavy with the weight of thick creepers. Above it all towered a great stepped pyramid, topped with a huge sun of beaten gold. The light of the true sun blazed off it in reflection, all but blinding me.

I gaped. Factoring the height of the pyramid, I worked out that the golden sun must have been almost half the size of *Dancing Girl*. That much gold could found a dynasty, or rescue one.

Javan paused, obviously taking in my reaction.

'This is our home,' he said proudly. 'This is Jav-va-chocqunel, the city of the golden sun.'

I could only nod in agreement.

'Magnificent,' Jondan said at my side, making me jump. 'The age of this stone… quite remarkable.'

I spared him a glance and shook my head as he traced his fingers lovingly along the nearest block of hewn stone, sparing not a glance for the king's ransom that loomed above us.

'Gold is plentiful, here?' I asked Javan, struggling to keep my tone light.

'Gold? It is shiny, but no use for making weapons,' he said. 'Too soft. We use it to make mirrors and decorations, but bronze is more valuable.'

'Yes,' I said hurriedly, thinking fast. 'Yes, bronze is better than gold. Steel is better still.'

Javan frowned at me. 'Steel?'

I eased my sword slowly from its scabbard, not wanting to give any threat, and showed it to him.

'Steel,' I said.

He took the weapon from my hand and examined it, a deep frown creasing his dark features.

'How is this made?'

Of course, I had no idea.

'In my land we have men called smiths,' I said. 'They… they are great magicians, who can work metal into blades a hundred times stronger than bronze.'

Javan nodded, and reluctantly handed the sword back to me.

'Come,' he said.

I wasn't at all sure I wanted to venture further, but with Javan's warriors around us I could see that we had little choice. All I wanted to do was trade, by which I meant rob them blind. A city this size, where gold was worth less than bronze, and steel looked like magic... oh, the money that could be made here!

Javan and his men led us deeper into the city, and all around us I could feel the weight of the years and a sense of all-pervading decay. The Dricheans might be the more civilised inhabitants of the Ghost Archipelago but all the same it was obvious that theirs was a failing, declining civilisation. Great cracks were visible in the stone buildings, and long beards of moss hung from every ledge and balcony.

I looked across an open plaza to a building that had clearly collapsed under its own weight, and saw young saplings pushing up through the fallen rubble. A huge snake wound around one, banded black and gold, and regarded me with pitiless eyes. Barefoot children ran out of a house to greet the returning warriors, clad in nothing but scraps of course-woven cloth.

'Your city is magnificent,' I told Javan. 'You must have many enemies, jealous of your wealth and civilisation.'

I heard Jondan cough loudly behind me, but I ignored him.

'The Tribals are a spear in our side,' Javan said. 'We are civilised and organised, but on this island we are few and they are many. Without our rangers to scout for us and warn us when they approach in force, we would be sorely pressed to hold them off.'

I nodded slowly in a way that I hoped looked wise.

'With steel weapons, you would be able to hold them

off with ease,' I said. 'Your rangers saw me fight, on the beach. You know what steel can do.'

Those things may not have been directly connected or entirely the whole of the truth, but Javan nodded all the same.

'How would we come by steel weapons?' he asked me.

'With gold,' I said. 'Gold is mostly useless, as you say, but there are those in my land who enjoy looking at the colour of it. A large enough amount of gold could, perhaps, persuade the magical smiths to conjure a few steel weapons for you.'

'We have much gold,' Javan said. 'The hills around here give little else.'

I swallowed in a dry throat, and forced my trembling lips to keep still and not betray the smile I felt. This whole island was made of gold! It was the legends come true, and Marek Price was here to claim the bounty of the Ghost Archipelago from these uneducated simpletons.

If only it had been that easy…

* * *

They feasted us that night, under the stars beside a great fire that burned in the open plaza at the foot of the pyramid. There was food and music and dancing, a throbbing rhythm of drums and pipes that set the Drichean women whirling in their loose, colourful garments. I was eating some sort of roast monkey, but it tasted good enough and their wine tasted better still. Curiously sweet, granted, but excellent none the less.

I was seated in the place of honour with the pyramid at my back, Javan on one side of me and Jondan on the other. In front of me were the gifts.

Oh, such gifts!

Javan had lavished me with gold, with sceptres and goblets and plate and rings and necklaces. I was wearing as much of the jewellery as I could fit on my hands and around my neck, and the rest of the treasure spilled out of a great leather sack that I kept close between my feet. I could buy ten ships with what that would bring, and hire the crews to sail them. I sat back in my carved wooden chair with a contented sigh. For that much gold I might even honour my side of the deal and bring them steel swords. Stranger things had happened.

I turned and gave Jondan a sly smile, but saw that he was asleep in his chair with his empty goblet dangling from limp fingers. Strange, he could usually hold his drink. My own head was heavy, I realised, and I looked around at the rest of my crew. Melissa was snoring on the floor, her wounded arm cradled against her body in its rough bandages, and Erik and Hallan were slumped in their chairs with their heads almost on their knees. Of all of them, only Headhunter was still awake, and he was reeling in his seat.

I squeezed my eyes shut for a moment and opened them again, and my vision swam. The great fire was a blur of light in front of me. How much had I had to drink, exactly?

'You are strong,' Javan said suddenly, a hard smile on his face. 'A mighty warrior. Your heart must be strong indeed.'

'What?' I blinked at him, swaying in my chair.

There was a horrible noise as Headhunter vomited in his own lap. A moment later he had passed out.

'Your heart will honour the sun.'

'I…'

I really didn't feel well. Not at all, and the look on Javan's face was only making me feel worse. Something was badly wrong.

'You think us fools and savages, easily cheated, but you are the fool,' he said. 'The rangers told me of the questions you asked, and of your greed for gold. We have greed too, greed for the hearts of strong warriors to appease the sun god. Come the dawn, you will see.'

I tried to rise, but my legs betrayed me. I grabbed at the arm of my chair but only succeeded in pulling it over on top of me as I fell to the ground. I stretched out a hand and my grasping fingers touched the sack of gold. Javan laughed, and the world went dark.

* * *

I woke with the dawn, light stabbing into my eyes as the first rays of the sun crested the horizon. I was high up, I realised, looking down on the canopy of the jungle. I tried to move and found my wrists and ankles lashed to a wooden frame that was holding me upright before a great stone altar. That stone was streaked rusty brown with old blood.

Fighting down panic I turned my head, looking for Jondan, for any of my crew. I was alone up there, atop the pyramid with the huge gold sun looming over me. I could hear chanting, coming closer.

I narrowed my eyes, fighting the pain in my head. Whatever they had drugged the wine with had left me with a savage headache, but in truth I had had worse. My father wasn't the only drinking man in the Price family, after all. I craned my neck and squinted, and now I could see Jondan and the others penned in a rough stockade hidden amongst the crumbling stone buildings below.

The tramp of boots was audible now, climbing the steps of the pyramid towards me. Three, maybe four men. I tested my bonds but I was held fast, although I realised suddenly that not only was I still wearing the huge quantity of gold jewellery I had adorned myself with the previous night, but also that my sword hung at my side, infuriatingly out of reach.

Of course, I realised. They want to sacrifice a warrior to this sun god of theirs, and what is a warrior without a weapon?

Oh, I had a weapon all right. I had a weapon they didn't know about.

I had Marta's legacy.

It was going to hurt, I knew it was, but I had learned my lesson on the beach. There, faced by overwhelming odds, I had drawn on everything I had, all at once, and blacked out in the resulting frenzy of killing. I couldn't risk that now. Instead I took a deep breath and pulled in just a little of my gift, enough to give me the strength to burst the ropes that held me. I grinned as the woven vines popped and gave but I stayed as I was, standing spread-eagled against the wooden frame until I saw Javan's head appear above the line of the steps. I waited until he was only three steps away, his head now level with my waist, then kicked him in the face as hard as I could.

I put a stab of my gift into that kick, enough to send him flailing back off the steps of the pyramid and into open space. There were two other men on the steps, some kind of priests I assumed from the leopardskins they wore over their clothes. Each had a long bronze dagger in his hand and a look of serene, holy murder on his face.

My sword flashed from its scabbard and I stabbed one of them through the neck even as I elbowed the other in the face, sending him tumbling from the steps with a wailing scream. Then I was off and running, pounding down the steps of the pyramid with my red blade in my hand.

I was halfway to the bottom when Javan grabbed me.

His leg was obviously broken from his fall, twisted under him at an unnatural angle, but his dark face was set in a snarl of hatred and he too had a dagger in his hand.

'The sun must have your heart!' he screamed, and plunged the dagger towards my chest.

I grabbed his wrist with my free hand and stayed the blade, cursing as I struggled to bring my sword to bear in the close confines of our deadly embrace. He gripped my wrist in turn, spitting hatred in my face. We were still on the steps, straining and struggling, and I knew any wrong move could send us both crashing to the bottom in a tangle of broken limbs.

Summoning my gift, I butted him in the face so hard I felt his skull shatter.

He slumped dead to the stones under me, and again I was off and running. I could hear shouting from below now as some of the Drichean warriors realised the sacrifice had gone awry. There were six of them charging towards the base of the pyramid with bronze weapons glinting in their hands. I leapt from the fifth step, sailing over their heads, and hit the ground in a neat roll that had me back on my feet and running towards the stockade before they realised what had happened.

I grit my teeth as I ran, feeling the blood already burning in my calves and forearms. The pain was building, searing my veins. I reached the stockade some twenty paces ahead of my pursuers and simply tore the wooden palisade apart with my hands, roaring defiance.

Headhunter was first out, his sword clutched in his huge hands.

'Fight!' I shouted, gasping through clenched teeth as the burning pain wracked my body.

So confident had the Dricheans been that they hadn't even stripped my crew of their weapons, and now they met the pursuing warriors with the fury of the betrayed. We had accepted hospitality from these people, and this was how they treated us?

I heard Erik yelling as he stabbed a man, then the six Drichean warriors were dead on the ground and Jondan was at my side.

'How bad is it?' he asked me, the concern plain on his grimy face.

'Hurts like all the hells,' I confessed. 'We have to get out of here, right now!'

He nodded and turned, and then I remembered the gifts. There was no way I was leaving that sack of gold behind.

I dashed back to the open space at the foot of the pyramid with Jondan's shouts echoing behind me, and found a great mound of ashes where the feasting fire had died in the night. The bulging sack of gold was still where I had left it in front of my fallen chair, and I grabbed it up in one hand with a grin of triumph.

'Our gold,' a woman's voice grated in heavily-accented trade. 'Not for you, man of ship.'

I turned to see her there, a fierce-looking warrior priestess wearing the skin of a leopard over her leather armour. She too had a sacrificial bronze dagger in her hand. Her eyes flashed with anger and she raised the blade.

I've never killed a woman. I didn't know if I could kill a woman.

In the moment it took me to think about that, Hallan stepped up behind the priestess and smashed her head open with her mace.

'We really should go,' the burly woman said.

I nodded my thanks to her.

A moment later someone sounded a long note on a conch shell, and then there were Dricheans pouring out of the stone dwellings all around us.

'We are leaving!' I shouted, and led my crew on a frantic sprint out of the city and into the waiting green.

The pain was growing by the minute. I might not be fighting anymore but now I was running, which I was unaccustomed to, and doing it with several stone of gold on my back in the bulging leather sack. Add to that the steaming heat and the swampy terrain, and I was having to draw more heavily on Marta's legacy than was wise.

It would fail me eventually, I knew. There was only so much power I could use, only so much pain the body could endure, and then both would fail. We had to reach *Dancing Girl* before that happened.

We had to.

We ran through the place where we had camped with the rangers two nights before, but other than the ashes of the fire there was no sign of them. I could hear things screaming and chattering in the green, monkeys and worse things racing away from the chaos we made as we splashed through pools and broke branches in our haste. Behind us the Dricheans were still coming, I had no doubt of that.

'Which way?' I shouted at Jondan. 'Which way?'

Surely he knew, he was the one who was supposed to be so in touch with nature.

He stopped his headlong flight for a moment, reached into the green sludge at his feet and lifted a stone. His brow furrowed in concentration while I almost chewed through my lip with impatience, listening to the Dricheans getting closer behind us. I could only hope that without their rangers they were as lost as we were.

'That way,' he said at last, pointing to a thicket of dripping ferns that looks like every other.

With no choice but to trust him, I led the crew in that direction, but the Dricheans were close behind us now.

We ran.

A spear flashed through the air behind me and stuck fast in the trunk of a tree, the shaft quivering. I fought the pain, tears stinging my eyes as I made myself run faster. It burned.

It burned so badly!

Eventually there was light ahead, a glimpse of white through the trees that I could only pray was the beach. We plunged out into the open sunlight at last and my booted feet caught in the sudden softness of the sand, almost spilling me onto my face. There was the boat, pulled up above the tidemark where we had left it.

The tide was out.

Of course it bloody was.

'The boat!' I shouted, my throat raw with pain. 'Get the boat into the godsdamned water!'

I could see *Dancing Girl* rocking at anchor, barely a hundred yards from the shore, could just make out the figure of Iain at the bow, waving. What use did he think that was, the fool?

The Dricheans crashed through the jungle behind us, and now I could hear drums pounding over the sound of the surf. The whole jungle was a cacophony of noise and fury.

It was no good, they would be on us in moments and my gift was all used up for the time being. If I had left the gold behind, if I hadn't wasted so much of Marta's legacy in carrying it, then perhaps I could have fought them. It was out of the question now, I realised. I could barely see for the pain as it was. I had to rest or I would drop where I stood.

It was hopeless.

The Dricheans charged onto the beach, twenty of them with their great bronze shields flashing in the sun.

The Tribals hit them like a stampeding herd.

They whooped and screamed as they came, thirty, forty of them, flint axes and sharks-tooth paddles in their hands.

Erik, Headhunter and Hallan were wrestling the boat into the surf while Melissa and Jondan dragged me down the beach, each helping to support the weight of the bulging sack that I still stubbornly refused to let go of. The edges of my vision were grey with pain and I could hardly stand, but I felt the relatively cool water wash around my ankles before they heaved me into the rocking boat.

'Oars!' I heard Erik order, and then we were moving.

From the beach came the crash of battle, the whooping of the Tribals and the sounds of the Dricheans' cheated rage.

I barely remember being hauled up the ropes onto the deck of *Dancing Girl* like a bale of cargo, the sack of gold still clutched tightly in my arms. By the time I came back to myself we were under sail.

Jondan was squatting in front of me where I lay near the bow, the soothing cool of the spray washing over my fevered body.

'We did it,' he said, a shaky grin on his face.

I looked down at the bulging sack on the deck in front of me, at the rings that glittered on my fingers and the ropes of gold that hung around my neck, and then back over my shoulder at the dark shape of the island that was steadily receding into the distance behind us.

'Aye, we did it,' I said.

We had done well. I had enough gold to rebuild Price Shipping, and once that was done I would mount a proper expedition to the Ghost Archipelago before it vanished again. I swore then to myself that I would find the legendary Crystal Pool and drink the waters that would, I was convinced, finally rid me of the curse of Marta's legacy and make me as great as she had been.

Jondan shook his head and put a rueful hand on my shoulder.

'I told you, you're going to get me killed one of these days,' he said.

I nodded, but I was barely listening. I would find the Crystal Pool, whatever the price I had to pay.

ISLE OF
THE SILVER MIST

BY
HOWARD ANDREW JONES

We were in-bound to the island, wind filling the sail of our little skiff. Our ship lay anchored in the clear blue bay behind us, and I had myself thinking it wouldn't be too long before we returned to her decks with a chest of shining treasure. Our luck had been great all the long way over, with clear skies and a wind out of the north-west, and I guess I thought maybe, just once, the gods were smiling on us. I should have known better.

Between us and the island loomed those tall, spiny brown reefs you see all over the Ghost Archipelago. They're dangerous in a storm, but with calm waters there was plenty of room to manoeuvre for its beach. Beyond the golden sand glistening in the sunlight lay leaning palms and the thick greens of the deep tropic jungle, ornamented with bright florals. And beyond even that was the worn grey stone height of a step pyramid.

That pyramid was our goal, and I figured, maybe, just maybe, we could get to the shore, get through the jungle, and snatch the treasures from the ruins before the sun set.

I was at the prow, right where a brave captain ought to be. Manning the tiller was my cousin Heln, whose bald pate and muscular bare chest were ornamented in blue and green tattoos. Working the sail was the ship's Wind Warden, his lover Lilandra, slim, trim, her silvery hair queued up tight at the base of her skull, her expression almost mournful in its calm. She was one with the wind, coaxing it to send us the right way. If Heln was my right hand, Lilandra was my left, and I'd been venturing the deeps with them long before the ghosts ever broke back up to haunt the surface again.

Normally it was us three who made landfall on an expedition, maybe backed by an extra sword arm or four. This time, though, we carried nine passengers, which meant we were brimming. Six were bearded men-at-arms, swarthy Tregellans complete with black lacquered cuirasses and matched helmets, a querulous lot I'd been at pains to keep my men from tossing overboard. Their leader was similarly equipped and just as large, but there was silver in his beard and steel in his gaze. That was Count Trovis, a man so used to commanding I'd been at pains to keep from heaving him into the deep blue myself.

With him was a slip of a boy, with only a little chin beard, his nephew Desron, the only good-humoured one of the lot, and Myria, a bronze-skinned, dark-haired vision. She was quiet and mysterious, as suits a sorceress, for so she was reputed to be. It was she who'd convinced the Count that there were treasures on the Isle of the Silver Mists, and that she alone could guide him there.

We weren't along out of the goodness of our hearts – Trovis had already paid out a handful of sapphires, and he had pledged us another on his safe return, plus a fair cut of all the treasure.

Me, I wasn't sure that we'd find any treasure. We'd profit enough from the sapphires. But even a rich man doesn't turn down the offer of more money, and none of us sailors were rich. I had a crew to feed, debts to pay, and maybe some wine and revelry and women to get acquainted with.

With Lilandra's help we were making grand time. I studied the shore while the Tregellan soldiers mumbled to themselves about what they'd do with their cut.

And then the closer reef started moving. I blinked. Unless you're inebriated or in the midst of a quake, reefs don't move, so I doubted my senses until I heard one of the soldiers shout. His hand rose and pointed towards the reef, asking Lilandra what that was.

It wasn't just the gliding reef that was problematic. Much as that was a mystery worth ruminating over, I was more worried that the gap between the reefs was shrinking. What had been an easy manoeuvre was growing more challenging by the second. There are certain understandings between you and the landscape, a gentleman's agreement like, that you're the one supposed to do the moving.

This island apparently hadn't heard that. A war galley's length of reef seventy-five feet high was inching north to south, straight into our path. As I shouted to Lilandra for more wind, a massive spear-shaped reptilian head climbed from the waves, dripping water. For a brief moment, I assumed this was a new problem. Then I realised it lay at the forefront of that reef. To make things abundantly clear, as the head rose a massive length of neck lifted behind it, connecting to the body of what we'd heretofore assumed for a reef.

'Sea monster!' the Count shouted. I hadn't before noticed his great gift for stating the obvious. He clambered towards me, his voice booming as though I was seated at the far end of a banquet table. 'We're heading straight for it! Turn or something!'

He was a lubber. You don't just turn a skiff like you would a horse. To our port was a string of little reefs and sandbars – no safety there. And there was no way to avoid the beast if we swung further to starboard. We'd just run smack dab into its aft quarters, rising now as a lengthy strand of tail.

'Orders, cap'n?' Heln shouted.

'Steady as she goes!'

Count Trovis gabbled at me about my stubbornness and stupidity, but I ignored him. Lilandra called to the winds, gesturing frantically with one hand while her other held to the mast.

She was good. That wind kicked in pretty as strawberry pie and sent us zooming past the monster. We passed only half a cable length out and I got a real good look at its head. A dripping mass of green seaweed hung out of one side of its mouth, and it chewed on this with no particular speed as it watched us dully. Above the huge green eyes was a rounded forehead and then a big flat skull. Apart from the reef-like back frill it looked about as dangerous as a turtle.

Well, a turtle long as the king's war galley. What I mean is that it didn't look like those drawings of beasties on map edges that are cracking ships open to snatch screaming sailors. It was just a giant grazer, as interested in us as a sheep is when a squirrel wanders past.

But as we drew even with the monster, three of the sailors whipped up their bows and started firing.

The thing kept chewing as the first arrows rebounded from its massive scales. I shouted at them to stop and Myria joined in.

'Fools!' she cried. 'You'll anger it!'

Their arrows didn't have any effect, or leave much impression, until the last shot struck its eye.

Its jaw opened wide and it let out a sky-rumbling roar. The sail rattled in its spars and the ship rocked. An arrow through a man's socket would surely have slain, but this hadn't even ruined the beast's eye – we saw the black shaft sticking out from the orb like a splinter in your hand.

The soldiers gabbled amongst themselves and the Count and his nephew shouted at them, belatedly, to stop.

In the stunned silence after the beast's second roar I heard Heln's low pronouncement. 'That's bad.' My cousin had a way with words. He put all his weight into the tiller, swinging us as close as he could to the real reef on our port side.

The beast started after us, each massive footfall conjuring a wave. Lilandra was singing up a mighty wind now, and it belled the sail and ballooned my sleeves.

We slipped past that second reef just before the head of a second beast began its rise. I saw a monstrous eye as the head soared up. A huge glob of masticated seaweed dropped right onto the deck. If it had decided to surface just a little sooner, we would have run straight into the thing. Yes, the other reef was another of the sea beasts.

I don't know what we'd have done if the second monster hadn't roared in answer to the first. The one that had started after us swung to regard the second and they both snorted at one another.

I kept my eyes on them both and they had quite a bellowing match as we rolled closer and closer to the shore. Fortunately, they didn't decide to join forces to smash us to paste and kindling. They were still grunting at each other as our prow drove into the beach.

I jumped to the sand and urged the men out to help drag up the boat. The Count was on me in an instant.

His voice was tight, and his yellowed teeth were bared in a dangerous smile. 'Captain Varn, you do not give orders to my men.'

I was having none of that. 'Your men just about got us killed, Count.'

'That is my affair.'

I shook my head. 'My boat. My crew, my rules. You hired me. That's how it rolls. That's the last time anyone attacks before I give the order, clear?'

'You know better than a soldier?'

'I know the Isles better than you.'

'You do not know them better than Myria.'

At mention of her name, the bronze-skinned beauty glided up, her ebon shoulder-length hair swaying with each step.

'Maybe not. But she was telling you to belay the attack as well. You'd do well to listen to your counsellors, Count. It's a long swim back.'

He growled something but turned sharply away, truculently commanding his men to help Heln and Lilandra drag in the skiff.

Myria gauged me with an unreadable look, then followed him.

The nephew drew close to me as I studied the jungle.

'You must forgive my uncle, Captain,' he told me with a head bob. 'He is old nobility, descended, on a lateral branch, from a line of kings. He is a good man, but he has trouble taking orders from those in… other classes.'

I nodded acknowledgement. His speech didn't do anything to endear the older man to me, but I liked the nephew a little better for it.

We left the skiff well up the beach so high tide wouldn't send it off on its own, stowed the sail, grabbed our gear, and headed into the deep green.

That temple had looked close from out in the bay, but there were a couple of miles of jungle between the beach and the ruins, and we didn't spot any trails. That meant hacking our own. Heln and I alternated taking point, hewing our way through the foliage with our machetes. The Count said he wanted to keep his men fresh for the fight, and there was no budging him. Lilandra kept her senses stretched taut. Sure, she was a Wind Warden, but she was sensitive to disturbances in the air, and if she concentrated she might be able to sense things that were interested in laying fang or claw into us. That was our hope, at least.

If you've never been to the tropics, you might have the idea that they're hot and you're always surrounded by weird birds and plants. It's true enough. There's constantly something off in the distance hooting or shouting. You spend enough time in these places and you get to recognise the difference between sorts of monkeys and birds, and know that one of the most threatening roars actually comes out of the maw of a hand-sized toad.

But there are new sounds on every single one of the islands of the Ghost Archipelago. You never know if that strange, spine-tingling ululation is from some bird or a lizard thing that's creeping up to kill you. Then there are the endless insects, and the sweat constantly dripping off of you, to which the insects are naturally drawn.

On the plus side, there are pretty flowers. If you take time to smell them, plenty are fragrant, which is nice, because when you're slicing through the jungle for a few hours it's a change to catch a whiff of a pleasant scent.

We were about two hours in when Heln stilled, crouching, his bald, tattooed head swivelling to take in the foliage ahead. One muscular arm motioned us down while the other was poised with machete ready.

Naturally we lowered, Lilandra's lean face screwing up in concentration. I did a quick scan over my shoulder to make sure the others obeyed.

Something heavy crushed through the underbrush, the ground shaking with each footfall. The thunder lizards in the Ghost Isles don't quite feel like an earthquake when they move, but you do feel like you're standing on the surface of a beaten drum when they near you. I'd been close to thunder lizards twice – one time a lot closer than I wanted – and I recognised the feel of their passage well enough.

The Count was demanding as usual when he rustled through the brush to whisper to me. 'What is that?'

I pressed fingers to my lips. The rest of the jungle had stilled, which should have been a big clue to stay silent.

I crept up to Heln, who had his hand up against a thick palm. I stepped around a fern and looked north-west.

The thunder lizard was damnably close. It could have peered right up into a second story and snapped you in two if you were dumping your slops. Fortunately, the thing was a couple of yards off and was moving diagonally away. I felt my heart thrum at sight of the thing, all different shades of green scale with occasional red patches, with huge clawed back feet and spindly clawed limbs thrust forward below the immense head, which towered over the trees it stomped past.

Suddenly it burst into speed and went rushing into the jungle depths. It let out an ear-shattering roar that rivalled a thunderclap and lowered its head. There was the crackling sound and thud of a tree falling, and then, over the silent forest, some light trilling vocalisations that set the beast roaring once more.

We stayed right where we were, thanks. I expected shortly to hear lots of crunching sounds as the thunder lizard closed on its prey, and was a little surprised when the trilling continued, moving east. We heard the beast following, letting out shorter roars, as if in frustration.

Finally, the sounds receded, along with the earth-rattling thud of the monster's steps. I felt it was safe to breathe when the creatures around us bucked up the courage to resume their own shouting matches.

'What was that all about?' the Count asked.

'A thunder lizard on the hunt,' I said. I might have explained further, but I didn't feel especially disposed towards it. I took the lead from Heln, and there was no missing the path the thunder lizard had made through the foliage. Its passage had crushed shrubs and grasses, so we followed. You can get worn down cutting your way through the jungle.

Pretty soon we saw what the crash had been about. The monster had bumped into and brought down one of those odd, scaly trees that grow in the Ghost Isles. They look a little like palms, but they're straighter, taller, and bigger around besides, about the size of a sturdy oak. They also have fruit that dangles down from their top leaves but it's not worth seeking out unless you're starving, because consuming one's about as much fun as eating a turnip-flavoured pinecone.

The tree was lying on its side, its shallow roots drooping and covered with big red ants. Two thirds of the way down it had pinned a man in green pants, who was struggling to free himself.

I let out a low oath, told Heln to keep watch, and hurried to help the poor fellow. Instantly I guessed what had happened – somehow, he and a group had been surprised and his friends had bravely lured the thunder lizard off so he could get free.

It wasn't until I drew close that I realised he wasn't wearing green pants. He was wearing a tunic down to his thighs, but after that were green, scaly legs, with clawed, scaly feet, and there was a green scaly tale to boot. I stopped short.

This was one of the serpent folk. I'd only seen them from afar, but I'd heard a lot of dark things about their practices. I'd seen enough about the world at that point to know half the stuff you hear is complete nonsense – the Tregellan claim that the Vilgani are cannibals and the Vilgani claim the Tregellan sell their own babies, while in truth both countries aren't guilty of anything more heinous than usual, apart from the Vilgani preference for ludicrous moustaches.

So I didn't necessarily believe that the serpent folk craved human flesh or that they could curse you just by looking at you. But I was a lot more cautious. I stepped all the way around the tree and looked down at the front end of the serpent man.

There was no mistaking him for a human from this side. Sure, there were human-like arms attached to the shoulders, and a torso, but the neck that sprouted up out of there might as well have been the top half of a snake, complete with a snake's head, albeit with a higher forehead.

It had been struggling until it heard me draw close, and now that head stared at me with its unreadable eyes in its alien, expressionless face, likely wondering what I planned to do. It was trapped, and I realised I still held a machete in one hand.

I'll be honest. I wasn't sure what I was going to do, either. We stared at each other for a moment that felt like a couple of hours, and we might have stared a little longer except that we heard the thunder lizard roar. It sounded a little closer.

I guess that's what made up my mind. I drove the machete upright into the dirt and advanced on the tree.

I reached down for the tree bole further away from him and grabbed hold of the tree bark. It was slicker than I expected.

I'm not a small man, but I'm no weightlifter. I can't say the trunk moved much despite my straining. I looked over at the serpent guy and he was still staring. 'Well,' I said at the same time the thunder lizard let off another roar. 'I can't lift it by myself.'

I wasn't sure he understood the words, but he must have understood my aim, because a moment after I bent to get to work, he pressed up against the tree with his back.

But one spindly serpent guy and one able sailor wasn't enough to move the tree. I glanced back and didn't see my people, and didn't want to call them out to the open anyway because damned if I didn't hear the pad of that thunder lizard. I heard the trilling, too, but the beast must have decided it wanted to come back for a sure meal and stop following the promise of one.

I had two choices. I could either abandon this serpent man to his fate, or I could let loose with a blood burn.

There's some Heritors who just love using blood burn. I'm not one of them. Sure, it comes in handy, but there's a reason 'burn' is in the descriptor. It hurts.

I'm still not sure why I helped him. Maybe it's because I'd gotten myself involved and that I don't like doing things halfway. It certainly wasn't because I overflowed with warm feelings for snakes. But I reached down into my core, sucked in a breath, and swore in Vilgani. Their oaths have a lot of poetry to them, you know?

And I knew a flush of strength at the same time it felt like a thousand fire ants suddenly chomped down on my skin. I actually shouted aloud at the pain.

But that tree came up, level with my shoulder, and then, as I braced my legs, higher than my head.

The serpent man scrambled away, stared at me, then jabbed over my shoulder with urgency.

I looked. Yeah, the thunder lizard was only a couple of cable lengths off, and his beady eyes were looking straight at us.

My new friend hightailed it into the jungle – and I mean this literally. I cursed again and dropped the tree, then ran west. I had the presence of mind not to run towards my crew.

The beast could have gone after the serpent man, but he came after me. The ground rattled with every stride, and when he roared it was a thunderclap.

I tore through the jungle, legs pumping, oblivious to the cut and scrape of spiny leaves and a sharp branch that sliced my cheek. I searched the ground ahead, desperate for something. Anything. Maybe a hole to dive into or a really big rock to hide behind – I didn't know, really, what could save me until I raced right up to the edge of a crevice.

A little stream twisted along the bottom of it. On either side, a whole slew of red and yellow flowers bloomed cheerily. The far side was a long ways off. Maybe ten metres.

Close as that thing was, I didn't have time for worry. I was already running at full speed, so I kept on straight for the edge, then leapt for it.

I heard the snap of great teeth just behind me, smelled the stink of that terrible maw. And then I was airborne and the far side rushed at me. I stretched out for it, aiming straight for a spiny green fern.

I didn't quite reach it. Instead I slammed against the wet, vine-draped earth on the far side of the crevice and scrabbled at the cliff edge.

I found no hand hold, and the next thing I knew I was dropping. I could see a ribbon of sky above the crevice where the trees gave way, and the thunder lizard leaning down, teeth bared as if in fury. I heard it start a roar, and then there was a sharp pain in my side and everything went black.

I woke to cool fingers brushing hair from my forehead. My vision was a little blurry, but I had the sense I was in a dark, moist place. Somewhere behind the figure near me, a red flame flickered. 'Where am I?' I asked. My voice sounded hoarse.

The woman answered in a husky, strangely sibilant voice. 'You are safe in the cave of my people.' She sounded familiar, and as I blinked I looked up into the striking green eyes of the Count's sorceress. 'Myria?' I asked.

Her lovely face tightened as though I had slapped her, and her fingers withdrew. 'No. I am Sora. Myria is my sister.'

At a furtive sound behind her, I tried to sit up and was overcome with a terrible pain in my side. I had to lie back down upon what I now realised was a bed of fronds.

'Be careful,' she urged. 'You broke your arm and many ribs.'

As I nodded slowly, I noticed my right arm was splinted and wrapped, and looking down my chest, I realised I was bare to the waist apart from some tight bandages. And I saw that Sora was in a red outfit that bared midriff and shoulders and was tight enough in all sorts of wonderful places so that a man wasn't sure where to put his eyes. Her hair was shorter, too, but otherwise she looked just like her sister.

The noise turned out to be one of the serpent folk, who deposited a woven basket heaped with those terrible turnip pinecone fruits beside me before withdrawing. I gathered I was supposed to eat them. Yay me.

At my look to the serpent man, Sora said, 'My people have ruled the scaled from the dawn times. But your people hunt and kill them. You did not? Why?'

I can't really explain my reasoning even now, and especially not then, half groggy as I was. 'He needed help,' I said.

'A simple answer. But a true one. I see this. My blood burns as yours does, and it gives me gifts. Yes, I was told of your feat of strength.'

'My crew. Where are they?'

She shook her lovely head. 'It is bad for them. They have hours at most.'

'What are you talking about?'

'My sister lured them to the temple, and they have been seduced by the sleep spell of the silver mists. Soon Myria will use their blood to fuel her ritual.'

Even in pain and groggy as I was, something didn't ring true. 'Couldn't she have gotten blood a little easier? Tregellan is months away by ship.'

'Myria has no shortage of blood. But she needs the blood of kings.' She touched my chest and I felt a chill that wasn't entirely unpleasant. 'And outlanders. She may have enough now to awaken the full power of the great necklace.'

'What happens then?'

'Then her power will grow like that of a goddess. She must be stopped, or she will kill your people and use her powers against mine.'

I looked down at my arm. 'I'd love to help,' I said. 'But I'm not sure I'm in any shape to do so. How long do we have?'

'Until tonight.'

She saw the despair I felt. I was practically helpless. Still, it was hard to believe that Heln and Lilandra had gone down so easily. 'You're sure they were captured?'

'We saw. What is your name?'

'Varn. Kellic Varn. Captain of the *Sea Witch*.'

'Well, Kellic Varn, there may be a way for you to help. But it is very dangerous.'

I've been led along enough times over the years to recognise a sales job. She'd shown me the problem, then the promise of a solution, then yanked so I'd chase after, like a fish swimming after bait. Still. What was I to do? My cousin and my friend needed me, not to mention the Count, his nephew and the soldiers. 'What's dangerous?'

'You have the blood burn. I have a drink. It might enhance your powers. Speed your healing. Right as rain, your people say.'

'Or?'

'Or it might kill you. Or worse.'

'What's worse?'

She drew her fingers through my hair, full lips shaping a sad pout. 'The blood burn pains, yes?'

'Yes, very much.'

'This will come with greater pain. And it may be that when you drink you transform into something that isn't human anymore. There is no telling.'

I can't say I was super excited to be trying it out. I glanced down at my bandages. 'Where did you get this drink?'

'From a sacred pool on a remote island. There is but a single dose. They say that those who are Heritors can drink it and live.'

There it was. I wanted to know what she planned after she got me to drink. All I knew for certain was that my friends were in danger. If I didn't hear a workable plan, I couldn't be sure my own risk was worth it. 'You want me to drink it. You heard about my strength, and want to use it.'

'We can be of use to each other. The fortress is surrounded by a great wooden barricade with sharpened spikes, and well-guarded. There is no way swiftly through them – unless someone were to rip through the old stone barricade below.'

'How many men do they have, and how many do you?'

'I have no men. I have the serpent folk. And we are three dozen. They have one hundred. But most of them will be scattered through the temple, and less than half are soldiers.'

'How many use magic?'

'At least four. But my archers will target them first. We will attack at dark, as the ceremony begins. If we strike the sorcerers, we have nearly won.'

It sounded to me as though she were readying herself for the victory party a little soon. Still. If she was telling the truth, and I thought she was, I didn't have many options. To aid my friends, I'd have to ally with these people. And I wouldn't be in shape to do so unless I tried her drink.

I sat up, managed not to moan as pain lanced through my shoulder and chest, and looked her boldly in the eyes. 'Bring the drink.'

She was good with theatre. She slipped away with a sway of rounded hips then passed through a beaded curtain. When she returned only moments later she held a gold, ruby-encrusted goblet. I guess she'd been pretty sure I'd take her offer.

As she brought it close, I saw it half full of a dark liquid that smelled of floral blooms. She presented it, her fingers lingering upon my own, and then I was staring at the goblet I gripped in my right hand, wondering if there were some other motive. If she'd wanted to drug me, she could have done it while I was unconscious. If she'd wanted me dead, she could have knifed me, or left me in the jungle.

What I didn't know was just how bad my chances were. I didn't trust her to tell me.

So I lifted the drink, toasting chance and the gods, then toasted her, then put the goblet to my lips and drank deep. It was sweet, like a first kiss and the blush on a maiden's cheek, and the sugared wine they give to children on Harvest Day in old Vornell.

Three good gulps and it was down me. I sat the goblet upon the stone floor and managed two blinks before the magic seized hold.

I thought I'd known what pain was before that. You ever been hit by an arrow? Imagine your body riddled with them. Maybe you've been lucky enough that's never happened. You ever get a dog bite? Imagine thirty dogs biting you at once, except with needle-sharp teeth. And then imagine that pain being trebled, and not just a single sharp moment, but one continual blast at the same level. I surely would have screamed, but I was struck so senseless I couldn't manage a breath.

When I fell backwards, writhing, so great was the agony that jarring my chest and my arm barely registered.

Within was a living flame that hungered to destroy me.

'Is it bad?' I heard her call, as if from far off. 'Do you feel much pain?'

I could say nothing.

But by and by the agony passed, and I can't say if it was minutes or hours. But it faded, and a strange strength filled me, such as I had never known. I breathed more easily, and as I shifted, testing my limbs, the pins and needles that enervated them left off and the pain departed. All of it. The arm trapped in the splint felt hale and hearty. And so I tore the cast away and flexed it. I sat up and breathed, and ripped off the bandages circling my chest. I sucked in a deep breath. No pain there, either.

'It worked!' She sounded relieved. Maybe she hadn't been as sure as she'd let on, for she made a strange gesture and rolled her eyes as she stared towards the cavern roof. 'Praise be the gods of the night!'

'Praise be,' I muttered.

She smiled at me. 'How do you feel?'

'Like it's time to see that temple.'

* * *

It was already dusk when we left the hiding place and moved silently through the foliage. The serpent folk strode ahead and behind, and didn't say a word to one another. Maybe a quarter of an hour passed, and then suddenly the greenery parted and we were in front of a narrow cave entrance, flanked by soaring, vine-choked stone columns. Sora led me past them and into the darkness, whereupon a serpent man handed over a torch, which flickered redly and threw our lurching shadows upon the wall. At a signal from her, serpent folk lit torches set all along the passage.

Two hundred paces further on, deep in the oppressive gloom, we began to pass slabs of rock and stone piled on the left side of the cavern.

'We've been moving the rock for a long time,' she said. 'But there was no way we could breach the final stones.'

And before long I saw what she meant. A slab of rock was crammed diagonally across the cavern. Its surface was carved with serpent folk in knee-length tunics raising their hands and bowing and carrying baskets of fruit, and a whole lot of squiggly characters that were someone else's idea of letters, I guess. The corners were cracked and broken, but the rest of the slab was intact. It looked very, very heavy.

'So,' said Sora, 'there it is. You have to move it.'

I gave it a good, long look. 'You're expecting a lot.'

'I'm expecting a little. Your strength, with ours. We need only move it far enough to squeeze past. And your friends need you.'

She could have gone without mentioning the whole friends angle again. But I stepped forward and watched as she pointed four serpent folk forward with me. They didn't look much stronger than the rest of the serpent folk, who might have been muscular, but were a little rangey. Sort of like me, I suppose, so maybe they were stronger than they looked.

The serpent heads swivelled to look at me as I crouched to put hands on one corner. The slab was tilted backwards just a little, or it would have been nigh impossible. The serpent folk aped – rather, copied – my movements, still watching with unblinking eyes.

I closed mine, partly so I'd stop seeing them but mostly so I could focus on the blood burn as I started to lift. It didn't budge, naturally, because I hadn't called on any sorcerous strength yet.

Then my pulse was racing and it felt again like fire raged through me, but the strength came. Even then it was hard going, but as I strained, the slab rose and I dragged it back. For all I know I might have been dragging the serpent folk too, because I couldn't tell if they were doing me any good, but by and by that old hunk of stone came along. Four spaces was all it needed, for Sora called us to a stop, then waved her serpent folk forward. She started into the darkness, saying something to her followers at the rear before hurrying off with the rest.

I would have started right after, but I was bent over, gasping for breath. The two she'd sent over to speak with me conferred briefly.

And then the shorter ran after the others, and that left me with one, staring at me and holding a torch.

'I have only words few of yours,' it hissed. 'You gave tree off me.'

'Oh,' I said. It was the one I'd rescued. I couldn't have told the serpent folk apart if I'd tried.

'Sora plans to give you dead hurt. Run off.'

I furrowed my brow. 'Why would she do that?'

'She gave you magic. If she kills you, she takes back. You run away.'

I shook my head. 'I can't do that. I have to save my friends.'

It only stared at me.

'Are my friends in there?'

'Yes. She will kill them.'

I asked my serpent folk pal why, but I didn't quite understand his answer. Something about their blood and magic. As he gabbled at me some more, I inferred that Sora and Myria had had a falling out. It wasn't so much that Sora opposed the idea of the ceremony at the silver waters, just the idea of the ceremony giving her sister the power.

I told my pal, who said his name was Zhleen, that I had to save my friends, and he said he had to save his, who were captured and to be sacrificed, and that's as close as we got to any agreement before we started into the cavern together. I couldn't be sure if we were allies now or just happened to be going in the same direction. I had clued in to the fact he limped a little, which was something, at least. I'd be able to tell him apart from the others.

The sounds of the conflict echoed back to us long before we reached the end of the cavern. There were shouts and screams and the clack of swords, which don't really have that romantic ringing sound you hear about in the songs.

All that noise was spuring me on. I believed Zhleen, and was worried Sora might already be killing my friends.

The tunnel came out at the edge of a large, clear space. To my left the crumbling temple loomed, steps climbing its face, its dark stone carved with innumerable serpent-folk faces. In front of it was a raised granite dais, looking over a long, rectangular pool framed by flagstone walkways. All along the walkway, columns of stone hung with flickering torches that supported a crumbling trellis.

The pool was the centre point, though. It bubbled, and in the lurid torchlight the steam rising from it took on a strange, silvery cast.

Everywhere the lizardfolk wrestled with bronze-skinned men and women in cloth of gold, in a bloody, no-holds battle. I searched through the ranks of struggling, stabbing figures, then saw a line of crude wooden cages on the pool's longest edge. And from within those cages I heard shouts, and saw human arms waving.

I snatched up a curved sword from a glassy-eyed corpse and sprinted for the cages. I was halfway there when I heard an explosive thunderclap behind me. On that raised dais, Myria and Sora were locked in sorcerous conflict. Myria still wore the ivory tunic dress thing I'd seen her in most of the voyage, and Sora had on that same garment that left only a little to the imagination. About Myria was a greenish glow, rising in a cloud above her head. A nimbus of lightning hovered over Sora's hands, then leapt from her fingertips as she pointed, piercing the green energy that shielded Myria.

She shrieked in agony, then sent a coil of that energy back towards Sora. I looked away just in time to sidestep a maddened man in cloth of gold jabbing at me with a spear. I cut the weapon's head off then kicked him off balance towards the pool. He screamed in fright as he tottered, then screamed, once, when he hit. He was silent after that, although the pool bubbled as it sucked him down, the way a dog slurps down leftover stew.

I decided then and there to avoid the water.

Heln and Lilandra were at the front of the first cage, and I could see the Count, his nephew and the soldiers crowding behind. Their armour and weapons were gone, though they still had clothes and footgear. A bunch of serpent folk were penned in the cage beside it, and I saw one of the serpentfolk hacking away at the tough ropes that bound the cage shut. Maybe it was Zhleen. He wasn't limping at the time, so I couldn't tell.

'We thought you were dead,' Lilandra told me.

There was no time for idle talk. 'Get back.' I raised the sword

From the dais arose a great gout of laughter that sounded an awful lot like the way villains laugh in stage plays, so you can hear them all the way back in the cheap seats. Loud, maniacal, depraved. One of the women had won the sorcerous conflict, I guessed. And given what I knew from Zhleen, I didn't figure it was good no matter who pulled through.

So I hacked once at the cords that tied the cage shut, but when that didn't work I tossed down the sword, gritted my teeth to the pain, and called on my strength. I tell you, after dragging that stone, ripping a bamboo cage open was child's play, and my friends and the Tregellan were soon swarming out. There were shouts of thanks and a hug from my cousin Heln, and naturally the Count asked if I'd seen where the treasure was, but I shouted them quiet and told them we had to get out. Now.

Like a lot of great ideas, that proved easier in conception than execution. Heln and the men grabbed spears and the curved swords that the dead natives were holding.

Over on the dais, Sora raised hands to the sky, calling out in a harsh, guttural language while groups of serpent folk heaved the bodies of the dead and dying into the pool. As they did that, Sora's eyes took on a glowing, silvery sheen. About her neck hung a sort of torc with pulsing rubies.

'Follow me,' I said, and made for the opening back of the dais from which we'd emerged.

Sora's chant rose to a crescendo and cut off as a massive bolt of white lightning shot down from the roiling heavens. I'd like to report that it blasted her into tiny pieces, but when it touched her, she tripled in size and turned towards us. We'd reached the end of the pool by then and were nearly to the dozen steps that led to the dais. She caught sight of us and extended a hand, crackling with energy.

Lilandra was waiting, though. She conjured a wind and with a wave of her hand sent a gust rolling at the mad woman atop the dais. It set her hair and garments sailing out behind her. The sparkle on her hands died as she staggered. We could just make out her shouting over the wind.

I couldn't speak serpent folk, but there was no trouble guessing the meaning behind her words, because they stopped heaving bodies and started for us.

We were past the dais and running for the dark maw of the tunnel when the first leapt with curved sword, or simply with claw and fang. They bore down three of the soldiers and there was nothing we could do. At my side, Heln parried a terrible swing aimed at my head and then I swung down at a serpent man who'd dived at his legs. The skull dissolved into red ruin and then I was face to fang with two new ones.

'Look out!' Desron cried, and drove his sword straight through the nearest. The serpent folk's companion turned in surprise, which left it open for me to take off its head, which bounded away into the darkness.

We heard Sora shouting as we reached the tunnel and started in. Lilandra paused at the threshold to send a gust of wind lashing at the serpent folk. The miniature whirlwind set them and their arrows tumbling.

Then we were running at full speed into the darkness, the torches that the serpent folk had set along the path flaring. There were only seven of us left, Heln, Lilandra, Count Trovis, his nephew, two of his soldiers and me. And we weren't much to look at, because our clothes were torn and we were streaked with scratches and blood, only a little of which was ours.

If I'd thought we were home free I was sadly mistaken, because from behind came a resoundingly loud hiss. Over my shoulder I caught sight of a vast and terrible snake head, nearly filling the tunnel. From where it had come I neither knew nor cared, but it was gaining on us. Somehow I didn't think it was there to spread good cheer.

We reached the slab I'd dragged clear, then resumed our sprint. Trovis and one of his soldiers were breathing like bellows.

I didn't think the snake would make it through, but as I looked back I beheld a curious thing. Instead of the snake, Sora stepped past the gap and then, before my eyes, warped and shifted and grew into the same serpent that had been after us.

The only good thing about that was that her delay bought us a little more time.

'Almost there,' Heln said. Maybe we were – a lighter darkness lay about ten paces on. I put on a final burst of speed and drew even with Heln. Lilandra was out in front and through to safety. Desron and one of the soldiers were even with me, but Trovis lagged, and his second soldier was still further behind.

The snake got the man. I saw it closing on him, saw its mouth widen, heard his scream as it closed down over him.

Desron, me and the soldier got past and that terrible death was apparently spur enough for the Count, because he came tripping out, right on our heels, looking as though he'd seen a ghost. Turns out a frightened man with the blood of kings doesn't look any different from a sailor who's been scared witless.

We'd made it clear, but a giant snake was still after us. I figured it wouldn't have much trouble tracking us tasty treats into the foliage. Barring sudden intervention from a hungry thunder lizard, we were all going to be night-time snacks.

We only really had one chance. On my right was one of those huge carven columns, draped with vines, right beside a huge palm.

I can't recall that there was any day, before or since, when I called up the blood burn so many times. I was almost dead on my feet. I wasn't sure I'd even stay conscious if I used my powers again.

But it wasn't like I'd be conscious if I were dead. So I shouted for the others to run and then dashed for the tree. I scaled the thing, bracing myself between it and the column beside it. With all the vines it wasn't too much different than climbing a net. Apart from the moment when the giant snake came slithering out of the cave below, I mean.

Sora in her snake form poked out her head and about six feet of neck, then let go with a flick of her tongue and scouted the darkness. Trovis shouted in fear, which was awfully obliging of him, because Sora let go with a hiss-like cry of laughter and then slithered on.

I put my back to the pillar, braced against the tree and pushed off it with my legs. And I called on all the strength in my power.

Ye gods, but the burn this time dizzied me. I felt like I'd had a couple of buckets of the worst grog this side of Tandrini. Behind me I heard a cracking noise and I couldn't be sure if it was the stone column, or my spine. The whole of my back was one long, throbbing ache.

Still the column didn't move. Maybe my idea hadn't been so great. It seemed to be taking forever. I couldn't even be sure if the snake was still behind him.

But something gave, at last. There was a tremendous cracking sound and the support against my back gave way. I hadn't meant to go with it, but there was nothing to grab, so down I went. I twisted in mid-air, turning far enough to see the final third of the snake slithering along beneath me. Only the upper half of the pillar broke free, in two separate pieces, and both smashed into that snake with a delightful crunching noise just before I slammed into the ground beside its enormous tail.

I didn't quite pass out. I just came close. Bright spots obscured my vision and my arm ached where I'd broken it earlier. Idly I wondered if I'd broken it again. I hoped not. Maybe I had that healing power still and maybe I didn't, but I was in no shape to try any more magic today.

I struggled to rise, then felt a strong grip on my good arm, and staggered to my feet.

Heln helped me stand, grinning, and Lilandra pushed stray hairs back in place, smiling at me, and skinny Desron panted with hands on his knees. I didn't see any sign of the snake, though.

'Did I miss her?' I asked.

'Direct hit, Captain,' Heln said. He was being downright expansive.

'Are you alright?' Lilandra asked.

I supposed I was. 'Where's the snake?'

'She's a snake no longer,' Desron said, and lifted one hand off his knee to point.

His uncle the Count was bent down near where one section of pillar was embedded diagonally into the ground. Something soft and terrible lay sandwiched between it and the soil.

Sure, Sora had tricked me, murdered dozens, and would have killed us all, but I still didn't like the sight of her like that, so I didn't stare too long. Count Trovis held up the silvery necklace that he'd somehow wrested from her body.

About that time, a dozen of the serpent folk crept out of the cave. I was spent, and the rest of us weren't doing so fine and maybe it would have been the end, but Lilandra snatched the necklace from the Count – who only managed an indignant shout – and with a puff of wind leapt to the top of the pillar and raised it high. I saw that its rubies still pulsed, as one, like the beat of some terrible heart.

At sight of the thing I'll be damned if the serpent men didn't, one by one, drop to their knees before Lilandra.

After that they walked in our train all the way back to the moonlit beach. I wasn't sure if they were escorts or what, because they were all carrying weapons, but they stood by as we pushed the skiff out towards the waves. Lilandra lingered behind and I saw Heln tense, as if he honestly thought his lover meant to linger behind and become queen of the serpent folk.

But soon as we had the skiff shoved off, she leapt gracefully and the wind caught her and set her down on the aft rower's bench. We looked back and saw the gleam of the serpent folk watching us, standing in a silent row. I wondered if any of them was Zhleen. I hadn't noticed any of them limping.

'The necklace is priceless,' Trovis was saying. 'Since there wasn't any other treasure I'll give you ten percent of whatever I can get for it. It will be a kingly sum—'

Lilandra lifted the necklace and sent it curling out over the waves, where it landed with a plop in the sand at the feet of the serpent folk.

Trovis let out a cry of rage and threw himself forwards. I think if I hadn't grabbed him, he might have dived after it.

He erupted with a torrent of terrible oaths, most of which he shouted at Lilandra.

Heln, unfurling the sail, scowled at him, but Trovis went on, undiminished. His words were unworthy of repetition. Suffice to say that they were full of invectives against the woman for her poor judgement.

I'd had enough out of him, so I smacked him with the flat of my blade. He dropped stunned into the bottom of the boat and I looked pointedly at the soldier and his nephew. 'Any objection?'

The soldier looked tiredly away.

'I am with you, Captain,' Desron said with a shake of his head. 'Your Warden saved us. And may the saints preserve us, I had no interest in taking that necklace along. Who's to say if it wouldn't have turned us all into great serpents? It would be hard to carry your bride across the threshold if you had no arms, yes?'

I'd never really thought about that, but his answer was good enough for me.

'Maybe the serpent folk can rule themselves now,' I said. 'Guess we chalk that one up as a loss.' I faced

Lilandra. 'You probably didn't want to be rich anyway, did you?'

'Not that way,' Lilandra said.

'Maybe next time,' said Heln.

And we sailed through a strip of moonlight and on for our anchored ship.

THE RIVER OF FIRE

BY
JOSEPH A. MCCULLOUGH

Thank you for reading *Ghost Archipelago: Tales of the Lost Isles*. The stories in this book take their setting from a tabletop wargame I designed called *Frostgrave: Ghost Archipelago*. In this game, each player takes on the role of a Heritor, recruits a Warden, and assembles a band of hardy adventurers to go explore the Lost Isles looking for treasure and, of course, the Crystal Pool. The game is designed to be fast, friendly, and fun, so if you have ever considered jumping into the wonderful hobby of tabletop miniature wargaming, check it out. For those who are already playing the game, we present this exclusive scenario, loosely based on the climactic scene in *The Serpent Engine* by Ben Counter.

* * *

The underground passageway ran on and on. The torches burned low, threatening to go out. Then, up ahead, a soft orange glow danced upon the walls. The passage ended and opened into a vast cavern, filled with stalactites and stalagmites. Through the centre of the chamber ran a river of lava, with small clouds of steam hissing up where water dropped on it from the ceiling. The river was filled with small islands, but your eyes were immediately drawn to the largest one. There, a ruined temple sat precariously above the burning river, a stone sarcophagus just visible amidst the fallen masonry. Could this be the tomb you've searched so long to discover?

Set-Up

This scenario is designed for two players and should be played on a table approximately 3' square. The table should be divided in half by a river of lava about 8" wide. In the centre of the table, on a small island right in the middle of the river, sits a ruined temple about 6" square. In the middle of this temple is a sarcophagus. The rest of the river should be filled with small islands and large rocks, so that it is possible to hop across the river at most points. The rest of the table should be covered with stalagmites and scattered ruins.

The players should each place two treasure tokens on the table. One of these tokens must be placed on one of the rocks or islands in the river of lava, but not in the central temple. The other treasure must be placed within 6" of the river, but not in the river itself.

The two crews will deploy facing each other across the river. Players roll to determine who chooses their starting edge, with the lowest roller taking the opposite edge. Each player then places all of their crew members within 6" of their starting table edge.

Special Rules

In this scenario, the central treasure is hidden inside the sarcophagus. To recover it, a figure must move into contact with the sarcophagus and spend an action to attempt to lift the lid. The figure makes a Fight Roll with a Target Number of 10. If the roll is successful, remove the sarcophagus and replace it with a treasure token and a large snake. The snake should be placed In Combat with the figure that opened the sarcophagus.

Any time a figure enters the river of lava for any reason it immediately suffers 5 points of damage and may move to the closest point of dry land. A figure may choose to voluntarily enter the river, in which case it takes 5 points of damage as above, and will take a further 5 points of damage at the start of each activation thereafter for as long as it remains in the river.

Any time a player rolls a 1 for their Initiative Roll, a stalactite falls from the ceiling. That player may nominate any one figure on the table and immediately makes a +5 attack against it as heavy rocks come crashing down.

Treasure and Experience

Heritors and Wardens gain experience as normal for this scenario. Heritors are also eligible to receive the following bonus experience:

+10 experience points if they stand in the ruined temple at any point during the scenario.

+20 experience points if the Heritor, or any member of his crew, successfully opens the sarcophagus.

AUTHORS

Ben Counter

Ben Counter is a veteran science fiction and fantasy writer with sixteen novels and a slew of short stories and novellas to his name, specialising in game-related fiction of the grimmest and most bloodstained kind. He is a fanatical miniature painter, an evangelical tabletop gamer and a Games Mastering guru, with a fascination for all things dark, gruesome and peculiar. He lives in the south of England where he is constantly surrounded by half-painted models and well-thumbed roleplaying books.

Jonathan Green

Jonathan Green is a writer of speculative fiction, with more than sixty books to his name. He has written everything from Fighting Fantasy gamebooks to *Doctor Who* novels, by way of Sonic the Hedgehog, Teenage Mutant Ninja Turtles, Judge Dredd, Robin of Sherwood, and *Frostgrave*. He is the creator of the *Pax Britannia* steampunk series for Abaddon Books, and the author of the award-winning, and critically-acclaimed, *YOU ARE THE HERO – A History of Fighting Fantasy Gamebooks*. He also edits and compiles short story anthologies. To find out more about his current projects visit www.

JonathanGreenAuthor.com and follow him on Twitter @jonathangreen.

Howard Andrew Jones

Howard Jones's debut historical fantasy novel, *The Desert of Souls* (Thomas Dunne Books 2011), was widely acclaimed by influential publications like *Library Journal*, *Kirkus*, and *Publisher's Weekly*, made Kirkus' New and Notable list for 2011, and was on both Locus's Recommended Reading List and the Barnes and Noble Best Fantasy Releases list of 2011. Its sequel, *The Bones of the Old Ones*, made the Barnes and Noble Best Fantasy Releases of 2013 and received a starred review from Publisher's Weekly. He is the author of two Pathfinder novels, *Plague of Shadows* and *Stalking the Beast,* and an e-collection of short stories featuring the heroes from his historical fantasy novels, *The Waters of Eternity.*

When not helping run his small family farm or spending time with his wife and children, he can be found hunched over his laptop or notebook, mumbling about flashing swords and doom-haunted towers. He's worked variously as a TV cameraman, a book editor, a recycling consultant, and most recently, as a writing instructor at a mid-western college.

Mark A. Latham

Mark A. Latham is a writer, editor, history nerd, frustrated grunge singer and amateur baker from Staffordshire, UK.

A recent immigrant to rural Nottinghamshire, he lives in a very old house (sadly not haunted), and is still regarded in the village as a foreigner. Formerly the editor of Games Workshop's *White Dwarf* magazine, Mark still dabbles in tabletop games design as well as being an author of strange, fantastical and macabre tales. His first Apollonian Casefiles books – *The Lazarus Gate* and *The Iscariot Sanction* – are out now, published by Titan Books.

Visit Mark's blog at http://thelostvictorian.blogspot.co.uk or follow him on Twitter @aLostVictorian.

David McIntee

David A McIntee is a writer, historian, and re-enactor. He was written novels, comics, and audio plays for many genre franchises, including *Doctor Who*, *Star Trek*, *Stargate*, *Space 1999*, and *Final Destination*, as well as comics adaptations of works by Ray Harryhausen and William Shatner, and biographies. He has also written and edited nonfiction on the subjects of military history, ancient Egypt, folklore, alien invasions, and treasure hunting. Away from writing, he is a martial artist, and historical fencer both in the Society for Creative Anachronism and in HEMA. Currently in his fourth lifetime, he is a true Renaissance Man, in the sense of being an unremitting debtor who fights duels with swords. He lives in Yorkshire, with his wife, who is also a part-time writer, and their cats. Any domestic arguments are usually settled with a few tourney rounds in medieval armour.

Peter Mclean

Peter McLean is the author of the Burned Man series of urban fantasy novels, *Drake*, *Dominion* and *Damnation*, published by Angry Robot. His debut epic fantasy, *Priest of Bones*, will be published by AceRoc Books in October 2018.

He lives in Norwich, England.

M Harold Page

M Harold Page, author of *Swords Versus Tanks*, believes in "write what you know", which explains the collection of occult tomes, the sword scar, and the battered suit of plate armour languishing in his hall closet. When he's not writing, parenting or tabletop gaming, his idea of a good time is fighting his friends with medieval weapons. He can be found most Tuesday nights teaching German Longsword at Edinburgh's Dawn Duellist Society.

Gav Thorpe

Gav Thorpe has a long history with the *Warhammer* and *Warhammer 40,000* universes, and has written many novels for the same. He is a New York Times best-selling author with the novella *The Lion*. His epic swords-and-sandals fantasy *Empire of the Blood* is available from Angry Robot. Gav has worked on numerous tabletop and video games as designer, writer and world creation consultant. He has also delivered writing workshops and appeared on numerous discussion panels at literature and genre events. He lives near Nottingham with his partner Kez and son Sammy.

Matthew Ward

After more than a decade of collaborative effort shaping Games Workshop's *Warhammer* and *Warhammer 40,000* universes, Matthew now crafts stories across all manner of realities. He firmly believes that there's not enough magic in the world, and writes for anyone else who feels the same way, as seen in the fantasy realm of Aradane (*The Tribute, a Matter of Belief, Shadow of the Raven & Light of the Radiant)* and intrusions into 'our' world from the land of Eventide (*Queen of Eventide, & Edges of the World).*

Matthew lives near Nottingham with his extremely patient wife and three attention-seeking cats. You can follow him on Twitter @thetowerofstars and find his creaking website at www.thetowerofstars.com.

Just don't get him talking about the hidden reaches of the London Underground. Life's too short. (Check out @ ColdharbourFeed on Twitter instead).

The Ghost Archipelago has returned, but only the bravest dare set foot on the mysterious Lost Isles.

In this fantasy skirmish wargame, players take on the role of Heritors, leading handpicked teams of spellcasters, rogues, and treasure hunters into the evershifting labyrinth of the Ghost Archipelago.

Using the same rules system as *Frostgrave*, this standalone wargame focuses on heroes who draw on the power in their blood to perform nigh-impossible feats of strength and agility.

Treasure and glory await for those that are willing to fight for it, but the Ghost Archipelago is an unforgiving place...

AVAILABLE NOW!

www.ospreygames.co.uk

Time is running out for
Yelen and Mirika Semova.

Though the sisters have earned an enviable reputation amongst
the explorers of the Frozen City, their lives are haunted by a
curse – the more Yelen uses her magic, the closer the demon
Azzanar comes to claiming her, body and soul. But Azzanar is
not the only one manipulating Yelen and Mirika...

When catastrophe separates the sisters, it falls to Yelen to
save them both. But in a city shrouded in deceit, who can
she turn to for help... and what price will she pay to get it?

AVAILABLE
NOVEMBER 2017!

www.ospreygames.co.uk